I0692056

Before We Fade Away

by

June Summers

This is a work of fiction. Names, characters, places, and incidents are either the product of the author's imagination or are used fictitiously, and any resemblance to actual persons living or dead, business establishments, events, or locales, is entirely coincidental.

Before We Fade Away

COPYRIGHT © 2018 by June F. Summers

All rights reserved. No part of this book may be used or reproduced in any manner whatsoever without written permission of the author or The Wild Rose Press, Inc. except in the case of brief quotations embodied in critical articles or reviews.
Contact Information: info@thewildrosepress.com

Cover Art by *Tina Lynn Stout*

The Wild Rose Press, Inc.
PO Box 708
Adams Basin, NY 14410-0708
Visit us at www.thewildrosepress.com

Publishing History
First Vintage Rose Edition, 2018
Print ISBN 978-1-5092-2047-2
Digital ISBN 978-1-5092-2048-9

Published in the United States of America

I hardly noticed their absence.
I must have sat on the porch for several hours, contemplating what lay ahead and what was in the past. How could I have allowed my family's murderer to enjoy his life all these years without any consequences for his appalling actions? I could've found him and killed him with my bare hands. He left me behind to find justice for my family. To search him out. To see that he paid. I was a fool for waiting all these years. Yes, originally, I was sick physically and mentally. Then I simply had no desire to live. I was a zombie, not knowing if I ate or drank, if I was dead or alive. Then when my brain finally accepted the tragedy, I tried unsuccessfully to kill myself several times. Was I supposed to stay alive for some reason, perhaps predestined to find this maniac? Then why did it take me so long?

I walked to the lake to cleanse my mind. I slowly waded into the cool water until it was up to my waist, then my neck, and then I was totally submerged. Should I stand underwater until my lungs could not escape the insurgent murky liquid? Should I end it now in defeat? No! I swiftly jumped up, spraying and splashing as my body broke through the water's surface. I rapidly swam back to shore. I was ready to live again.

Praise for June Summers

Ms. Summers' first novel, *LET FREEDOM RING*, published by The Wild Rose Press, June 22, 2016, received a five-star rating from both *Amazon* and *Long and Short Reviews*.

Dedication

To Glory, my right arm
To Wendy, forever in my heart

Chapter One
The Nightmares

Mid-October, Dani

When I awakened at three a.m., my sweat laden pajamas clung to my cold and clammy skin. I was tired of this crap. Every single night for the past two weeks, I had these terrible nightmares. They started with my walking through a neglected orange grove. The pitch-black sky enveloped the grove, but apparently, I had a flashlight because I could see in front of me. The distant, live oak trees shivered in the howling wind while a steady rain soaked my T-shirt, which gripped uncomfortably to my trembling body. The dry, brittle branches of the dead orange trees surrounding me jutted out in all directions, scratching my arms and face as I passed. Overgrown, tangled weeds creeped up my legs like a thousand dancing spiders. Sand spurs burrowed into my socks, painfully pricking my ankles.

Suddenly, I was gazing at a huge, abandoned house. The window shutters faltered on their hinges, and the house looked as if it hadn't seen paint in a lifetime. Leading up to the expansive porch were broken stairs with rusty nails sticking out the edges.

As I stared at the structure, wide eyed and breathing heavily, a sweaty hand grabbed my shoulder. I stood perfectly still, expecting a knife to stab my rib

1

cage or a gunshot to shatter my skull. In a movement more stupid than courageous, I turned around to confront a grimy, old man, his face blackened with soot.

He whispered, "Y'all lookin' for somethin'? Kin I hep y'all?"

Then abruptly, I was inside the decrepit house, following the old man down a long corridor whose walls were covered with blood. "What is this place? Where are you taking me?"

The stagnant, smoky air made it difficult to see and breathe. I was so terrified I moved closer to the old man, his rancid body odor pervading my nose.

"Come along, now." He led me into the kitchen, where a myriad of knives, hatchets, and daggers hung precariously from heavy chains attached to the ceiling. As I walked beneath them, blood dripped and seeped into my wet hair and T-shirt. The old man shone a flashlight around the room, casting light and shadows on the broken cupboards, the cracked ceiling, and the rusty appliances.

I covered my eyes. "Why are you showing me this?"

Suddenly, I heard horrid screams. The old man shone the light in the direction of the noise. "Lookie there, lookie there!" The beam focused on a maniacal man wielding a large ax, hacking away at a mangled captive tied to a chair. Blood splattered wide as the sharp blade severed bone and flesh.

Thankfully, I woke up.

The nightmares aren't always the same. Sometimes the old man cries. Sometimes he laughs hysterically. We always end up in the battered house. Then the scenario changes. Tonight, he led me into the kitchen. Last night, I was in the living room where a raging fire leaped from the fireplace, scorching everything in its path. Portraits of malformed children hung on the wall, their twisted and maimed bodies covered in blood. A woman draped over the arm of a high-back chair lay with her scalp severed and her brain seeping through her fractured skull.

My name is Danielle Reynolds. Since nothing horrible ever happened to me, I don't know why I have these nightmares. I've had tragedy in my life, but nothing to warrant enduring horrid visions night after night. I'm a normal, young woman living an unexciting life. I work part time as a sales clerk at the Sea and Surf Shop in the attractions area on Route 535. My boss looks at me strangely because I'm forever yawning.

This lack of sleep also affects my class work at Valencia College, where I major in criminal justice. I had all A's and B's, but my grades have slipped lately. I haven't told my dad yet. He pays for most of my tuition, but I help with what I earn at work. I live with my dad Andrew and my brother Frankie. My dad owns an auto body shop in Nawinah. My mom Michelle died of breast cancer when I was ten and Frankie was two. Dad and I still miss her very much. Frankie is too young to remember her. I wish she were here to talk about these nightmares.

One thing is strange about my family, although I'm not sure if *strange* is the correct word. On Halloween night in 1971, my grandfather, Daniel Reynolds, killed his boss and his boss' entire family, pregnant wife, six children, and a grandmother. The whole country tried to locate him. He was even on the FBI's most wanted list, but he was never apprehended.

Dad had told me what he remembered. "I was a kid when it happened. My best friend, Travis, was one of the murdered children. After your grandfather disappeared, Grandma Anna raised me. She was only a secretary for Matthew Plimpton, a lawyer in Nawinah at the time. We struggled financially while I was growing up. As soon as I turned fifteen, I got a job at Spencer's Auto Body Shop. When Mr. Spencer got very ill, he sold me the shop."

So sure, according to what Dad knew, I had a monster for a grandfather, but I didn't even know him.

I finally got back to sleep about five a.m. I went to work that day and then to my best friend Emily's house to spend the night. We watched television for a few hours, but I was so tired I could hardly hold my eyes open. We went to bed, hoping I'd sleep through the night. I fell asleep immediately, but after a couple of hours the nightmare began.

Same old thing—in the orange grove getting soaked in the rain. This time the old man's skin was charred and his hair singed as if he'd been set on fire. He was covered in blood, dripping it on me as he touched my shoulder. I guess I screamed because I woke up with Emily shaking me and calling my name. "Dani! Wake up. You're having another nightmare."

I sat up in the bed, sweating, sobbing, and trying to catch my breath. Emily grabbed a handful of tissues. "Dry your eyes, and wipe your nose. Let's talk about this."

Probably louder than I should have, I hastily responded, "No! I don't want to talk about it. I just want these nightmares to stop."

4

"I don't mean to talk about the nightmares. Let's try to come up with some solution."

She made us hot, herbal tea and settled next to me while we both silently sipped our drinks. Five minutes later, she advised, "Here's how I see it. These nightmares are not going away by themselves. They even seem worse. Has anything happened at college or at your job lately that might cause them?"

"Everything has happened because of these nightmares. Nothing happened *before* them. That's what's so confusing. I didn't get the D in psychology until *after* the nightmares started. My boss didn't call me into her office because I was always yawning until *after* the nightmares started!"

"Since you're sure nothing in your life has happened or changed, you *must* get some help. Talk to your college counselor. He'd definitely be more knowledgeable about what's happening to you than we are."

The next morning, I went on Emily's computer and made an appointment to see Mr. Beatty on Monday morning after class.

Chapter Two
The Massacre

October 31, 1971

Law enforcement worked tirelessly on the case of the murdered Cunningham family, but it remained unsolved for decades. From the evidence, questioning eyewitnesses, and piecing innumerable clues together, they did their best to determine what happened on that Halloween night.

The evening began when Mary Cunningham and Ida Mae Cunningham, Mary's mother-in-law, took the Cunningham children trick or treating.

Betsy Ann was the eldest child. "Mother, I'm not dressing in costume this year. I'm thirteen now, and I'm too mature for that silly custom."

Cletus was eleven and the oldest boy. "I want to be Jed Clampett from the *Beverly Hillbillies*. I'll attach floppy, cardboard ears to Blackie's natural ears, and he'll be Jed's Bloodhound, Duke."

Nine-year-old Daisy divulged, "I'm dressing as Jeannie from *I Dream of Jeannie*. That was my favorite television show."

Travis, who was six, loved baseball. "I'll be Jim Palmer, the Baltimore Orioles' pitcher. I know, I always dress like him. That's because he's the best ball player ever."

Four-year-old Lily constantly needed to be the center of attention. "I'm a princess." She danced around in her lovely, pink lace and netted dress with the shiny crown atop her golden locks.

As for two-year-old Silas, he didn't care what he wore as long as he was included in the fun. Grandma had made a charming, white bunny costume for him.

Since the children had school the next day, Mary didn't keep them out late. Around seven fifteen, rain began to fall, soaking the children's festive costumes. As the group left the home of Rhonda Dixon, one of the ladies in Mary's prayer group at the Nawinah Presbyterian Church, Rhonda had heard Mary say, "This rain is coming down too heavily. This is the last house we're stopping at tonight."

Officials surmised the family arrived home before eight p.m.

"Bath time, children," Mary said as she and Betsy Ann readied the younger three for bed. "Since it's a special night, you older kids may stay up a little later to sample some of your treats."

Ida Mae prepared her evening chamomile tea. "I've started a new novel, and I'm retiring to my room to read this fascinating book."

Mary replied, "Well, I plan to enjoy a cup of hot coffee in the living room until Bill gets home. His secretary called earlier to inform me he'd be late."

Bill Cunningham, standing well over six feet with dark brown hair, worked late the night of the tragedy. Bill's secretary had hurried into his office. "Mr. Cunningham, I've just received an emergency call about a fire reported at the Wesley Road Orange Grove."

7

Bill jumped out of his seat. "Call Dan immediately. Tell him I'll pick him up on the way to the grove." He grabbed his jacket from the coat rack and rushed out the door.

Nothing was ever proven, but rumor was some disgruntled pickers had set the fire. Bill and Dan Reynolds, Bill's chief foreman, arrived at the fire location shortly after the fire department. Several hours were spent putting out the flames. The fire department left the scene around nine fifteen p.m. Bill, Dan, and a few of Bill's workers stayed longer to confirm no sparks remained. Shortly before ten, Bill said to Dan, "What do you say we go back to my house for a few drinks? It's been a long day."

The practice of enjoying drinks together was not unusual for Bill and Dan. As well as being Bill's foreman, Dan was Bill's best friend. Mary and Dan's wife, Anna, co-chaired the annual rummage sale at the Presbyterian Church.

With rich, dark hair and deep brown eyes, Dan Reynolds was nearly as tall as Bill Cunningham and similar in stature. While on the job, he, like Bill and all workers at Gunderson Orange Groves, wore the official navy blue company uniform with the gold orange tree emblazoned on the chest pocket.

Dan and Bill often confided in each other about their personal lives. Bill was not one to gossip, but a hushed rumor in Nawinah speculated that Dan and Anna were having marital issues. How the rumor started was unknown. However, during the social hour after the ladies' prayer meetings, the women would often discuss the personal lives of those members not in attendance.

****

Just after sunrise the next morning, an anonymous telephone call came into the Nawinah Sheriff's Office. The caller sounded very agitated but did not give his or her name. The conversation was so inaudible and muffled Trudy Prout, the desk clerk who took the call, couldn't determine if the caller was male or female. Trudy thought the caller said, "There's trouble at the Cunningham House. Better send the sheriff right away."

Several times in the last few years, Sheriff Albert Bailey was called to the Cunningham House to check out complaints regarding drifters breaking into an outbuilding or the smaller Gunderson House on the property. Setting far back from the road among the tall, juniper trees and thick ground foliage, the property provided a perfect place for the homeless to find shelter.

When Trudy contacted Sheriff Bailey, he thought, "With all the rain last night, prob'ly some ol' bum decided to sleep off a drunk. Maybe Trudy jist wasn't payin' attention when she took the call. Sometimes she's too busy readin' her gossip newspapers. I don't want to fire the woman 'cause she really needs her job to support her two youngins, bein' that her ol' man was killed in that plant accident. But she has to start payin' attention."

"Hell, since it ain't no emergency, I'm gonna stop at the Donut Oven and git me some coffee and one o' those frosted lemon donuts."

About seven thirty a.m., Sheriff Bailey drove his cruiser down the long, winding drive lined with neat rows of blooming flowers and lofty shrubbery. His thoughts were concentrated on Edna, his wife of thirty-five years. *Edna is makin' her delicious pot roast tonight. I got a hankerin' for some.* As was evident by his bulging belly, the sheriff loved his food and looked forward to every meal.

Approaching the residence, the sheriff noticed an eerie silence. His professional senses took over, and the thought of food was cast aside.

Awful quiet out here. Why ain't no ceilin' fans runnin' on the porch? And where is Blackie? He's always barkin' when I come down the drive. How come the youngins aren't raisin' a raucous gettin' ready to catch the school bus? This is strange..."

Concerned, Sheriff Bailey got on his radio to Chief Deputy Edgar Fitzsimmons. "Ed, whare are ye right now?"

After a crackling reception, the deputy responded, "I'm at the Dobson place on Drake Road."

"You'd best git out to the Cunningham House. I'm not sure what's agoin' on, but somethin' jist ain't right."

"Okay, I should be thar in about thirdy. I'm finishin' up here now. Somethin' got inta Mrs. Dobson's chicken coop, and thar are dead chickens layin' everwhere."

"You'd best git here sooner. Forget about the chickens."

After hanging up his radio, Sheriff Bailey exited his cruiser while keeping his eyes on the house. He cautiously walked to the porch, climbed the stairs, and knocked on the front door.

No answer.

Then he shouted, "Hello! Bill? Mary? Anabody

home?"

Still no answer.

He knocked again and yelled even louder, "Bill? Mary? Are ye here?"

Still no sound came from inside the house.

He tried the doorknob. The door was unlocked. Drawing his weapon and pointing it ahead, he pushed the door with his gun and walked onto the black and white tile foyer.

"Hello. Bill? Mary? Anabody home?"

The sheriff stood in the entranceway of the big house, repeating Bill and Mary's names and hearing only the echo of his own voice as it reverberated in the empty hallway.

"Bill? Mary? Are ya in here?"

****

The sheriff was still inside the Cunningham House when Chief Deputy Fitzsimmons parked his cruiser near the porch. Just as the deputy was exiting his vehicle, the sheriff came bursting out the front door, tripping down the stairs, and dashing past the deputy into the thick bushes on the side of the house. He must have stayed hunched over vomiting for a full five minutes before catching his breath. "Ed, somethin' horrible has happened! They all dead! All nine of them—all dead! Thar's blood everwhere!"

Chapter Three
Plan of Action

Dani

On both Saturday and Sunday nights, the nightmares grew more intense. I was exhausted Monday morning when I got to my nine o'clock communication class. Like a zombie, I walked through the halls with mud colored circles under my eyes, watering and burning from lack of sleep. The strands of my normally shiny and styled, dark hair lay limp on top of my head. I looked and felt like hell.

After my class, I met with my counselor, Mr. Beatty.

"So what can I do for you, Danielle? You look like shit. Have you been pulling too many all-nighters?"

I shook my head. "I've been pulling all-nighters, but not by choice. I'm having horrific nightmares every night. Do you happen to know anybody who could tell me why and how to stop them?"

The teasing smile left Mr. Beatty's face. "When did these start?"

"A little over two weeks ago. I'm physically, mentally, and emotionally exhausted. Before you ask, nothing has happened to cause them. Nothing traumatic. Nothing tragic. Nothing at all."

"Hmm." He puckered his lips and tapped his finger

on his desk. "Did you ever have anything like them previously?"

"No, never. The last time I had a nightmare I can remember was when I was eight years old, and little, green men came through my bedroom window to eat me. That was one, single nightmare. It never repeated itself. These keep going on and on, getting worse every night."

Mr. Beatty leaned back in his chair. "I know someone who might be able to help you. She's a psychiatrist in Orlando. Her name is Dr. Grace DeMarco. She's dealt with issues like yours before. Let me give her a call." Mr. Beatty called Dr. DeMarco and made an appointment for three that afternoon.

I went to the coffee shop for some caffeine to keep me awake. I had my communications book with me to study. My stomach was doing flip-flops from the caffeine, so I bought a turkey sandwich, hoping it would help the nausea and keep me awake. As hard as I tried to keep my eyes open, they kept drifting shut. Finally, I gave up and moved to a back table. Laying my arms on the table and resting my head on my arms, I dozed off until a nightmare caused me to bolt upright, sending my textbook crashing to the floor and half the coffeehouse staring at me. Embarrassed, I picked up my book and scurried out of the shop.

****

At Dr. DeMarco's office, I filled out the new patient paperwork and then opened my communications book, pretending to read. Letting my eyes gently close, I dozed for about ten minutes until my name was called. I was led to a small room where an attractive woman stood behind a polished wooden desk against a huge window looking out at several tall buildings. Dressed in a gray suit with a silk, magenta blouse, she wore her auburn, shoulder-length hair in a very flattering style.

"Good afternoon, Ms. Reynolds. I'm Dr. Grace DeMarco. Please have a seat. Mr. Beatty briefed me about your problem. However, I'd like to hear your version."

I told her about the nightmares, told her I didn't know why I was having them, no stressful events in my life, no sexual abuse, and no other traumatic events, nothing that might cause them. I talked for a solid twenty minutes without interruption. When I stopped, I took a deep breath and waited for her response.

She folded her delicate hands on her desk. "If you agree, I'd like to hypnotize you. Something in your psyche has alarmed you and won't release itself. We need to find out exactly what it is and why it has suddenly become an issue. Recurring nightmares oftentimes can be explained once we determine what your mind is harboring. It could be something you've buried in your mind, and we simply need it to resurface. Perhaps it's an experience you had as a child too horrific or embarrassing to remember, and the nightmares are trying to push it into the present. These nightmares can also become dangerous and lead to accidents because of insufficient sleep. Some doctors say nightmares can cause epilepsy. You probably have already experienced the lack of focus, motivation, and concentration. I can't guarantee hypnosis will be the answer, but it's the first step we should take."

Dr. DeMarco moved forward and rested her elbows on her desk. "What do you think, Danielle?"

I'd never been hypnotized before. One time in my

psychology class, we had a guest professor who hypnotized volunteers. They'd do foolish things when they were under hypnosis. The professor told one student he'd wake up and be Justin Bieber. The entire class laughed when he awakened and sang Bieber's *Boyfriend.* He sounded more like a beaver than Justin Bieber. I felt sorry for him, making an ass of himself. I surely didn't want that happening to me.

My situation was different. I wouldn't be hypnotized for entertainment, and I'd have no audience to ridicule me. So I agreed and scheduled an appointment for nine the next morning.

When I arrived home, Dad was still at work. I removed pasta sauce and meatballs from the freezer. I put them on the burner to defrost and water on the stove to boil the pasta. Turning on the television and sitting on the couch, I thought I'd watch something mindless until the water boiled and the sauce warmed. I must've drifted off to sleep because I was again in the heavily overgrown area of an orange grove with the old man approaching me, crying tears of blood. He grabbed my arm and pulled me behind him. "Come, Danielle. Follow me."

As I stumbled through the weeds and fallen tree branches, he kept supporting me. This time he led me to a magnificently tailored yard with a cobblestone path leading to a gorgeous, white house with gables and turrets. When he turned to look at me, he appeared so sad I no longer was afraid. Instead of him pulling me, I walked beside him to the mansion. I let him open the ornate, heavy door, and I followed him inside. Then the terror began.

As soon as the door closed, I heard piercing wails

from every corner of the house. The walls, the floors, the ceilings were splattered with blood. The smell was so obnoxious I covered my mouth and nose with my arm. The man led me into a room filled with bludgeoned bodies in unnatural positions. As the bodies reached for me, I felt someone shaking me. "Dani! Dani. Wake up."

Dad was shouting at me. "You left the food on the stove and fell asleep. The water has almost evaporated, and the sauce is boiling over."

I jumped up, sweat dripping down my brow, not completely awake, and glared at Dad.

He scowled at me. "You can't let this happen. You could've burned down the house."

Now aware of my surroundings, I apologized, "I'm sorry. You're right. I shouldn't have sat down. I should've known I'd doze off."

Dad's voice became more sympathetic. "Well, I took the water and sauce off the burners. It's no emergency anymore, but this has got to stop."

"It will. It will. I saw a psychiatrist today. She wants to hypnotize me to find out why I'm having the nightmares. I have an appointment tomorrow morning. She said it could be dangerous if I don't get answers. I guess this was a perfect example."

After discussing my quandary, Dad agreed to accompany me to see Dr. DeMarco.

Frankie got home from his friend Dylan's, and we ate dinner. I cleared the table and started the dishwasher. After a long, hot shower, I went directly to bed, hoping to sleep. As suspected, I was in the dilapidated house again trying to escape bloody, mutilated children coming toward me. Walking backward and unaware I was at the top of a staircase, I lost my footing and fell, toppling down the stairs. I felt the sensation of plummeting in space, but before I hit the bottom of the stairs, I woke up sweating and screaming. Gripped with fear, I looked around the room, unaware of where I was. Both Dad and Frankie rushed into the room. Dad embraced me, holding me against his strong body while I sobbed. Poor Frankie. He stood at the bottom of the bed, not knowing what to do or say.

"Dad, what can I do? Every time I close my eyes, the nightmares start."

He held me close. "We'll find an answer. If this hypnosis thing doesn't work, we'll try something else. We'll ask that psychiatrist for sleeping pills. I still have some pills from when I dislocated my elbow. Let me give you one for tonight."

When Dad went to get the pill, Frankie timidly came closer. "Are you okay?"

I didn't want to burden the poor kid with my issues. "Yeah, I just need sleep. I've been having some bad dreams. Remember when you dreamt those monster trucks on your bookshelf came to life and attacked you? My dreams are similar, only they keep coming back. It's like seeing a scary movie over and over again, but each time seems like the first time, and you're just as frightened. Dad's pill will help."

Unsure if I was telling him the truth, he continued to stare.

I fell asleep not long after taking the pill. It worked to some degree. I had flashbacks instead of outright nightmares. I'd wake up, realize where I was, then fall back to sleep.

Chapter Four
The Cleanup

November 1, 1971

After Sheriff Bailey exited the Cunningham House, he gained his composure and rushed to his cruiser to call his office. "Trudy, call Wade Perkins right now. Tell Wade to git out to the Cunningham place on the double. And git in touch with Phil Drummond. Tell him to bring the camera and the crime kit. Everone of those Cunninghams have been killed!"

Sheriff Bailey exited his cruiser. He leaned his back against the vehicle, slouching with both hands covering his face while sobbing quietly.

Nervously, Fitzsimmons approached him. "Sheriff, should I go in thar?"

The sheriff removed his hands from his face. "No! We got to wait for the coroner and Phil. I don't want nobody stepping in thar 'til we git some pitures."

Fifteen minutes later, Deputy Scott Adams' cruiser came speeding down the Cunningham drive, screeching to a halt next to the other police cars. He jammed the vehicle into park, jumped out, and sprinted over to the sheriff, leaving the driver door wide open. "Sheriff, what happened? Trudy told me I'd better get here right away."

The sheriff was still breathing heavily. "Scott,

thar's been a massacre in that house. The coroner and Phil are on the way. I don't want nobody steppin' in thar 'til the crew is here."

Adams stared at the sheriff. "What do you mean?"

A tear flowed down the sheriff's cheek. "Every one of them was killed. Oh, my Gawd!"

Adams hastily took off his deputy cap and flung it to the ground. "No! No!" He paced in circles while he shook his head.

Nawinah was a small town where everyone knew one another. Deputy Adams and Bill Cunningham had been buddies since both were on the Nawinah Tigers high school football team. They still went to the football games as spectators to cheer on the current team.

Dr. Wade Perkins, the county coroner, and two assistants arrived twenty-five minutes later, preceded by Deputies Phil Drummond and Glen Myers.

The sheriff addressed the new arrivals. "In all my years of public service, I ne'er seen anythin' as gruesome as the scenes in that house. What kind a human could do such a turrible thang? The entire family was slaughtered! Children, babies, all killed."

Dr. Perkins, Chief Deputy Fitzsimmons, and Sheriff Bailey put on paper shoe coverings and rubber gloves. With the sheriff leading the way, the trio entered the house. The place had an eerie silence about it, and the stench of death saturated the stagnant atmosphere. The sheriff pushed open the partially closed French doors into the living room.

On the wine-colored sofa draped across its tightly stretched fabric arm was the body of Mary Cunningham. She lay with her long, strawberry blonde hair cascading loosely over the edge of the sofa. Unnaturally, she stared at the ceiling with her lifeless blue eyes and gaping mouth. Her dress was hiked to her bosom, exposing her pink, lace panties and swollen, pregnant belly. From wounds gouged into her slim body, streaks of dried blood covered her gingham dress, her ample chest, and the mangled flesh of her stomach. Murky bloodstains darkened the already deep red sofa.

The coroner stared in disbelief. "What kind of a monster would do this?"

On the floral-patterned carpeted floor beside the sofa, lay the still body of Bill Cunningham in his blue Gunderson uniform. His face had been bludgeoned beyond recognition with brain matter and bone fragments scattered as far as six feet away from the body. Deep gashes nearly severed his head from his neck, revealing his sliced windpipe and cauterizing blood vessels. A pool of settling blood had not yet been completely absorbed into the surrounding carpet.

Chief Deputy Fitzsimmons put his hand over his mouth. "Oh, my Gawd! This is the work of a devil!"

Sheriff Bailey, seeing this horror previously, didn't look directly at the bodies but stood silently as the other two men gazed in disbelief.

The sheriff exited the room with the others following. "The grandma's bedroom is toward the back of the house."

As he pushed open Ida Mae's bedroom door, her body lay naked on the blood-soaked bed with her left arm and leg dangling over the side. Her yellow, soiled nightdress lay crumpled on the floor. The corpse was brutally eviscerated from the neck to the graying pubic area.

Dr. Perkins crossed his arms over his chest. "What did they do to this poor woman?"

Sheriff Bailey refused to look at the body but stared out the window.

Fitzsimmons kept shaking his head. "Awful, awful."

Next Sheriff Bailey led the trio to the kitchen. The upper part of Betsy Ann's youthful body lay limp, and her ashen face was smashed on the table's hard surface. An overturned, turquoise tea mug rested next to her with a partially wrapped candy bar soaking in the puddle of tea. Betsy Ann's blonde hair was crimson with the dried blood surrounding the gaping wound in the back of her head.

Across from Betsy Ann was the body of Cletus. His buttocks were still on the chair, but his long arms outstretched and reached for the kitchen floor. His hands had multiple cuts and slices on the palms, and his face was riddled with angry bruises and abrasions. Beside his battered left hand lay a broken soda pop bottle with its contents spewed on the floor, the brown liquid mixing with the coagulating blood.

Dr. Perkins walked over to the bodies, bending to get a closer look. Fitzsimmons took a couple of steps backward. Sheriff Bailey stared out the kitchen window.

Fitzsimmons took the initiative and left the room. "I've seen enough."

The trio ascended the winding staircase in the main hall. At the top, the sheriff signaled to the right. "We'll go to these rooms. Thar ain't no carnage down the left hallway."

They skipped Betsy Ann's bedroom, the first on

the right, and entered Daisy's room. Daisy, an avid reader, sat upright in her favorite chair with a book on the life of Martha Washington open on her lap. Her mouth was stuffed with wadded pages from the book while other pages were strewn on the blue carpet. Dried vomit, spittle, and blood had seeped into her clothing, the book, and the chair fabric. A bullet hole with crusted blood contiguous to the wound was in the middle of her forehead.

Dr. Perkins stared at Daisy. "Why do this to an innocent child?"

The next room was Lily's bedroom. Sheriff Bailey remained in the hallway while the other two entered the room. Lily's delicate body lay prone across her miniature table, her tiny, china tea set broken and spread on the floor. Her mutilated dolls were pushed off the shelves with their body parts scattered about the room. The head of one doll was forcibly stuffed into Lily's mouth, tearing her flesh at the corners. A bullet hole was in the middle of her forehead.

When Dr. Perkins and Fitzsimmons exited the room, the sheriff was still staring at the window down the end of the hall. Dr. Perkins touched the sheriff on the shoulder. "Which room next, Al?"

Startled from the touch, the sheriff hastily pointed to the room across the hall. "That's Travis's room."

Travis's slumped corpse was constrained against the wall with his desk supporting him. His arms and neck were affixed with heavy, black tape. His body was sandwiched between the posters of Baltimore Orioles' pitchers Mike Cuellar and Jim Palmer. Bullet holes were in the foreheads of Travis, Cuellar, and Palmer.

The sheriff left the room. "I can't take no more.

I'm goin' outside afore I pass out. Little Silas is in the next room."

Soaked in urine and covered in fecal matter, Silas' naked body lay on his race car bed. The fetid odor was so unbearable Dr. Perkins and Fitzsimmons covered their noses and mouths to keep from gagging.

Fitzsimmons shook his head. "If'n I didn't see this, I wouldn't believe it."

When the coroner and the chief deputy joined the sheriff outside, Bailey was leaning against his cruiser with his eyes cast to the ground. "Doc, I'm gonna send my boys in with y'all now to do the dirty work."

With the team donning paper slippers and rubber gloves and carrying the needed equipment, everyone but the sheriff entered the house. They went through each room methodically. A bullet was recovered from deep in the wall of Travis's room behind the poster of Jim Palmer. A bullet casing was also found underneath Daisy's chair. Countless photos were taken of each body and the area surrounding them. The coroner examined the bodies as completely as possible at the crime scene. More in-depth examinations would be completed at the county morgue. Every spot of blood on the carpet, walls, furniture, and household items was tagged, and samples were taken. Every surface was examined for fingerprints and footprints. The team did not finish their morbid task until early the next morning.

The body of Blackie, the dog, was later found in the woods with his throat cut. An autopsy on his body revealed he had ingested a large piece of raw steak.

The sheriff's department learned a few more details about the events of that Halloween night. They knew the shootings were done with a handgun firing .380 caliber bullets. They found no match to the bullet with any gun confiscated after the murders. They also believed the Cunningham family knew their killer. No evidence of any break-in was found at any window or door. No broken windows or screens. No tampered locks. Bill and Mary Cunningham were probably killed first with both sharp and blunt, heavy instruments. Ida Mae was presumed the next victim. She had also been raped and sodomized after she was murdered. The investigators believed Betsy Ann and Cletus were murdered in the kitchen before the killer ventured upstairs to shoot and mutilate the other children.

State crime scene investigators were called in to help solve the crimes, but they had no more luck than the local sheriff department. After several years of investigations without any success, the case became a cold case file.

Chapter Five
Professional Help

Dani

The next morning Dad battled the heavy traffic into Orlando. At Dr. DeMarco's, the receptionist led us into a larger room than the day before with a puffy, beige couch, a brown leather recliner, a small, metal desk, and a couple of waiting room type chairs. The soft blue dress worn by Dr. DeMarco dazzled her eyes. I introduced her to Dad, and she explained the hypnosis procedure.

"If you become too stressed while under hypnosis, I'll immediately bring you out of your trance. Danielle, sit in the recliner. Don't cross your legs or arms. You may be in this position for a while, and having them crossed could become uncomfortable. Gently clasp the arms of the chair. Mr. Reynolds, why don't you sit on the sofa? Danielle, I'll sit next to you.

"Please relax and close your eyes. Imagine the tension in your body slowly vanishing. It is freeing each body part one at a time, starting with your toes and working up. Visualize your body becoming lighter as the tension fades. Relax your toes, your feet, your calves, thighs, hips, stomach, and so on until you're completely relaxed. Imagine soothing, flowing water rushing over your feet and ankles, cleansing them of tension. Take slow, deep breaths, ridding your mind of any stress or anxiety. You're beginning to have a pleasant feeling of drowsiness. You're getting a sense of deep relaxation in a safe and serene environment. Nothing is interfering with your restful state. We are now going to venture back to your youth."

My body was relaxing completely. In the background, I heard Dr. DeMarco's calm voice as my mind seemed to turn inward. A floating sensation took over me, like I was not even sitting in the chair anymore, but soaring in the air. Dr. DeMarco's voice became distant. I forgot it was even there, yet the soothing sound somehow continued. As I relaxed even further, I was no longer aware of where I was, why I was there, or who was speaking. I was simply content in a state of profound relaxation and deep tranquility.

Then somewhere far away I heard someone calling my name. I didn't want to hear it. I wanted to stay in that peaceful state of serenity, but the voice kept calling me until I couldn't ignore it any longer. I felt my body falling back to reality. The leather of the recliner wrapped around me. The voice seemed to be screaming, and I opened my eyes. Dad and Dr. DeMarco were staring at me.

"What happened? Why are you looking at me like that?"

Dr. DeMarco put her hand over mine. "Danielle, you were hypnotized for about twenty-five minutes, but I saw no trauma in your body expressions. While in your hypnotic state, I asked you many questions about where you were and what you were doing. You said you were in the best place in the world, having the happiest time of your life. You saw your mother. Tears of joy were in your eyes when you spoke of her, but no fear or trauma."

"I don't remember any of it. What does it mean? I only remember floating in air and being suspended in time."

"By your reactions under hypnosis, it's my professional opinion that nothing in your personal life, past or present, is causing your nightmares. You didn't appear to harbor any devastating experiences from your past. We can now rule out one of the most typical causes of nightmares."

So nothing happened to me when I was a child: no dirty, old man ever accosted me; I never got lost in the woods; I never got jumped by a monster when I went to those haunted houses on Halloween. "So what do I do now?"

"I'd like you to stop in the lab next door. I'll give you a script for a blood test to rule out any physical condition. In the meantime, I'll also give you a script for some sleep medication. You may feel lethargic tomorrow, but you should be able to function. Until we're able to determine the reason for your nightmares, it'll enable you to get some rest. If I find no medical reason for your nightmares, we'll go into phase two of the analysis."

I stiffened and sat upright. "What's phase two?"

She looked first at me, then at Dad. "I want to get the blood work results before recommending any further treatment. However, if the tests come back negative for any physical issues, we should proceed with this next step."

I was getting apprehensive, not knowing what she would recommend.

Dad asked, "What is this next step?"

She cleared her throat. "I plan to suggest an unconventional treatment, but I want to consult with my colleague beforehand. In most cases, we don't consider it an option. However, finding no basis of any trauma in your background, nor any event triggering your nightmares in your recent history, we need to look at an alternative treatment."

Both Dad and I were getting impatient. Why doesn't she simply tell us what it is?

Dr. DeMarco leaned forward in her chair and looked directly into my eyes. "I want you to see a medium."

I opened my mouth wide enough to insert a football. Dad had the same shocked look on his face. Was I hearing her correctly?

We waited for Dr. DeMarco to explain. "Yes, it's unusual, but if it works, your nightmares will stop. I'll work closely with the medium to monitor you during the procedure."

Perhaps I closed my mouth. Maybe not. This was insane! Voodoo. Exorcism. Witchcraft. All of these things ran through my mind.

Dad seemed as skeptical as I was. "I don't know. I never expected you to say *that*. We aren't into the *occult*. We're a good Catholic family."

Dr. DeMarco immediately responded, "I know it sounds irregular, but believe me, I have great confidence this will work."

I wasn't exactly sure what treatment a medium would give. "Uh, what happens? What do they do? Do you see ghosts? Do you talk to ghosts?"

"No, it's nothing like that. Unlike hypnosis, during

a séance you are completely aware of your physical surroundings. It's not specifically about *you*. It's about someone else *and you*.

I was still confused. "What do you mean?"

"When you are hypnotized, we try to discover what in your psyche causes the problem. What a medium does is to determine why someone else is invading your space, so to speak. Some people try to contact a deceased loved one through a medium. Oftentimes, how successful the connection is depends on both the deceased and the one trying to contact him or her. And of course, the capabilities of the medium."

I was still skeptical. "A deceased? But I'm not trying to communicate with any dead person. I'd like to see my mom again, but I never thought about contacting her through a medium."

Dad had been sitting with a puzzled look on his face, taking in our conversation. "Besides contacting someone who died, what other purpose could it have you haven't told us about?"

Dr. DeMarco continued her explanation. "Sometimes it works in reverse. Sometimes a deceased person tries to contact *you*."

Startled, I jerked upright in the chair. "What? You think my mom is trying to contact me?"

"Perhaps not her but someone else."

"But who? Why?"

"That's what a medium can determine. This is not in my area of expertise, but it has worked in other cases."

Dad took my hand. "What do you think, Dani? It sounds bizarre, but if it can help you, maybe you should try it."

I lifted my hands and covered my face. "I don't know! I don't know!"

"You want to get rid of the nightmares. I'll go with you to the session. Dr. DeMarco will also be there."

"What if I'm too frightened whenever this dead person comes around? I'm not sure I can handle it."

"I think you can. Remember that break-in at Emily's house? The two of you were only thirteen and alone in the house. You took control of the situation, called 911, and stayed on the line until the police arrived. You were afraid, but you did what you had to do. I know you can handle this."

I finally acquiesced. "Okay, I'll do it," convincing myself more than Dad or Dr. DeMarco.

Dr. DeMarco made an appointment with Nafia Celik, the medium, for Friday evening. Before going home, we stopped at the lab for the blood work and picked up the script for the sleeping medication. I was to take a pill an hour before bedtime. Since I was so exhausted after dinner, I took the pill and went directly to bed.

I'm not sure how long I had been asleep before the dream started, not a nightmare but also not pleasant. My body was floating in air. Not peaceful. Not relaxed. I was shivering, but I was sweating. Then I felt like I was falling through space, plunging swiftly toward the earth. Before I crashed, I popped my eyes open. Still shaking, I went to the bathroom, got a drink of water, and then crawled back into bed. I took deep, relaxing breaths while my mind wandered for a while. Then I fell back to sleep. I was at the large, white house again. However, it was very peaceful. The birds chirped melodiously, the air smelled fresh and clean, and a gentle breeze fluttered my hair against my cheeks. I ambled through a garden full of radiant flowers. Their fragrance enveloped me as I stepped on the narrow, cobblestone path, the flowing sound of nearby water rippling through my ears. As I walked, I was humming, enjoying the sights and sounds around me. Then I heard another faint, far away sound, which gradually grew louder.

Unexpectedly, the garden opened to a meadow where large, flat rocks lay in a semi-circle. Seated on each rock was a child. In the middle of the circle was a petite woman with long, blonde hair. When I looked more closely, I saw her face was extremely red, as if she had a terrible sunburn. When I entered the semi-circle, all the children and the lady looked up at me. They each had red faces, and they were crying. "Why are you so sad?" I asked the lady.

I tried to go closer to comfort her, but when I reached out, she disappeared. The children began to wail. "No, no. It's okay. Please don't cry."

When I approached them, they too disappeared, and I was left all alone in the meadow.

The next thing I knew, Dad was awakening me for breakfast.

Chapter Six
Rumors and Speculations

1971

Sheriff Albert Bailey spent the rest of his career arduously trying to solve the horrendous murders of the Cunningham family. He spent countless hours going over every clue year after year. Periodically, he submitted the partial fingerprint found on a whiskey glass to the National Fingerprint Database, hoping for a match. He frequently went back to the Cunningham House, searching in vain for anything his staff had missed.

His wife Edna worried about him. His favorite pastime had been eating her homemade meals, but he began skipping meals or pushing his plate away half full. "Al, what is it? You never eat anymore? Should I make an appointment for you to see Dr. Kettering? I'm worried about you."

"No, dear, I'm just not hungry. Maybe I'll warm it up later."

In the evening, the sheriff often wandered by the lake, keeping his thoughts and feelings to himself, no longer sharing them with Edna. One night he did not return from his walk. At midnight, a worried Edna went searching for him. She found his lifeless body resting against a hollow log. The coroner ruled he suffered a massive heart attack.

Upon Sheriff Bailey's passing, Edgar Fitzsimmons was next in line for the sheriff's position. However, the Cunningham tragedy had devastated Fitzsimmons so much he no longer wanted to remain in law enforcement. Six months after the murders, he resigned. "I'm movin' back to help my pop run the family hardware business. He's gettin' up thar in years and can use my help."

Deputy Scott Adams finished Sheriff Bailey's term and was re-elected several times thereafter. Being that Bill Cunningham was a good friend of his, Adams also tried unsuccessfully to solve the brutal murders.

Dan Reynolds, Bill Cunningham's best friend and chief foreman, became the primary suspect. Since he'd accompanied Bill home that evening, his presence already in the house would account for the absence of broken locks or windows. However, as the authorities soon discovered, Dan Reynolds couldn't be found. His bank accounts were cleaned out shortly after the incident, leaving his wife Anna with little money to raise her son Andrew. Checks were cashed on their joint accounts from varied locations throughout the south.

Still, if Dan Reynolds was the murderer, what was his motive for killing the Cunningham family in such a coldhearted, brutal manner? Expensive jewelry and up to one hundred thousand dollars in cash were stolen from the library safe. Did Reynolds kill for money? Perhaps Dan was jealous of Bill's success. Was it more than a rumor purporting Dan and Anna Reynolds were having marital problems? Was Bill Cunningham really the father of the baby Mary was carrying in her womb?

Perhaps Mary and Dan were having an affair. Was that the reason for the problems in Anna and Dan's marriage? Did Bill Cunningham find out about the affair?

If Dan Reynolds wasn't the murderer, then who was? Maybe it was one of the drifters who spent nights in the Gunderson House. Bill Cunningham's body was found with his pockets empty. His wallet and all the money on his person were stolen. That money plus the contents of the safe were a substantial amount of loot for a drifter.

Bill Cunningham had no real enemies. He was friends with all his counterparts. Was it possible one of them secretly held a grudge against him?

Bill's grove workers were satisfied with his leadership. He paid them well for jobs well done. However, what about those employees suspected of setting the fire at the Wesley Road Grove the night of the murders? Were they so upset they'd kill the entire Cunningham family?

After all the investigations and speculations, the main suspect was still Dan Reynolds. Despite a nationwide search and his face shown on television across the country, he somehow eluded any sightings, let alone capture.

Chapter Seven
Over The Top

Dani

Dr. DeMarco had called to inform me the blood work had come back negative regarding any physical reasons for my nightmares. Thus, my appointment with the medium was still scheduled.

The medium's house did not look like a haunted house as I expected, just an ordinary small, white bungalow with stucco siding and blue-green trim. A bushy oak tree loomed in the tiny front yard, and a cement walkway led to a small, open porch. When Dr. DeMarco arrived, the three of us walked to the door. She rang the doorbell, and I heard footsteps against the floor surface inside. Then the door opened.

A slightly plump woman, barely up to Dad's shoulders, was robed in a deep red and purple garb tickling her ankles and flowing like a bird from her elbows. She had black, straight hair streaked with strands of gray and falling past her shoulders. She peered at us with her sparkling, ebony eyes nestled in a buttery, sand-toned face.

"Good evening, Dr. DeMarco, Danielle, Mr. Reynolds. Please come in."

When I shook the medium's hand, I was surprised how warm and smooth it was, not rough and boney like a witch's hand. She led us through a double doorway into the living room, filled with heavy furniture and dim lighting. We then went into a small dining area with a kitchen off to one side. No cobwebs. No monsters. She opened a door opposite the kitchen, and we entered an elongated, narrow room. The only source of light came from a floor lamp in the corner, its beam reflecting upward and casting unnerving shadows on the ceiling. The windows' heavy, black drapes cascading to the floor begged to wrap around and suffocate me. I was afraid to speculate what was behind the door in the wall facing us.

The medium signaled us to sit around a small, square table covered with a deep purple cloth imbedded with sparkling, gold flakes. Thick, brocade fabric covered the accompanying chairs. I gazed around the room, getting more nervous by the second. Dad sat to my left and Dr. DeMarco to my right. The medium sat across from me. Dad, knowing how terrified I was, clasped my hand.

The medium spoke in a low, slightly accented voice. "My name is Nafia Celik. I'm originally from Turkey, but I've lived in this country for most of my life. I'm a psychic medium dealing with the paranormal. I have fine-tuned my extrasensory perception so I can interface with the spirits in the afterlife. Oftentimes, I can feel and hear the thoughts, the voices, and the mental sensations created by the energy of spirits. This means I rely on the presence of non-physical energy outside myself for information to help me. I make connections with and deliver messages from people no longer living to those still alive. I can receive information directly from the dead and from the spirits."

As she spoke, my thoughts darted haywire. *No way. This is some kind of hoax.* Yet Dr. DeMarco, a very educated woman, must not agree. She told me to come here.

Nafia Celik continued, "I'm not a charlatan after your father's money or even after fame and fortune. My calling is to help people find that connection with the deceased vital to their well-being. Would you like to ask me any questions before we begin?"

I wanted to be anywhere else but in that room. "Here's the thing. I don't know why I'm here. I don't know what deceased person I'm supposed to contact. I merely want to get rid of the nightmares. But I must tell you, my mind can't even comprehend how you can talk to the dead, or if you possibly can, what it has to do with me."

"I understand your skepticism. This is overwhelming, and you're hesitant about the experience. However, I'm certain I can help you. From what Dr. DeMarco has told me, we've both concluded you have a spirit from your past urgently wanting to speak to you. You'll continue having the nightmares unless you find out what this spirit wants."

Her marble eyes looked at me sympathetically. "Let's begin."

Nafia went to the lamp and turned it to the dimmest setting. After she was seated, she gave her instructions. "Please remain in your seats at all times with your hands on the table, palms down. Don't speak. I will address the spirit and relay to you what he or she wants to communicate. Let me warn you—the atmosphere may become very intense as the spirit is summoned. I

37

have no way of knowing how much energy will be released."

Oh, the thoughts going through my head. I shook so much the table moved. *That* wasn't the spirit. My heart pulsated so fast it could jump out of my chest. Perhaps I should put up with the nightmares. At least I woke up from them. This was something else, something far beyond my imagination. Dad gave me a reassuring look. Dr. DeMarco appeared like she was already in some sort of trance. She had her eyes closed and her head slightly tilted upward.

Half chanting, half speaking, Nafia raised her hands in the air. "Oh, spirit of the dead, you who are tormented and seeking relief, you who tried time and again to communicate with Danielle through her unconscious mind, I reach out to you. I want to help you find peace to put your soul to rest. Join us this evening, and we will help you in your quest. I welcome you now. Please come forward so we will know why you feel such unrest."

Nafia began to speak in some strange, gibberish language. First her speech was soft, but her voice grew louder, saying weird, bizarre words.

Without warning, the room felt so cold I wanted to take my hands off the table and rub my arms for warmth, but I was afraid to move. As Nafia chanted, the heavy drapes on the window began to rustle and flap extending a visual invitation they wanted to smother me. I arose from my seat, but Dad grabbed my arm and pulled me down. Nafia hadn't stopped chanting during my escape attempt. I waited for the windows to crash in or the door to blow open.

Then she started *wooing*, like the sound kids

sometimes make when they're trying to terrify someone. It worked for me.

"Spirit, I feel you. You are troubled. We want to help you. Spirit, come to us."

The drapes flapped, and the table literally lifted off the floor. That *wasn't* me. As Nafia spoke, an eerie sound saturated the atmosphere, like a faraway train whistle. I sat as still as possible with the turmoil surrounding me. The whistling sound grew so loud and high pitched my ears hurt.

Then the noise abruptly stopped. The flapping of the drapes subsided, and the room was still and cold. Nafia spoke softly, "Spirit, you are here. Tell me what you want." She was silent as she waited.

Something different was happening. She spoke again, "Spirit, I am trying to reach out to you. I sense you are a man. Do you know Danielle? Why are you calling to her in her dreams?"

Silence again.

"Please, reach out to me." Nafia extended her arms upward. "Please, tell us what you need."

Again she was silent.

"Yes, yes, I hear you. No, do not leave yet. Please wait."

Abruptly, she dropped her arms to her side and slammed her head on the table. At first, I thought she was hurt, but she soon lifted her head, her eyes still closed. When her eyes burst open, she looked bewildered. Dr. DeMarco put her hand on mine. "Wait. She'll speak shortly."

So I waited.

Soon Nafia became aware of our presence. She stared at me. Then like a bomb explosion, she blurted,

"Your grandfather is trying to reach you."

I almost fell off my chair. "What? That's impossible. I didn't even know him. What does he want with me? He's a murderer. If I knew him, I wouldn't want to even speak to him."

Dad reassured me. "Take it easy, Dani. Let her explain."

"I felt his spirit. He was able to identify himself through the transcending, but he couldn't stay. He kept fading away. I felt his urgency to contact you, for he was very troubled."

I shouted, "He's troubled! What about me?"

Nafia tried to ease my concern. "Danielle, we do not always know the reason behind a spirit's need to communicate with the living, but if he is going to such great lengths to get your attention, it must be urgent. You can't ignore it."

"How can I ignore it? He haunts me in my nightmares every night. What kind of a grandfather would do that to his grandchild?"

"I can't answer that, but until you recognize his need and confront whatever issue he's having, your nightmares will continue. This is difficult for you, but we need to reach out to him again. Since he was able to communicate once, it may be easier for him a second time."

I covered my face with my hands, forcing myself to think. Could I go through this again? If I didn't, I'd probably have these nightmares forever.

When I looked at Dad, he had tears in his eyes. "Everyone said your grandfather was a murderer, but the father I knew wasn't capable of those heinous crimes. He was a loving man, not violent in any way.

At first my mother supported his innocence completely, but as time went by, she had doubts. Their bank accounts were cleared out, and she never heard from him after the Cunningham murders. She thought at least he should've contacted her to explain himself. But never a word. No phone calls. No letters. She naturally came to doubt his innocence. But me? Never. I knew the man who played baseball with me, who stayed constantly by my side when I was ill, could never be a murderer. I saw how he treated the Cunningham children. No way could he hurt them. But I was just a kid, and with him being my father, I couldn't convince anyone of his innocence, not even my mother. So, Dani, not only would you be doing this for my father, but you'd be doing this for *me*. *I* need to know why he's trying to communicate with you."

So many thoughts were filling my head. "Okay, okay, I'll do it."

We arranged to return to Nafia Celik's the following Wednesday evening. I worried about what would happen with the nightmares before then. I still took the sleeping medication, but I didn't like the way it made me feel. I couldn't concentrate in class or keep focused at work. In a sense, I looked forward to Wednesday to get it over with as soon as possible.

Chapter Eight
Try, Try Again

Dani

We returned to Nafia Celik's house on Halloween night. The sidewalks were filled with kids dressed as monsters, ghosts, and witches, parading house to house to demand their contraband. As for me, I was on my way to talk to the dead. How ironic.

The same ritual took place: Nafia's trance, drapes moving, and frigid air. I kept my eyes closed and my palms flat on the table even when the table shook. I was determined to be as calm as possible, which wasn't easy with my heart racing like a cat chasing a mouse and my body shaking like a baby's rattle.

Nafia began chanting, "Oh, spirit of Daniel Reynolds, we beseech you to come forth. Tell us what you need to be at peace with your passing. Present your spirit to resolve whatever issues you have with the living. We want you to be at rest."

I sensed when the spirit was in the room. I couldn't see or hear it. The feeling was certainly the most bizarre I've ever had.

Nafia became very quiet, eyes closed and arms raised upward. She began talking in tongues, pausing now and then as if she was listening to some response. This strange conversation went on for several minutes with the atmosphere staying caustic. When Nafia came out of her trance, she gradually lowered her arms and opened her eyes. "Your grandfather is very sad and needs your help."

And I am thinking to myself, how can I help a dead man?

"He says he's innocent of the crimes for which he's been accused. He wants you to vindicate him."

"What! Excuse my language, but how the hell can *I* vindicate him?"

"Danielle, this is very difficult for you to understand, but sometimes the dead need our help to move on and find peace in their afterlife. He didn't convey why he's chosen you, but he feels you can help him find the peace he desperately needs."

I was still shaken from this revelation. "What does he want me to do? I don't know anything about what happened, only what Dad has told me."

"He says he's known you for a lifetime, even though you don't know him. He has watched over you throughout your life and was by your side many times when you needed him. He wanted me to remind you of the time when you were eight years old and almost run over by a truck. He was the one who pulled you to safety."

I covered my mouth with my hands. How would she know anything about that incident? My mind shot back to my experience, recalling how I barely escaped getting run over by a huge delivery truck. I remembered leaving the grocery store and starting to cross the street when the truck came barreling down on me. The next thing I knew I was on the sidewalk next to the store, unaware of how I got there. I thought I must've unknowingly jumped backwards. My legs and elbows were scraped and bleeding, and the people in the grocery store came to help me. They called Mom and Dad, who took me to the hospital to make sure I had no broken bones. No way would Nafia Celik know anything about that episode. I could tell from Dad's expression he too was completely baffled. From what the people at the grocery store had said, I was by myself and jumped out of the way of the truck on my own.

Nafia continued to summarize her conversation with my grandfather. "He is pleading with you to clear his name. He can't rest until he knows his loved ones, both alive and deceased, know he is innocent of the horrid accusations. He apologizes for frightening you and putting you through this ordeal, but he knows you have the mind and capabilities to come through for him."

Dr. DeMarco sensed this experience was way beyond my comprehension. "Danielle, I'd like to help you through this. Why don't we meet tomorrow to decide a plan of action?"

Dad quickly answered, "How about if Dr. DeMarco comes to dinner at our house tomorrow night? We can talk about it then."

Chapter Nine
Danielle Reynolds, Detective Extraordinaire

Dani

I had no nightmares that night. Not even a dream. In all the excitement, I hadn't even taken the sleeping pills. It was the most blissful night's sleep I could ever remember. I woke with the alarm ringing at six thirty, feeling more rested than I'd felt in a long time. I was ready to conquer the world. I could solve any crime. Danielle Reynolds, detective extraordinaire.

I had to shake off the confidence in myself and get to class. A big day was ahead of me. Class, work, crime solving. Oh, yeah, crime solving. It started to hit me. How was I supposed to solve a crime I knew nothing about? If professional law enforcement, who had forensic science available to them, were unable to solve this mystery, how could I? I didn't have any credentials or support at my disposal. I only had a dead grandfather telling me he was innocent.

As I prepared for class, I made a somewhat haphazard plan. The first thing was to find out as much as possible about the murders. Since the crime happened so long ago, who'd even remember the details? Was anybody still alive? What about the police? Computers existed then, but the internet and any of today's sophisticated technology were not available. I often watched the television show, *Cold Case*. The detectives go back many years to solve crimes. A dark room lined with high, metal shelves all filled with white boxes housed the evidence for each cold case. A number and a name were handwritten with a thick, black marker on each box. Perhaps the Nawinah police had such a room with a box of evidence from the Cunningham murders. I'll start with the police department.

I had classes until noon, then work until five. I got home about five-thirty and helped Dad prepare dinner for our meeting with Dr. DeMarco. Dad was taking the steaks off the grill when she arrived.

After dinner I began the conversation. "The first thing I need to do is to research the crime and find out all I can about it."

Dad suggested, "Why don't you run this entire scenario by your criminology professor? You don't need to tell him about your personal connection, but perhaps you can work this into a class assignment."

"That's a great idea. It falls into our current course study. We're each reporting on a crime of the twentieth century, like the Lindbergh kidnapping or the Jimmy Hoffa disappearance. I bet he won't mind me researching a local crime. I won't mention Nafia Celik. He'd never believe me. I barely believe it myself except since last night was nightmare *and* drug free, I'm beginning to think maybe there was something to it."

Dr. DeMarco apologized, "I was fairly certain Nafia could get to the crux of your nightmares. However, I didn't know she was eventually going to lay this heavy burden on you."

"You know, Dr. DeMarco, I'm excited about it.

Without the nightmares to burden me, I'll be able to concentrate. I guess my grandfather did know who to call on after all."

We ate dinner and discussed my plans more in depth. After coffee and dessert, Dr. DeMarco got up to leave. As she was going out the door, she advised, "Oh, by the way, call me Grace. Dr. DeMarco is too formal."

I looked at Dad. Did I see a twinkle in his eyes? I think there's romance brewing in the air. I gave Dad a haughty smile.

After Grace left, Dad asked, "What's that look for?" He knew I noticed his demeanor around her.

That night I went online to learn all I could about the Cunningham case from any public records. I learned the full names and ages of the victims. I found out the names and responsibilities of those in law enforcement who worked on the case. I also read articles clearly pointing to my grandfather as the murderer. However, I still needed more facts, not speculations or opinions. Hopefully, the police department could help.

From Thursday until Monday I had no nightmares. It was glorious to sleep through the night. In Monday's criminology class, we discussed the crimes of the twentieth century. Professor Belinsky assigned the various crimes to different class members. He gave me the D.B. Cooper case, which was the 1971 unsolved mystery where an unidentified man hijacked a plane and extorted two hundred thousand dollars in ransom. He then parachuted out of the plane to an unknown fate. I asked Dr. Belinsky, "Sir, can I talk to you briefly after class? I have a proposition."

Perhaps I shouldn't have phrased it quite that way. I heard giggles from the girls and *yahoo's* from the guys. One guy snickered, "*I'll* gladly meet you after class, Danielle."

After everyone left the classroom, I approached Dr. Belinsky. "Do you remember a local crime in Nawinah in 1971 where the entire Cunningham family was murdered?"

"Oh, yes, I recall that case. Wasn't the family killed by Cunningham's foreman?"

"The case was never officially solved. The killer was never located."

"Oh, I didn't know. That'll make a great case study, but I must caution you. This will require more extensive research than simply searching online, and you may not be able to finish the project within the allotted timeline."

"I'm aware of all that. I'll do whatever you suggest."

"I guess I can extend your deadline as long as I get updates regularly with information and progress reports. Also, when the others have completed their case and go on to another project, you'll be required to work on the next assignment as well."

"I can handle it."

"Well then, Danielle, I'm very excited about this. I'm sincerely looking forward to the outcome. Good luck." He gathered his books and walked out the door.

Chapter Ten
Criminology at Its Best—Or Worst

Dani

The next morning, I went to the Nawinah Police Department to see if they'd release the files on the Cunningham case. Large, balloon-like lights on short posts were out front with *POLICE* in thick black letters painted on the white background. I entered the double glass doors and walked to the glass faced counter. A policewoman was shuffling through some papers. "Can I help you?"

I didn't exactly know what to say. "Uh, I'm a college student at Valencia taking criminal justice classes. I'd like some information on a local, unsolved case from 1971."

She stopped looking through the papers and came to the counter. "All unsolved cases are confidential and not released to the general public. What was the case?"

"It was the murders of the Cunningham family."

"I know the case, but we can't release anything on it."

"If the case is so old, what harm would it be for me to see the files now?"

"I don't make the rules. Police records can't be released to just anyone. It'd be too easy for that information to get into the wrong hands. If you were

49

involved in a case and had retained an attorney, it's possible the attorney could get the information. Do you have an attorney?"

"No, I don't." I'm sure my disappointment showed.

"I'm sorry. Maybe try the library or the internet. Several crime books also include information on that case."

"Thanks for your advice."

Disappointed, I walked out the door. What next? Would the library have anything more than what I had gleaned from the internet?

Metal benches lined each side of the walkway outside the police station. I sat on one, thinking about what to do next. I looked at the notes I had made previously and tried to develop a plan. I should've expected this. Why would they give records to a naïve, college student? Was I getting into more than I could handle?

As I sat staring at my notes, I saw a pair of shiny black shoes stop about a foot away and point toward me. I focused on the shoes then slowly moved my eyes upward to a man in a dark blue, police uniform. His piercing, blue eyes were set in a pleasant face with high cheekbones and a nose a plastic surgeon would copy. Strands of dark brown hair poked out beneath his police cap.

"Can I help you? Are you okay?" He had a clear, velvety voice.

I looked straight into those baby blue eyes and prattled, "I really wish you could, but I'm not any type of law enforcement officer, so I guess I don't have a right to find out the information I want to know, and I don't know how to get it, and I already committed to many people I would find it for them. Now I'm going to disappoint not only myself but so many other people. I don't know what to do about it. So there!"

"Whoa! Do you want to run that by me again? No! Never mind. Can you just tell me a shorter, less speedy version?"

"I'm sorry. I'm just so frustrated. I need information on a murder case from several years ago, but the policewoman inside said I'm not authorized to look at any of the evidence."

He looked so tall and handsome standing in front of me. "That's correct. Police files are not open to the general public. Were you personally involved in the case? Your attorney can get that information."

"No, I wasn't involved, and I don't have an attorney."

"Is there anything else I can help you with? Perhaps buying you a cup of coffee?"

I squinted my eyes half closed. Was this guy hitting on me? Truthfully, I didn't mind. He was really cute. Normally, I don't let any guy I just met buy me coffee, but maybe it wouldn't hurt to accept his offer. Perhaps he could help me get some information. After all, he was a policeman.

I smiled as I stood. "That's a good idea. I could use a cup of coffee."

I sat at a booth in the nearby restaurant, and he went to the counter, bringing back two cups of coffee and two blueberry muffins.

He placed my coffee and muffin in front of me. "I hope you like muffins. I'm starving, and I didn't want to eat alone."

I took a sip of the hot coffee. "So, what do I call

you? Officer?"

"Officer Joel Adams. Please just call me Joel. And may I ask your name?"

"I'm Danielle Reynolds. And please just call me Dani."

"So, Dani, why is it so important to get information on this case of yours?" He seemed genuinely interested.

I went into some detail telling him about my criminology assignment. Of course, I didn't tell this stranger about my dead grandfather. He most certainly would've left the restaurant immediately, thinking what kind of wacko he had picked up. I tried to express the urgency of finding out information simply from the standpoint of college credit. I talked for several minutes, explaining my situation. "What do you think? Is there any way you could possibly help me?"

He held his coffee mug and looked deeply into the liquid as if he could see his answer in the swirling steam coming off the coffee. "This is weird."

"What's weird? I just asked if you could help me. Why is it so weird?"

"No, no, not that. I didn't mean your request was weird. I thought you might ask me for help. The weird part is I'm *very* familiar with that case."

"What do you mean? You must be about twenty or twenty-five. Why would you be so familiar with it? It happened before you were born."

"I'm twenty-four, and the weird part is my grandfather was a good friend of Bill Cunningham. My father talked about that case many times."

Well, if he'd thrown a pie in my face, I wouldn't have been more surprised. Who would have thought I'd meet someone also connected to this case? And his grandfather!

I looked at him with a blank stare. "You're kidding."

"No, I'm very serious. My grandfather was a deputy with the Orange County Sheriff's Department when the murders occurred. He became sheriff with the death of the then current sheriff."

My mouth was still open as I gawked at this Joel Adams. "Then your grandfather was Scott Adams?"

"How did you know?" He now seemed as surprised as I was. I could see the wheels in his brain definitely moving. "Wait a minute. What did you say your name is?"

"It's Danielle."

"No, what did you say your *last* name is?"

I glared straight into those blue eyes. "It's Reynolds."

"Ah, that's it! You're related to the butcher who killed that family."

I quickly corrected him. "First of all, I'm *not* related to any butcher. I *am* related to Daniel Reynolds, Mr. Cunningham's best friend. He was my grandfather, but he wasn't a butcher, and he didn't kill that family."

He studied my angry face. "Dani, you do realize I know how that crime went down. I've heard about it all my life. The man bludgeoned those parents to death, shot those kids in the head, and committed necrophilia on that old woman."

"Hey, I just met you. I don't plan to argue with you. I also don't want to go into this any further. There are some facts of which the police aren't aware that prove my grandfather is innocent."

He put his elbows on the table and moved closer to

me. "I don't mean to sound condescending, but how can a young college student know more than the entire Orange County Sheriff's Department?"

He was annoying me. "I don't need to explain anything to you. I know something the police didn't know then, and no one is interested now because they already convicted my grandfather without a trial."

With my lips tightly sealed and my chin raised, I leaped out of my seat. "Thanks for the coffee, Officer Adams."

"Wait!" He caught my arm as I passed his bench. "What are you talking about? Please. Sit back down. I'm sorry. I didn't mean to offend you."

I remained standing, looking toward the exit with him holding my wrist.

"Come on; sit down. I'll be civil. Let's talk about something else. Really, I'm sorry."

I hesitated. He *was* cute. Maybe I'll see what happens next. I sat back down.

His peace offering, "So, do you want another cup of coffee?"

"Okay."

"Let's pretend we just sat down in here. Forget our other conversations. So. Dani, where do you go to school? Do you have any brothers or sisters?"

"Valencia College. Believe it or not, I'm majoring in criminal justice." I guess I said that a little sarcastically. "I have a younger brother, Frankie. He's almost thirteen. I live with my dad. My mom died of cancer a couple of years ago. Is there anything else you need to know in your interrogation?"

"I'm not interrogating you. I like you and want to know a little about you."

"How do you know you like me? You don't even know me. I might be the granddaughter of a vicious killer. Maybe I'm just like him."

"Aww, come on, Dani. I'm really sorry. Please, let's not fight the first time we meet."

I looked into my empty cup. "Where's my second cup of coffee?"

He hastily jumped up. "I'll go get it right now."

I chuckled to myself as he walked back to the counter. I guess I shouldn't be too hard on him. The entire country had the same opinion about my grandfather as he did.

He came back with two more cups of coffee. "Friends?"

I smiled. "Friends."

For a while we sipped our drinks in silence. "So what about you? When did you join the police force? Do you have a family? I assume you're not married, or you shouldn't be having coffee with me."

"I'm not married. I've been with the Nawinah Police Department for three years. My dad is also a policeman with the department. I have two sisters, one older and one younger. My younger sister, Sabrina, might have gone to school with you."

Sabrina Adams. That name did sound familiar. "I think she was in my biology class in tenth grade. How is she?"

"She's at Florida State on a lacrosse scholarship and wants to go into sports medicine."

"That's great. I remember she was very athletic. Good for her. What about your other sister?"

"Lindsay is married to a navy guy. They live in Norfolk. She has a little boy Ethan."

We continued the small talk for quite some time. We didn't venture near any discussion about the Cunningham case again.

Eventually, he stood. "I have to get back to the station. I'm on duty in a few minutes. I really enjoyed talking to you. Do you think we could do this again sometime?"

"Yes, I would like that."

"How about if we go to dinner this Friday? I can tell you all I know about the Cunningham case without giving any confidential information. I promise I won't say anything to upset you. I'm so sorry. I really would like to see you again."

I agreed to the dinner date, and we exchanged phone numbers.

Next I went to the library. The source documents on the case had been converted to microfilm, and the microfilm data had been transferred into the library's computer system. I found some additional facts from what I had accessed online. I searched the Orlando newspapers, and I read excerpts on the case in numerous books. For several hours, I continued to read and take extensive notes. The information I accumulated would help me with my class assignment, but I didn't find anything to clear my grandfather. I decided to go home and discuss my findings with Dad.

After dinner Dad and I went over the notes. He read them thoroughly and asked several questions. "I don't have anything else to offer. That's definitely more than I knew. Remember, my dad took off right after the crime, and I never saw him again. There was no opportunity for him to tell me anything different from what those newspapers stated. You don't have much to go on to prove his innocence, do you?"

"That's my quandary. I know he must be innocent. Otherwise, these nightmares and this business with Nadia Celik amount to nothing. Since the nightmares have stopped, and since we know something happened during those séances, I truly believe he didn't commit those crimes."

"Oh, Dani, I agree with you. I just don't know how you can prove it."

Chapter Eleven
Step By Step By Step

Dani

I had another dream that night, not a nightmare, but very vivid. It gave me the answer to what my next step would be.

I was near the familiar, old mansion, anxious but not afraid. I climbed the rickety steps to the porch, looking at my feet so I wouldn't trip on a broken plank. When I reached the top, someone called my name. A man looking very much like my father stood on the porch. He was dressed in a blue uniform with an orange tree embroidered on the pocket.

I was not the least bit afraid. "Are you my father?"

"No."

"Then who are you? You look like my father."

"I'm your grandfather." Sorrow filled his voice.

"Why am I here?"

"You have come to save me." He spoke poignantly.

"How can I do that?"

"You must see for yourself."

"I must see what?" I still didn't understand.

"You must open your eyes and see." He raised his hands and pivoted from side to side.

"I don't know what I'm supposed to see."

"Come. Come." He turned and walked through the dark, open doorway, disappearing inside the old house. I think he expected me to follow him, but then I awakened.

The next morning the dream was still vivid in my mind. Before I joined Dad at breakfast, I knew what I had to do.

I told Dad about the dream. "I wasn't afraid at all, but Grandfather had a sense of urgency about him, as if I needed to save him soon. And he did say *save* to me, whatever that means. I thought a lot about this after I woke up. I have to go to that house."

Dad paused his eating and shook his head. "I've heard that derelicts hang out there. Also, the place must be falling apart after so many years of neglect. It wouldn't be safe."

"I need to do this, Dad. He told me to come. I know that's what he meant."

"Well, you can't go alone. Can it wait until this weekend when I'm off work?" He was concerned for my safety.

"I've got another plan. Let me think about it, and I'll let you know tonight, okay?"

"Okay, but don't try anything foolish today."

As I was leaving, I heard him telephone Grace DeMarco. I assumed he was updating her on my plan, but I think he was calling her on a regular basis lately.

I put my plan into action after work. Officer Joel Adams wanted to make it up to me for the way he reacted when we first met. I decided how he could redeem himself, and I called him before I left the parking lot. His phone rang twice.

"Officer Adams."

"Officer Adams, this is Dani Reynolds. Remember me?"

"Of course, I remember you. How could I forget? I didn't expect a call from you this soon. Are you canceling our dinner date?"

"I'm not canceling it, but I'd like to change it."

"Do you need to make it for some other day?" I heard disappointment in his voice.

"No, I want to do something else instead." I thought he'd be curious.

"What might that be? A party? A movie?"

"No, nothing like that." I teased a bit.

"You have me interested. What do you want to do?"

"I'd rather tell you in person. Is there a time we could meet for coffee again? It won't take long."

We met that afternoon at the restaurant near the police station. Joel was already seated when I arrived. "Can you tell me now what you're planning for Friday? You really have me wondering."

I took a deep breath and began. "I want you to keep an open mind. I don't know you very well, but I have a feeling you might want to do this as much as I. Since I sincerely need somebody's help, I think you're that somebody."

"Okay Dani, get to it."

"First of all, please don't say anything until I finish. It's very important you understand this is not something I've imagined or thought about casually."

"Will you just tell me, *already*?"

"Okay, okay. Remember, silence until I'm finished."

I paused and took another deep breath. "You know

my grandfather was accused of killing the Cunningham family, and your grandfather tried to find and convict him. Even though we're on opposite sides, we both have a genuine interest in finding answers. I'm about to tell you something that you'll find extremely difficult to believe. At first, I too was very skeptical."

"I thought we weren't going to talk about this."

"I changed my mind. Now listen and don't speak."

I told him about the nightmares and the séances. Then I told him of my class assignment. Lastly, I told him about my recent dream of seeing my grandfather at the old house. True to his word, he said nothing while I spoke. His facial expressions must have changed a hundred times during my recitation.

"Now comes my plan for Friday night. You're a policeman, so you've confronted dangerous situations during your career. I don't know if this plan is dangerous, but just on the chance it might be, I'd like to have someone along who's more equipped than I am."

He was still staring at me, not saying a word. I dropped the ball. "I want to go to the Cunningham House, and I want you to come with me."

He said nothing. I should've known. Nobody would believe a wild story like I just told him.

"Uh, wow! You really are serious, aren't you? Wow! Uh, can you give me a minute?"

He arose and walked out the door. I had scared him off. He could at least have said goodbye. I went back to drinking my coffee, trying to decide what to do next. A few minutes later as I was looking down at my cup, someone sat down across from me.

Joel had returned. "I'll do it."

So I hadn't scared him away after all.

It was his turn to explain. "Look, you blew my mind, whether you meant to or not. I still don't know what to think. I do believe you're passionate about this case. I don't know if everything you told me is true. Like you said, we don't know each other very well. You might be some sicko trying to lure me to a deserted location to take advantage of my innocence, or you might be telling me the truth. But you and your story have intrigued me, whether you're a sicko or just a concerned granddaughter. Besides, I definitely want to find out what happened at that house."

"You mean you'll go with me?"

"Yes."

Chapter Twelve
The Reality of a Nightmare

Dani

I told Dad about Joel, and I said he'd accompany me to the Cunningham House. Dad commented, "If he's a policeman, it's probably best for somebody like him to go with you instead of an old man like me."

Time to bring my observation into the open. "Dad, you aren't so old. Just ask *Grace*."

"What do you mean by that, young lady?"

He knew exactly what I meant, but I wanted to tease him. "I know how you call her all the time. I suspect you've also been meeting secretly."

"We haven't been meeting secretly. It's just I haven't had the opportunity to talk to you about her. You've been so busy with your own issues." His face turned serious. "Are you okay with this?"

"I'm happy for you. I know how much you loved Mom, but I also know she'd want you to get on with your life. I like Grace. This is good for both of you."

On Friday, Joel picked me up at seven-thirty for the trip to the Cunningham property. I introduced him to Dad, and they talked briefly while I grabbed my cell phone and wallet.

When we got in his truck, I asked, "So, you know where this place is?"

"Yeah, a couple of guys at work have been there. It's on Lake Gossett. They said the drive leading to the house is overgrown with weeds and small trees. I won't be able to drive the truck to the house. We'll have to walk part of the way."

"I know that."

He turned toward me. "How did you know that?"

"Remember, I told you about all those nightmares. I could probably describe the place better than your buddies."

He kept driving as he stared at the road in front. "Like I said the other day, I'm not sure whether I believe everything you've told me, but I'm doing this with an open mind because I hope to find answers too."

I gazed at his handsome profile. "That's enough for me."

The sun had already set when we started our journey. He took the highway out of town and drove about four or five miles. He then turned onto Milligan Road, a narrow two-lane county road. Roughly every quarter mile, I saw lights in a house back a hundred feet or so from the road. We'd seen only one other vehicle since we'd been on that road. Joel drove for another two and a half miles on Milligan, then he slowed. "A turn-off should be on the right. The guys said we'd see a pair of large, oak trees with a drive between them. There's no road sign. Can you grab the spotlight in the backseat and shine it out the window?"

Finding the flashlight, I rolled down my window and directed the light out the opening. He drove for perhaps another quarter mile.

"There they are!" I squealed.

Joel slowed and turned between the two trees. The

truck maneuvered the wild growth and the ruts in the broken pavement for about a tenth of a mile. Then the brush became too thick to drive through. "We'd better get out and walk. I don't want to ruin my truck. Give me the spotlight."

I handed him the light and exited the truck. Even though Joel was with me, I felt apprehensive. Did we make a mistake coming here? I stood near the door waiting for Joel to get to my side. "Do you mind if I hold your arm?"

With the beam of the spotlight, I saw him smiling. "Not at all."

I hooked my right arm through his left arm as we walked the broken drive. Sharp branches and twigs reached out to scratch our faces. Luckily, our long-sleeved shirts and jeans deterred attacks on our legs and arms.

Finally, we reached the enormous house, surreal in the eerie spotlight beam as it bounced off the rotted wood siding. The November breeze whistled through the neighboring trees, sounding like the cries of a baby. I snuggled closer to Joel as we both stared in awe.

"What do you want to do now?" Joel whispered, as if our nemesis was listening while lurking in the shadows of the nearby brush.

"I guess we should go into the house." I trembled while holding securely onto his arm.

He tightened his arm around me. "Are you sure?"

I needed to get in that house. "Yes."

Joel led us up the warped, front steps, moving cautiously as he tested each step, and we hung onto the precarious railing. The weathered floor boards on the porch were besieged with holes and gaps. Joel instructed, "Stay behind me. I'll try the boards before putting all my weight on them. Then you step in the same places where I step."

The boards creaked as his weight pressed on them. He hesitated with each placement of his feet. Sometimes he had to move to the right or left where it felt more secure. I mimicked his every move. At the entrance, the screen door was unhinged on top with part of the upper half lying on the porch several feet away. The stain and varnish were worn off the wood door, which was closed and missing a doorknob. Several boards were nailed across the entranceway, thwarting our entrance into the house.

"We can't go in this way. We'd need to pull these boards off. As a policeman, I can't do that, whether this house is abandoned or not."

"Okay, let's see if we can find another way inside."

I waited while Joel checked the large windows on the porch. They too were boarded up. Then we descended the stairs and trampled around the house, crushing the high vegetation. As he shone the spotlight over the surface of the huge structure, all the first level windows were boarded up. When we reached the back porch, it too was inaccessible.

I was disappointed. "What can we do now?"

Joel stepped back several feet. "The house is built over a crawlspace. An access to that space should be somewhere. Let's look for an entrance."

We worked our way around the house again and finally found a short, wooden door leading into the crawlspace. Joel opened the door without difficulty and shone the light inside. The space was filled with debris of all kinds—furniture, discarded clothing, empty cardboard and Styrofoam food containers, plastic bags, and other putrid garbage. The offensive odors of mold and decay permeating the cramped space forced me to put my hands over my mouth to avoid upchucking my earlier dinner.

Joel asked, "Can you do this?"

I pulled my T-shirt over my nose and mouth. "I'll be okay."

As Joel shone the light around the space, we saw a small opening above us leading into the house. I spotted a wooden ladder against the wall and held the light while Joel dragged it to the opening. The ladder was about four feet high, but the first step was broken with only a metal rod in its place. After he had it opened and stabilized, he climbed the ladder, heaving his muscular body through the opening. I handed him the light, which he set on the floor inside so it shone in a way not to blind me as I climbed. Joel pulled me upright after my body cleared the hole.

We determined we were in a pantry. One shelf held dusty, broken dishes and small, rusted appliances. The other side held remnants of boxes and packages of food, all askew and lying empty and riddled with holes. Another shelf held a few rusty cans of food with their labels chewed off. Hundreds of cockroaches scattered to hide as the light hit them. The door into the kitchen lay on the floor, looking like it had literally been pulled off its hinges. I had a creepy feeling immediately as I stepped through the doorway. I whispered, "This is where the two oldest children were murdered."

Joel focused the light on the wooden table in the center of the room. "Look. Those bloodstains are permanently embedded in that table and floor."

We left the kitchen and walked a narrow hall toward the back of the house. The door at the end of the hall was open. The single bed was broken, and the other furniture was in disarray. Dark, rust colored stains covered the bedding. I felt such empathy for the grandmother who had lost her life on that very bed. "Oh, that poor woman."

We then found the more expansive, main hall and entered the dining room. Dust and cobwebs hung off the chandelier, and mice dirt scattered about the table. A few chairs were overturned. The china cabinet against the wall held what remained of the fine china. Bug skeletons occupied the few unbroken plates and cups.

Leaving the dining room, we went across the hall to the library. Hundreds of dusty books lined the shelves. A bulky, mahogany desk was positioned in the back of the room. Next to the fireplace rested a weathered and cracked leather chair. A side table next to it held a brittle, yellowed newspaper folded in such a way I saw the date. "Joel, this is the very newspaper from the day of the murders. It's the *Nawinah Chronicle* from October 31, 1971. Isn't that amazing it's still here?"

Joel came forward to look at the newspaper but didn't touch it.

Exiting the library, we entered the living room through the French doors, whose panels were broken with glass scattered on the floor. The wood furniture had intricate scrolls and carvings on the cabriole legs and arms. The deep colors or wide floral designs of the chairs and sofas were extremely faded. The entire end of the main sofa in the middle of the room was stained brown. The patterned carpet near the sofa had also become a deep brown. I touched Joel's arm. "This is where Mary and Bill Cunningham were killed. How very sad." I paused as we exited the French doors.

Joel asked, "Are you okay? Do you want to leave?"

Silent tears flowed from my eyes. "No. We have to do this."

Next, we entered the children's playroom. Except for forty years of dust and dirt, the room looked somewhat normal. Most of the toys were gone, and those that remained were broken or rusted. I picked up one doll from the floor. Her head and arms were spongy. I quickly replaced it back on the floor, wiping the liquidized rubbery flesh from my hands onto my jeans.

We crossed the hall to an enclosed porch. The drapes were hanging unevenly from their rods. Termites had feasted on the rattan furniture, but no signs of foul play were evident.

A spiral staircase ascended from the middle of the front foyer. "I guess we need to go upstairs." I dreaded the thought of what was on that floor but knew I couldn't leave without seeing for myself.

Although the iron was rusted and the wood cracked, the banister was still functional. Joel focused the light ahead of us as we climbed, being careful not to get our shoes caught in the torn carpet.

The first room on the left of the stairs appeared to be the master bedroom. What furnishings remained, though faded, still looked elegant. To persuade myself as well as Joel, I said, "No sign of any violence seems to have occurred in this room."

We looked in the other rooms along the left hall.

They too had been spared of any bloodshed.

In the first room to the right of the stairs the plaid bedspread had a grimy, greasy body print on it, but no blood. The bedroom was feminine but not frilly. "This was probably Betsy Ann's room,"

The room directly across the hall was a boy's room, dusty but also with no disarray or bloodstains. The bedding was dirty, and the blankets and bedspread hung off the side of the bed. Probably this house had been a shelter for many homeless people, but I again saw no evidence of foul play. "I think this was Cletus' room. His body was found in the kitchen." Again, Joel was silent.

In the next room across the hall, blood stained the worn blue chair near the window. Crumpled and yellowed pages from books were strewn about the room. The books once occupying the bookshelves now lay scattered over the dusty, blue carpet. "Daisy was an avid reader. I'm sure this was her room."

The walls of the next room were decorated with loosely hanging, yellowed remnants of posters depicting baseball players. Baseball memorabilia were scattered on the floor. "Oh, this was my dad's friend, Travis's room."

The next room we entered was a little girl's room. Broken dolls were spread on the floor. Blood had changed areas of the shabby, pink carpet to a dark rust. Pieces of shattered miniature china rested on the small child's wooden table permanently stained with blood. "Lily must have been killed at her little table."

One more bedroom was on this side of the house. As we entered, I knew it was the little boy, Silas's room. I couldn't hold back the tears as I envisioned his last hours.

I had enough. We left the house through the crawlspace. I was relieved to get into the open air but also distressed, thinking about what had happened to that poor family. I stood for several minutes breathing in the fresh air with my eyes closed and my head raised to the sky.

My mind was so confused. My grandfather needed me to see the horror in that house, but I still didn't know what he wanted of me. I thought he was innocent, but how was I to prove it? Seeing the inside of the house only made me wonder more what kind of person could possibly inflict so much suffering on another human being. Yet it did nothing to exonerate my grandfather.

Joel put his arm around me as we stood looking out at the darkness. "What do you want to do now?"

"Do you think we can find a place to sit for a while?"

"This house is on a lake. I've got a blanket and some cold sodas in the truck. Let me get them, and we'll pick a spot near the water."

"Great, except I'm going with you to the truck. I'm not staying here by myself."

After retrieving the blanket and sodas, we found an area near the lake under a big, oak tree where the foliage was at a minimum. Joel laid the blanket while I took two sodas from the cooler. We sat on the blanket and leaned against the tree, our thoughts going in their own private directions. Mine were reliving the scenes inside the house and unwillingly imagining where each member of the family was killed. Finally, we both stretched out flat on the blanket and silently looked at the sky through the mesmerizing motion of the leaves. We fell asleep.

I'm not sure how long I had slept when something awakened me. I jerked upright. Joel was still sleeping. I listened intently, but all I heard were the sounds of the night—crickets, the fish jumping in the water, and the rustle of the oak tree in the night breeze.

I got off the blanket, picked up the spotlight, and walked along the shore a few feet before switching on the light. I shone the beam over the lake. The brightness reflected like diamonds as the ripples rose and fell. It was so peaceful. No wonder William Cunningham had built his house near this lake. I walked along the shore a little farther. Shining the light in front of me, I saw a wooden bench and next to it, a galvanized bucket half full of water and small fish. I focused the light around the area and found a path leading away from the wooden bench. The path was clear of weeds and other vegetation. Since I was far from the Cunningham House, I doubted the path led to it. After walking a few more yards, at the end of the path was another house. It wasn't a large house and was fairly normal in structure, but it was also in need of major repairs. Then I remembered reading that two houses were on the Cunningham property. This must be the house of William Cunningham's childhood. No mention had ever been made of any carnage occurring in this house. I climbed the front steps onto the porch and tried the doorknob. It easily opened, and I cautiously walked inside, shining the light all around.

The rooms were dusty, but small and cozy. I had the impossible feeling that somebody lived there. I found clothes scattered throughout a small bedroom and stacks of dishes piled in the kitchen sink. I went to the wall and flicked on the light switch. Nothing. No electricity. Probably vagrants had taken over the place. Nobody was left to care. Although, I should let Joel know. I didn't know whether the police did anything about the homeless living in abandoned houses. I'd tell Joel, and he could take it from there.

I left the house to go back to Joel. As I neared the bench by the lake, I heard a crunching sound off to the side of the path. I stopped and turned the spotlight in that direction. At that moment, out of the brush came this horrid, freakish monster coming toward me.

Chapter Thirteen
Things Aren't Always What They Seem

Dani

At the sight of the monster, I screamed and ran toward Joel, tripping on rocks and tree roots and almost dropping the spotlight. "Help! Joel! Help!" The spotlight focused haphazardly in all directions as I stumbled. Finally, Joel came bounding toward me. I dropped the spotlight and jumped into his arms, clinging tightly and almost knocking him over.

"Hey. Hey. It's okay. It's okay." He held me and rubbed my back.

I gained a little composure. "There's a monster back there. He's coming after me."

"Take it easy. You're safe now." He tried to calm me down. Picking up the spotlight, he led us back to the blanket. I clung to his arm so tightly I probably stopped his circulation. "Let's sit down. You can tell me what happened, and why you ran off on me."

"No. We have to get out of here before he comes back. We have to go *now*."

"Dani, it's okay. I have my weapon. If he comes near, I can shoot him."

I calmed down a little, still sobbing and shaking.

He took my face in his hands and gently turned it toward him. "Tell me what happened."

I told him how I was startled out of a deep sleep by something and walked along the lake because it was so peaceful. I told him about the house near the lake and how on my way back to tell him homeless people lived in it, this hideous monster came after me. "Can we leave now?"

I clung to him like a magnet while we walked to the truck. Every few steps he looked at me with his calming smile. He opened the truck door. As I hoisted myself into the high seat, the monster I had seen earlier crept from the thickets near the back of the truck. I scrambled into the truck so fast I bumped my knee on the dashboard. Joel let loose of the door to grab for his gun. "Hold it right there. Don't come any closer!"

The monster extended both of his arms in front of him, hands facing toward us. He stopped when Joel yelled. Joel was alert but confused. "Who are you? What are you doing here?"

I had turned sideways to observe the creature through the open door. He lowered his arms to his side, still not speaking. I looked intently at him. He wasn't a monster at all—just a weird looking man, well over six feet tall. His matted hair fell several inches beyond his shoulders. His filthy, gray beard reached to the middle of his chest. The scratched and scarred roadmap on his face supported his bulky, beak-like nose. The ragged edges of his pants reached a few inches below his knees, and his gnarled toes protruded from the holes in his shoes with thick, discolored toenails curling into the toes themselves. His shirt sleeves were torn at his boney elbows. The eyes were what frightened me most, being wild, almost maniacal, as if they could stare directly into a person's soul.

When the man didn't respond to Joel, he repeated, "Hey, man, I asked you a question. Who the hell are you? What's the matter? Can't you talk?"

The man simply stood there. Maybe he couldn't talk. He looked between Joel and me with those crazy eyes. We waited for him to do or say *something*. Joel was getting nervous. He started to inch toward the man. "Answer my question."

In a deep, gravelly voice, the man asked, "Which one?"

Joel looked surprised. "Which one *what*?"

Still in that eerie voice, the man enquired, "Which question? You asked me four different questions."

He caught Joel off guard. "Uh, I guess you're right. I did."

I could see Joel slightly lowering his gun and relaxing a bit.

"I guess you can first answer who you are."

The man then looked directly at me with those intense eyes. "I...am William Cunningham."

Chapter Fourteen
Danielle Meets Bill

Dani

I had been staring at that monster of a man standing beside the truck with Joel pointing the gun at him. When he said his name was William Cunningham, I fell off the truck seat, catching myself on the door handle as I stumbled. I looked directly into his intense eyes and said in a very bold voice, "You can't be William Cunningham. You're dead."

"Young lady, I'm dead in many ways, but my body is very much alive. It may be broken and old, but much to my dismay, it is still alive."

As he spoke, the gravelly sound of his voice seemed to disappear. Those eyes that seemed so wild and penetrating now appeared filled with pain and torture. He truly was William Cunningham, the man who supposedly was killed in his home in 1971. That man was standing before me, and I was thoroughly confused.

By this time Joel had lowered his gun, looking back and forth between the man and me. He looked as baffled as I was.

Still staring at him, I asked, "But what happened? Why aren't you dead? No, I don't mean it that way. Everything, the newspapers, the law enforcement agencies, they all said you were dead. I don't understand."

"Miss, can I ask you a question?"

He took me off guard. "Uh, sure?"

"Something is familiar about you. You're not like most of the others who've come here over the years, the thrill seekers, the horror mongers. I can sense you're different. May I ask your name?"

"Danielle Reynolds."

"Ah, I thought so. Daniel Reynolds was my best friend. Was he your uncle, your grandfather?"

"He was my grandfather."

"Poor Daniel. He lost his life because of me. He's one of the many crosses I bear."

"What do you mean?"

"It was I who was supposed to be in the house with my wife, but he and Mary were murdered together." Tears crept down his scarred, dirty cheeks channeling through the grime. "I was supposed to be the one who was killed. Instead, the fiend who murdered my family also killed my best friend. His face was so disfigured the authorities thought I was the victim."

Excited, I turned to Joel. "See, Joel. I told you my grandfather was innocent." I turned back to William Cunningham. "Please, sir, would you tell me what happened that night? I really need to know."

"Child, I sincerely would like to talk to you. I'd also like to know about you and your family, but I'm very tired."

"It doesn't need to be now. Can I come back tomorrow? You don't know how much this means to me."

He was silent for a while, staring at me. "I suppose no harm can come in your returning. Go to the lake house tomorrow afternoon. I know you know how to get there. You know very much about both of my houses. I followed you tonight."

He then turned and walked into the deep woods out of sight.

Joel and I watched as he vanished in the night. When he was gone, still not saying a word, we climbed into the truck. As he turned onto Milligan, he slapped the steering wheel. "How intense was that."

"I can't believe he's alive. Who would've thought he survived? And my grandfather. He is definitely innocent."

Joel glanced over at me as he was driving. "I've got to hand it to you, Dani. You were so sure your grandfather didn't kill that family. I guess you aren't a wacko after all."

I simply looked at him and smiled.

It was after midnight when Joel pulled in front of my house. "I must say I've never spent an evening quite like this in my entire life. I'd like to see you again."

"I thought you were going back with me tomorrow?"

"I can't. I'm on duty."

We arranged to meet the next day after he finished his shift. Before I had a chance to open the truck door, he grabbed my arm, reached over, and kissed me on the cheek. I hesitated, then turned swiftly toward him and lightly kissed him on his lips. I hurried out the door, and when I reached the house, I turned back to smile at him.

Dad was asleep on the couch when I got home. I wanted to let him sleep, but I was so excited about what happened I had to awaken him. I gently shook him.

"Dad, wake up."

Drowsily, he opened his eyes, blankly staring at me.

"I have so much to tell you. I'm going to fix some tea while you become coherent."

He was sitting upright on the couch when I brought the tea. I recounted the entire evening, giving him a few minutes to take in what I had told him. "I need to go back again this afternoon. Will you go with me?"

"Of course, I will. Oh, what a tragedy. I can't imagine what his life has been like."

"I know. That's why I think it's a good idea for you to accompany me. I think he knew me. At least he knew we weren't there to harm him or destroy his property. That's why he came out of the woods. Perhaps he was in my nightmares too, just like grandfather."

Later that morning, Dad and Frankie were drinking coffee when I came into the kitchen. I grabbed a cup and sat with them.

"So did you sleep well?" Dad asked.

"Yes, I did. It was a dreamless, nightmare-less sleep. How about you?"

"Not so well. Our conversation last night made me reminisce about my dad and Mr. Cunningham. I'm so glad we'll be able to prove my father's innocence. I don't know if there's anyone left on this earth who cares, but *I* care."

"Oh, Dad, I care too," I said.

"I care too," said Frankie.

Surprised, I turned to Frankie. "I'm so sorry. I never thought how you might feel. He was your grandfather too."

"It's okay. I know you've been having a rough time lately. You're right, though. I think about Grandpa a lot. I used to wonder if I'd turn into a murderer too. When you were having those bad nightmares, I thought maybe I was the one who caused them because I was like Grandpa."

"Oh, Frankie, you had nothing whatsoever to do with them. And since you know Grandpa wasn't a murderer, you can say you want to be like him. Dad, do you think Frankie can come with us to see Mr. Cunningham?"

"Frankie, do you want to go?"

Frankie's eyes brightened. "Oh yeah!"

We left for the Cunningham property about two o'clock. Since Joel's truck had flattened much of the weeds, Dad's SUV handled the rough drive fairly well. The area didn't look as haunting and unnerving by daylight. We followed the path Joel and I had taken the night before. When we came to the big house, we stopped and stared at its enormity and decay.

"Wow!" Frankie exclaimed. "That's really big and ugly!"

I reminded him, "It wasn't always like that. It used to look like a beautiful, white castle."

"It sure doesn't look like a castle now. It looks like a haunted house."

We walked to the lake and took the path toward the Gunderson House. As we neared the house, we saw Mr. Cunningham sitting on the bench near the lake. "It's Danielle from last night, Mr. Cunningham."

Mr. Cunningham turned his head in our direction and stood. As we drew near, a big smile broke through his craggy face. "Andrew? Is that you?"

"Yes, it's Andrew." Dad hurried toward him.

Mr. Cunningham reached Dad and gave him a big, bear hug. Dad returned the gesture with no thought of Mr. Cunningham's grimy appearance. "Andrew, I can't believe it's you. You look exactly like your dad."

Frankie and I both were taking in this touching scene with tears in our eyes.

Mr. Cunningham ended the embrace. "Come. Let's go into the house where we can sit. Forgive me. I'm not used to visitors, but this visit is important to your family and me. We must talk."

The three of us sat on the tattered couch in the living room. Mr. Cunningham sat on a faded chair across from us. "Andrew, tell me about yourself and your family. This must be your son. He too looks like Daniel."

Proudly, Frankie spoke, "Sir, I'm Frank Andrew Reynolds."

"Well, Frank Andrew Reynolds, I'm very pleased to meet you. May I shake your hand?"

Frankie went across the room and shook his hand. Dad's eyes seemed filled with pride as he watched.

Dad began to tell Mr. Cunningham a brief version of our lives. "At first my mother didn't believe my dad was a murderer. However, soon our money ran out. She assumed he was withdrawing it from their bank accounts. She didn't know what to believe. Do you have any idea what was going on?"

"Please, tell me more. When you're done, I'll explain everything I know."

"You probably remember my mother worked as a secretary for Attorney Matthew Plimpton. She didn't make much money, and it was difficult for her to support us."

Dad then told how he came to own Spencer's Body shop. Then he talked about Mom.

"My wife Michelle got cancer and died a few years ago. She was the daughter of Ben and Lucille Gleason, who owned the pharmacy at Lester and Barnett. They were killed in a plane crash before our children were born. My mom died when Danielle was a baby, so they never knew their grandparents. Frankie is twelve and goes to middle school." Dad looked affectionately at Frankie. "He's a good kid. Danielle, we call her Dani, was named after my dad. I never believed he killed your family. I was proud to name her after him. Dani goes to college part-time, majoring in criminal justice."

Mr. Cunningham acknowledged, "Son, you didn't have an easy life, did you? But I see you have a strong and loving family. I'm proud of you, and I'm sure your father would've been equally proud of the man you've become."

"Sir, I don't want you to relive that tragic event, but can you tell us anything to help us understand what happened to my father?"

Chapter Fifteen
Reliving a Nightmare

Bill

I was very pleased to see Daniel's son and grandchildren. I'd been apprehensive the night before when the young lady asked to come back. However, it was time. Time to find answers for me and for them. I began to tell them what only I knew about my world's worst tragedy.

"There have been many people over the years invading my property, but I frighten most of them away. Some are simply thrill seekers, thinking they're brave, young hellions and wanting the experience of seeing a murder scene. Most of them came in the seventies shortly after the tragedy. Lately, it's just been bums looking for a place to get out of the weather or to partake of their drugs and alcohol. As you can see, I'm not a handsome man. If I'm in the mood, I might even get my shotgun out and shoot into the air. They disappear then.

"A few scoundrels have even entered the house where my family spent their last hours, which is off limits to everyone. I have not entered it since that horrible day after their deaths. Originally, I was upset when you, Danielle, and that young man found the crawlspace entrance. I was there at the time, though you were unaware of my presence. I've learned to be invisible when I choose. However, I noticed something different about you. Thus, I let you enter the house. When you came out, I saw how upset you were. I knew then you were somehow involved in my tragic life.

"I stayed close by while the two of you walked to the lake. I watched as you entered this house, where I now live. When you came out, I was torn whether to approach you. I wanted to find out more about you, but once I came forward, there'd be no turning back. I didn't know if I was ready. But here I am, a man in his late seventies, when would I be ready?

"Years ago after discovering the fate of my family and my best friend, I was so devastated I didn't want to live."

"So how did my grandfather get killed?" asked the boy.

"Well, on Halloween night, after your grandpa and I stayed to help put out a fire in one of my groves, we went back to my house for a couple of drinks. Before we entered the house, my wife Mary said, 'You boys both jump in the shower before you step one foot into my house.' She was a very neat woman.

"We used the outdoor shower and changed into clean uniforms while Mary fixed us drinks and sandwiches. She had taken a new bottle of Jack Daniel's from the liquor cabinet and filled three glasses with whiskey and ice.

"Around ten-thirty, I thought I heard something outside. I decided to check what was causing it. I took my rifle from the gun rack and went to the kitchen for a flashlight. Cletus and Betsy Ann were still eating their Halloween candy. 'Finish your snack and get to bed.

School tomorrow.'

"Finding no source for the noise outside, I started back to the house. Suddenly, I heard the sound again and stopped to listen. That's the last thing I remember."

"So what happened to you?" interrupted Frank.

"Well, I don't know how long I was unconscious. When I awoke I had a terrible headache and every bone and muscle in my body throbbed. I didn't know where I was, but the place was dark, damp, and reeked of decay. In my weakened state, I struggled to escape. I finally gained enough strength to get off the ground and walk around. Eventually, I found a door. When I pushed it opened, I saw my garage several yards in front of me. I had been in the crawlspace of my own house.

"That night the killer must've hit me on the head when I had gone outside to investigate the noise. He also must've kicked or pounded my entire body. I had a couple broken ribs. I believe my skull was fractured or perhaps, a severe concussion. After he beat me, he must've dragged me into the crawlspace, believing I was dead."

I then recounted how I got into the house after awakening in the crawlspace, finding all doors and windows locked and eventually, entering from the crawlspace opening. "I won't describe the horror inside that house. It is much too painful."

Danielle consoled, "Oh, Mr. Cunningham, I can't imagine how horrible it was for you. I was deeply affected when I saw what had happened over forty years ago. But you, your entire family. I am so, so sorry."

I couldn't speak for a while. The memories of the gruesome scenes began to play in my head. When I finally gained my composure, I told them about finding the newspapers.

"After seeing my children's rooms, somehow I got out of the house. The smells, the silence, and the visions of what I had seen were unbearable. I went on the front porch and sat on one of the rockers, crying until I could cry no more. When I lifted my head, I saw three separate packets of newspapers at the bottom of the porch staircase. As I stared at them, I recalled reading the Sunday newspaper the day before and leaving it next to my chair in the library. I calculated that it was then Monday morning. Therefore, I was bewildered as to why three newspapers had been delivered. I retrieved them and took them back to the rocker.

"The first one I grabbed was dated Monday, November 1, 1971. The next one was dated Tuesday, November 2, 1971. But that couldn't be. You can't get a newspaper *before* the date occurs. It had to be a mistake. The third one was dated November 3, 1971. I opened that newspaper to the headline, *NO NEW CLUES IN CUNNINHAM MASSACRE*. Then I knew it was real. My entire family had been murdered."

I had to stop. I was too emotional to go on. The young boy went into my kitchen. When he returned, he handed me a glass of water. "Here, Mr. Cunningham. Drink this. It'll help."

I drank the entire contents. "I'm so sorry. No matter how many years have passed, I can never forget."

Andrew said, "Bill, we understand. You have had so much to deal with. If it's any consolation, we're here for you now."

I wanted to finish explaining to them about Daniel. I took a deep breath. "After the reality sank into my brain, I took the newspapers and made my way to Mom's house, this house, and passed out in my old bedroom. When I awakened that evening, I reread the newspapers. It was then I became aware that Daniel was dead. The police thought my body lay on the floor next to Mary, but it was Daniel. It was Daniel, my best friend. That monster had put me in the crawlspace and made it appear to the investigators that Daniel was I. Oh, what that madman did to him."

I explained my state of mind during the years since the tragedy, barely surviving the first few months, not caring if I lived or died, trying to kill myself several times. I described how I eventually lived off the land, hunting wild animals, eating the wild, edible vegetation or the vegetables from Mary's garden I continued to grow, and fishing in the lake. Not living; just existing. Never seeking out people; never wanting to associate with anyone.

"Days turned into weeks, weeks turned into months, and months turned into years. And I have turned into this ugly, broken old man."

Chapter Sixteen
The Time Is Now

Dani

I couldn't imagine what that poor man had endured. To discover what had happened to his family and his best friend. To live out his years in the way he had. Dad, Frankie, and I were speechless. But I had to know more. "Mr. Cunningham, do you have *any* idea who could've killed your family?"

"No, Danielle, I don't. I've accused every single person I've ever known. I wasn't aware of any enemies capable of such appalling acts. I respected all my workers, and I thought they felt the same about me. As for friends and acquaintances, I don't know anyone who despised me enough to kill my entire family. This was not a random act by some derelict who chose us by chance. This savage knew me personally, somebody very vindictive, or somebody who wanted to hurt me like he imagined I'd hurt him. All my life I've tried to figure out who that person could be."

Dad responded, "At least we definitely know it was *not* my dad."

Frankie presented his idea. "Mr. Cunningham, my sister is studying criminology. Her assignment is to find out more about what happened to your family."

"Frankie, can I explain why it's a class project

before you give him your idea. I don't want Mr. Cunningham thinking the murders of his family were so trivial I'd reduce them to a class assignment."

"Sure, go ahead."

"For several weeks, I'd been having horrible nightmares. I went to a medium to find what was causing them. She determined my grandfather was trying to contact me. In another dream he urged me to come here. I didn't know what I'd find, but I knew I had to obey."

Mr. Cunningham looked astonished. "That's amazing! Almost impossible to believe, but I do believe you."

"Can I tell my idea now?" Frankie asked. "Maybe Mr. Cunningham could write down the names of all the people he knew at the time of the murders. Then Dani can question them to see if they can give her any clues. Lots of them are probably dead, but maybe some of them aren't. Maybe their families might be able to help."

Mr. Cunningham agreed, "Frankie, you have an excellent idea."

I noticed Mr. Cunningham looked fatigued. I think Dad noticed it too. "I'm sure you're getting tired, Bill. We'll leave you to rest and to do the job Frankie suggested."

After saying our goodbyes, we left Mr. Cunningham and arranged to return the next Saturday, giving him a week to make his list.

****

Joel called that evening, and we met for dinner. As I told him about our meeting with Mr. Cunningham, he listened without interrupting.

"Do you think I can go back with you next week if I'm not working?"

"I don't see why not. Mr. Cunningham didn't seem to have an issue with you last night. In fact, he called you a nice young man."

"Hey, he's really a smart man. He knows a good guy when he sees one."

I couldn't help but laugh. "Oh, you are full of it."

We had a great dinner. The steaks were cooked to perfection, and the company was amazing. When he drove me home, he walked me to the door.

I hesitated before entering my house. "Thanks again for dinner."

He grabbed me by my shoulders and pulled me toward him. He gave me the softest, most tender kiss I've ever had, taking my breath away.

He caressed my back as he released me. "Thanks for that great kiss." After he walked to his truck, I stood on the porch and watched him pull away. "I think I could go for that guy."

Locking the door behind me once I entered the house, I looked around. All was dark except for a small lamp by the couch. "Dad, Frankie, anybody home?"

No response.

In the kitchen, I switched on the light. A note was on the counter.

Dani,

I'm out with Grace. I should be back around midnight. Frankie is staying over Dylan Marshall's house tonight. He was excited to talk to his friend about his day. Don't wait up. See you for breakfast.

Dad
****

91

When I got home from work the next day, I wrote my criminology report. With much to write, I had to watch how I phrased it so I wouldn't allude to Mr. Cunningham yet. I wasn't sure what would happen next regarding him.

Joel and I went to dinner Tuesday. I've never had such an easy time talking to a guy before. He seemed to be everything in one package: good looks, good bod, great personality, good job, *and* good listener. Even though I had only known him for a short time, I felt like we were old friends. Perhaps more than friends. Was I ready for that?

Dad and Frankie were in bed once we got back to my house.

"Do you want to come in?"

"Are you sure it's okay with your dad?"

"Well, it's not like I'm going to have sex with you tonight. I'm just going to offer you a soda. I'm sure he's okay with that."

Joel blushed and stuttered, "I didn't mean that."

He stayed about an hour, and we had a couple of sodas. And we kissed. I must say the sex thing crossed my mind when we were passionately kissing, but good girl that I am, I held back from ripping his pants off.

When Joel left, he gave me a long, goodnight kiss. I went upstairs and took a very cold shower.

The next day in criminology class, Dr. Belinsky asked me to stop by his desk after class. Since my reports were so different from everyone else's assignments, did he think I should scrap the Cunningham case and do D.B. Cooper instead?

"Danielle, your accounts on the case are intriguing. I'm amazed at what you've uncovered in such a short time. I'm anxious to see your next installment. Keep up the good work."

I was shocked! And I thought I was in trouble.

I invited Joel to dinner Friday night to discuss the plans for Saturday. Dad also invited Grace. Dad made his delicious lasagna. I swear he should've been a chef instead of an auto mechanic. We went into the living room after dinner for cake and coffee.

"Tomorrow we should take some food to Mr. Cunningham," Frankie suggested. "We can also fill a cooler with some cold drinks."

We made a few more plans, then Frankie went to his room to play computer games. Joel and I went on the back patio and left Dad and Grace in the living room.

As we sat on the outdoor loveseat, I shivered from the chilly air. Joel removed his jacket and positioned it around my shoulders. At first, we talked about Saturday, enjoying the cool, night air and each other's company.

Joel turned to me and broke the silence. "Dani, you'll probably think I'm an idiot, but I've never felt the way I do about any other girl like I do about you. I think I'm falling in love with you."

I looked straight into those big, blue eyes. "If you're an idiot, then I am too."

I put my arms around his neck and pulled his lips to mine. Our kisses were getting a little too passionate. I was thankful I heard Grace's car pull out of the driveway before I did something I might regret.

Chapter Seventeen
The Investigation Begins

Dani

Frankie and I went to the grocery store Saturday morning to buy soda, snacks, paper goods, and ice. Grabbing cookies and donuts from the bakery, I wanted Mr. Cunningham to experience a real treat. Joel arrived fifteen minutes early and helped us load the car. I also took a pen and a large note pad. We stopped at a restaurant on our way to pick up fried chicken.

Dad parked his SUV on the Cunningham property, and everyone helped carry the goodies to the Gunderson House. Mr. Cunningham was sitting on the bench near the lake when we arrived. He took the chicken from Frankie. "Son, this smells delicious!"

Frankie agreed, "It's my favorite chicken."

"I bet it'll be mine too."

We spread two tarps on the ground and put the food, paper goods, and utensils on one. We filled our plates with food, took a drink from the cooler, and found a seat.

Mr. Cunningham finished a chicken leg. "Oh, my, this food is delightful. It's been a long time since I've had anything like this. Thank you very much."

The leftovers were taken to the kitchen for Mr. Cunningham's future meals. Then we settled in the living room for our discussion. Mr. Cunningham began by reading his long list of names.

"*My acquaintances and friends*: Some of these people were also members of the Nawinah Presbyterian Church, but I've listed them separately because they were either in the Men's Club, a good friend, or had a special connection to the community.

"*Church members:*" These are church members who I only knew casually."

Between his friends, acquaintances, and church members, he rattled off a list of one-hundred-three names! I know because I counted them afterwards. I couldn't believe it. How could he remember all those people? Not only did he remember their names, but he also remembered what they did for a living. This man was amazing. And he wasn't done yet.

Mr. Cunningham paused after reading the first few portions of his list. "Now I'll read the employees of Gunderson Ltd."

If I was surprised with his memory of friends, church members, and acquaintances, he blew me away when he told us about the Gunderson employees. Not only did he list his professional staff, but he mentioned every office, maintenance, and warehouse worker. Then he surprised me further by giving us the names of all his orange pickers and foremen. This man's memory was uncanny! Another hundred names.

"This last list contains those who worked for the sheriff's department." And he spouted off another nine names.

When Mr. Cunningham finished reading all the names, he laid the papers on the end table and took a big gulp of his soda.

I was stunned. "Sir, how did you remember all those names and so much about them?"

Frankie also commented, "You are really a smart man."

Mr. Cunningham took several more swallows of the soda. "No, Frankie, I'm not a smart man. I've just had years to think. I've gone over every one of these names, trying to figure out who'd want to harm me and my family, and I've been unable to come up with anybody."

I wanted to give him some hope. "You have help now. I'm not sure how yet, but we're going to find out who killed your family."

"I know you have good intentions, but it's been so long. I suspect more than half of those people are deceased. Many of them have perhaps moved from the area. You're taking on an insurmountable task."

Joel also wanted to convince him. "We have more resources than in the seventies. With more people working to find answers and more ways to find them, I'm confident we'll be successful."

Dad looked at his watch, then stood. "I think we've worn out Mr. Cunningham. Bill, do you mind if we come back next Saturday?"

"I'd be delighted."

I took the name list from Mr. Cunningham. We said our goodbyes and walked back to the SUV.

****

We invited Joel to the next Saturday dinner to bring our ideas and plans together and determine our next step. Dad also invited Grace. After dinner, we gathered in the living room.

Joel offered his suggestions. "I'm friends with a

detective on the force. I'll check with him to see if he can access the evidence removed from the crime scene. They didn't have the technology in the seventies to do DNA profiling. If we get the case reopened, we can have the samples tested to see if a match can be found in the National DNA Database. Perhaps fingerprints were found that might exonerate Dan Reynolds *and* William Cunningham. Fingerprints are kept on file forever. I'll get in touch with my buddy tomorrow."

Dad added, "We'll be busy the entire week with Mr. Cunningham's list, determining who is still alive and what knowledge or connection they might have."

Grace questioned, "Won't it be difficult investigating with everyone thinking Mr. Cunningham is dead? The more we dig into any clues or evidence, the more questions will be asked by the authorities *and* those who we approach. If Mr. Cunningham doesn't come forward, what reason can we give for an extensive investigation?"

"What about Dani's class project?" Frankie suggested.

Grace shook her head. "That's not a good enough reason. We need to do more digging than what a class project would require. Getting the police involved makes it essential for Bill to come forward."

"I'm sure I can look at the collected evidence, but if I want to check into any fingerprints or DNA, I'll need a reason," added Joel.

"So, do we need to persuade him out of hibernation to tell his story?" asked Dad.

Grace expressed her concern. "I'm worried about his ability to accept the magnitude of changes in the world enough to meld into mainstream society."

Dad stated what worried him. "What about the impending media coverage with the opening of the case? How will that affect Bill?"

However, everyone agreed his coming forward was imperative to finding the murderer.

I divided the name list between Dad, Grace, and me. I took the page consisting of Mr. Cunningham's friends and acquaintances. Grace received the church members. Dad took the Gunderson Grove employees and the sheriff's department. During the week, we looked online and in the local phone books for addresses and phone numbers. Sometimes we went to an address to see if that person still lived there. It took hours of hard work. When we got together with Joel, we came up with a few possible suspects. We decided to leave all the names on the list but highlight who we wanted to further investigate if nothing materializes from other research to exonerate them.

I told Dad and Grace of my priorities. "Mitch Ramsey, Mrs. Ida Mae Cunningham's foreman when she ran Gunderson Groves, was fired because he was stealing from the company. Dave and Amy Patterson owned the competitive orange groves. Charles Taggart was Mr. Cunningham's financial advisor. We should highlight him because he knew so much about Mr. Cunningham's financial matters. I got a strange feeling when talking to Greg Shuster, owner of the company which built some of the outbuildings for Mr. Cunningham. He seemed envious of Mr. Cunningham.

"That's it for me. Who's next?"

Grace began on her list. "Clarence Billings, an accountant, who sometimes worked with Art Stafford, Mr. Cunningham's accountant, should be considered.

Arnold Phillips was the foreman for Patterson Orange Grove. My last one is Lora Parsons, a counselor at the high school who seemed to know so much about the Cunningham children. None of them was old enough to attend the high school, so her interest seems unusual."

Grace looked up from her list. "That's all I have."

Dad was next. "I believe everyone who worked for Gunderson Groves should be highlighted. Mr. Cunningham claims he had no disgruntled employees, but do you think if they were, they'd admit it? I've singled out a few of them as being more important than others. Art Stafford was Bill's business and personal accountant. Bobby Cooper was the accounting assistant. With my dad gone, Waylon Smitt was appointed chief foreman. As for the warehouse and maintenance workers and the orange pickers, we might look the closest at the foremen. If I were just a picker, I wouldn't want to kill my meal ticket. Cunningham paid good wages, and the work was steady.

"Next, the sheriff's department. I couldn't find anything at all on Chief Deputy Edgar Fitzsimmons. When I called the sheriff's department, they looked through their records and said he quit the department in April 1972. Mr. Cunningham said he was from Alabama. I thought he went back there but couldn't find anything about him. Trudy Prout was the desk clerk at the sheriff's department. She had a boyfriend named Horace McIntire. I couldn't find anything on Prout. Maybe she lives with McIntire. I wasn't able to reach him. I'll try again this week.

Dad folded up his list and sat down. "That's it for me."

Joel then informed us about his progress. "My

friend, Detective Sean Sullivan, got permission to look at the evidence collected at the crime scene. Surprisingly, he found several boxes fairly well preserved. Clothing, bedding, toys, knives, drinking glasses, pieces of carpet, and so many other items. Sean and I went through it all, even the horrible crime scene photos. We looked through everything but didn't find anything to determine the killer. Sean told me he'd put the fingerprints in the national database to see if a match can be found. As for DNA profiling, it might be possible to extract samples from the stains on some of the items. However, until the case is reopened, the profiling can't be done, which is another reason to convince Cunningham to go public. Otherwise, I don't think we can present enough to the captain to justify reopening it."

Chapter Eighteen
Expect the Unexpected

Dani

On our next trip to the Cunningham property, we recapped to Mr. Cunningham what we had discussed the night before. Although I was disappointed at how little information we'd learned about the names on his list, he was impressed with our accomplishments. He was saddened by the death of so many of his friends. "I have no opinion regarding who should be at the top of the list. I'll leave that decision in your hands and at your discretion."

We decided Dad should approach him about coming into mainstream society. "Bill, we discussed something we think will help considerably in finding answers. We'd like you to think seriously about it before you respond."

Mr. Cunningham came to attention, squinting. "What is it, Andrew?"

"In order to have the case reopened, we must give a reason to do so. Thus far, we were unable to find any new evidence beyond what had originally been accumulated. We feel if law enforcement knew you survived and my father was killed, they'd be forced to reopen the case."

Mr. Cunningham stared out at the lake.

Joel decided to help Dad by revealing the technical aspects. "If the case is reopened, we can get the DNA on the evidence reviewed. There's a big possibility we might find a match."

Mr. Cunningham wrinkled his already lined forehead. "What is DNA?"

"It's a very powerful tool in solving crimes. DNA collected from a crime scene can either link a suspect to the evidence or even eliminate an innocent person. It can be collected from virtually anything, such as cigarette butts, postage stamps, or hair strands. When I viewed the evidence collected from your house, many samples were taken. Sometimes DNA can be found on evidence decades old. If we can get the case reopened, we can have those items checked."

Mr. Cunningham was silent for a while. "You have given me some very compelling reasons, young man. At my age, I don't know if I can take the strain of what society requires. Yes, I'd like to find that fiend who murdered my family, but after hearing how many of my friends have died, who's to say he hasn't died also? God would be punishing him now." He put his head down covering his face with his hands.

No one spoke, trying to decide how to convince him to come forward.

Suddenly, Frankie walked over to Mr. Cunningham, gently put his hand on Mr. Cunningham's bended shoulder. "Sir, what about my grandpa?"

Mr. Cunningham withdrew his hands from his face and took Frankie's hand. "Ah, son, your grandfather." He held Frankie's hand and looked into his eyes. "You're right. What about your grandfather?"

Then he spoke enthusiastically, "He was my best

friend, and he didn't deserve to die in my place or to be accused of these murders. Something needs to be done to clear his name whether the real villain is dead or not."

He dropped Frankie's hand and grasped the chair arm to stand. "I'll do it. I'll come forward."

We all punched our fists in the air, shouting, "Yes!"

When we quieted down, Dad said, "The first thing, even before Mr. Cunningham goes public, is to get an attorney. This situation is way beyond our legal expertise. Sir, Matthew Plimpton's son Douglas is still with the Plimpton law firm. Should we contact him?"

"Oh, yes. A few years before the tragedy, I had met with both Matt and Doug to discuss my financial situation. Mary and I made new wills, making Matt the executor should we precede him in death. With an additional backup, we designated Doug as executor in case Matt preceded him in death. So Doug would definitely be the one to talk to."

We left Mr. Cunningham to ponder his decision and prepare for his public disclosure.

****

Dad made an appointment with Doug Plimpton for the following Wednesday. We all rearranged our schedules to attend. Plimpton's office was a large, white, historic house tastefully converted into an office building. Dad pulled into the driveway and parked against some shaded, leafy trees. The five of us filed out of the SUV and entered the reception area. Dad signed us in while we took available seats on the plush blue and green furniture. Ten minutes later, the receptionist opened the glass door and asked those with

Mr. Reynolds to follow her to the conference room. "Please take any seats. Mr. Plimpton will be with you shortly."

We sat in the posh, navy leather chairs pushed against a polished conference table. A carafe of steaming coffee sat on a credenza at one end of the room. Glasses filled with ice water rested on coasters at each seat. We had left the seat at the head of the table for Mr. Plimpton. Within a few minutes, he sauntered into the room, carrying several file folders. A tall, stocky, balding man with a white, trimmed beard and mustache and wearing a very expensive navy suit, he set his files on the table near his seat.

Dad and Joel, who were sitting on opposite sides, stood while Mr. Plimpton was putting his papers in order. Dad extended his hand. "Good afternoon, Mr. Plimpton, I'm Andrew Reynolds."

Mr. Plimpton grabbed Dad's hand. "Pleased to meet you, Andrew. By chance are you related to the late Anna Reynolds? She was my father's secretary years ago."

"She was my mother."

"Small world. She was a very good worker."

"May I introduce my associates?" Dad introduced each of us. Joel was wearing his police uniform. Mr. Plimpton observed him but made no comment.

After the introductions, Mr. Plimpton quizzed, "Frankly, I have no idea what this meeting is about. My secretary said you had set up an urgent appointment to include several interested parties. She was told it concerned William Cunningham and his family. Am I correct?"

'That's correct," said Dad. "We didn't want to go

into any detail with her, since this is a sensitive matter." Dad hesitated, looking around at us before proceeding. "We have reason to believe Daniel Reynolds, my father, was not the man who murdered the Cunningham family. We'd like to have the case reopened and need some legal advice."

Dad gestured toward Joel. "Joel's grandfather was one of the deputies who worked on the case, so he too has a vested interest. Since your firm dealt with the Cunningham legal matters, I'm sure you heard all the rhetoric about why my father was guilty. However, we have proof he had nothing to do with those murders."

Mr. Plimpton pursed his lips and wrinkled his forehead. "It's been a while, but if I remember correctly, Dan Reynolds cleaned out the family bank accounts and was never seen in the area again. The consensus at the time was he committed the crimes. What do you have to disprove this?"

Dad looked Mr. Plimpton directly in the eye. "Daniel Reynolds was also killed in that house that fateful night."

While leaning back on his leather chair with hands clasped in front of him, Mr. Plimpton stared at Dad. He abruptly came forward and sat upright. "That's preposterous! Only one man's body was found at the crime scene—that of William Cunningham. You're wasting my time." He got out of his chair and collected his folders.

"Please sit down, Doug," Dad pleaded. "As I said, we have proof."

Mr. Plimpton stood with his folders in his arms. "What proof could you possibly have? One man's body was found in that house, and you're saying after all this time you have proof your father was also killed there?"

"It's true only one male body was found, and that body was my father."

"Don't be ridiculous. Bill Cunningham was killed alongside his wife. I've heard enough." He walked toward the door.

Before Mr. Plimpton opened the door, Dad raised his voice. "Bill Cunningham is still alive."

Mr. Plimpton stopped, his hand on the doorknob, and turned his head sideways. "What did you say?"

"I said Bill Cunningham is still alive."

He removed his hand from the doorknob, returned to his seat, put the folders on the table, and plopped in his chair, staring at Dad.

Dad took a long drink of the ice water. "Bill Cunningham is still alive and has been living on his property since the murders being seen only by vagrants and trespassers until now. He's an old and broken man, but very much alive."

"And how do you know about this miraculous resurrection?"

"Dani, why don't you tell Mr. Plimpton about this?"

I summarized my experiences to Mr. Plimpton, leaving out the nightmares and the séances. "Mr. Cunningham has agreed to come forward and do what he can to correct this injustice. We'll see him on Saturday to update him on what we've done regarding the case. We want to tell him what you consider to be in his best interest."

Mr. Plimpton leaned back on his chair again. His eyes wandered over each of us. "Young lady, you have told an incredible story. I'd think you were all psychos.

However, since a psychiatrist *and* a policeman are present, maybe you *are* telling the truth. To think all these years we thought Bill was dead. You've shocked me more than I've ever been shocked before. This is, however, very unique, something with no precedent. I need to examine this carefully and not make any rash decisions. Before we decide on anything, I'll review my files on the Cunningham family. I advise you to do as you've been doing. See Mr. Cunningham on Saturday and return next week for a longer appointment. Please be sure to include him. Do not let anyone else know he's alive. This will end up being a sensationalized case. The national press will have a field day."

Dad responded, "We plan to keep him at our house to acclimate him. We don't want to bring him forward until he's ready to handle the huge change."

Mr. Plimpton arose from his chair again. "This has definitely been an hour beyond belief. I'll be much more prepared since the initial shock is over. Forgive me if I appeared rude. Please stop by the receptionist's desk and set up a two-hour appointment."

We scheduled the appointment for a week from Wednesday, hoping Mr. Cunningham would be able to join us.

Joel and Grace came over Friday night. Joel told us about the fingerprint investigation.

"After the murders, the fingerprints of each member of the Cunningham family were taken on the cadavers in the coroner's lab. From the living room, the three cocktail glasses all had Mary's prints on them. Also, one glass had prints the authorities thought were Bill Cunningham's, since those on that particular glass matched the ones of the male corpse. The authorities

107

also assumed your grandfather was nowhere around to voluntarily submit his fingerprints. Thus, the third glass had prints suspected to belong to him."

Grace interjected, "It sounds like this monster did a great deal of planning before committing his violence."

Then Joel told us some encouraging news. "The third glass having your grandfather's fingerprints on it also contained a partial print at the very bottom which did not match any of the family members or your grandfather. Sean and I think the authorities discounted it because not enough was available to isolate a particular individual. Modern technology might be able to identify it.

"The prints on the empty Jack Daniel's bottle presented another oddity. Mary had poured the liquor from this bottle. However, all fingerprints were wiped clean. We figure the killer didn't wipe off the glasses on purpose. He must've held that one glass in a weird way intentionally leaving any other prints still undamaged, yet not showing his own print in its entirety. He probably planned all along to implicate your grandfather as the murderer."

Chapter Nineteen
Nobody Said It Would Be Easy

Dani

Dad, Frankie, and I took sandwiches to Mr. Cunningham after mass on Sunday. We sat on the front porch enjoying our lunch. Dad told him of our meeting with Mr. Plimpton and how we had scheduled another appointment for next week. He then brought up the issue of Mr. Cunningham leaving his property. "This is entirely up to you, but we'd like you to stay at our house so we can help you understand all the crazy things going on in the world. Lifestyles have changed drastically; sometimes for the better; sometimes not. We've a modest home, nothing fancy, but I think you'll be comfortable. We feel like you're family and would be honored if you'd accept our invitation. As far as when this should occur, we don't want to pressure you. However, if you come forward sooner rather than later, we have more time to find the bastard."

Mr. Cunningham leaned back on his chair. "I realize this change is necessary. You've given me the impetus to make it. I want this monster punished more than anyone. Of course, I'm fearful of the world out there. I'm an old man. It'll be difficult to grasp new concepts and new ideas. Until Danielle came on my property, I had resigned myself to a life of solitude, but the deaths of my family wouldn't allow me to be at peace. And if I'm ever to have solace in what remains of my life, no matter what the inconvenience, I need to make this change."

Mr. Cunningham stopped speaking and closed his eyes. He seemed to be considering the turmoil about to upset his current, quiet lifestyle.

Frankie softly uttered, "I'll help you learn how to use the computer, and there's lots of cool shows on TV we can watch."

Mr. Cunningham smiled, but tears misted his eyes. "I'd like that very much, Frankie." He then addressed all of us. "I'll be ready next Saturday. I have some planning to do first. I'm going back into the house for one last time to collect anything I want to save."

"Would you like us to go in with you?" I asked.

"No, I need to do this myself. I need to say goodbye."

We left shortly after Mr. Cunningham made his decision. A very emotional week was ahead for him. His entire life was about to change—again.

That night I sat on the back patio thinking about Mr. Cunningham. Relaxing on the swing, I gently moved it back and forth. I closed my eyes and rested my head on the back cushion. I must've dozed off, for I heard children playing and water splashing. My eyes remained closed, but I saw kids in our backyard pool throwing a big, red ball to two men in the pool with them. One of the men looked like Dad. I got out of the swing to ask him why he was in the pool with those kids when I heard a woman's voice. Then someone called my name. "Dani?"

I opened my eyes to see Grace and Dad standing

over me. Dad apologized, "Oh, I'm sorry. I didn't know you were out here. It's such a nice evening, we were going to enjoy it for a while."

Groggily, I sat straight. "Oh, I must've fallen asleep. Dad, I had a weird dream. You and some other man were swimming in our pool with a bunch of kids playing ball. I haven't had these weird dreams in a while."

Dad had an odd look on his face. "Strange, when I was a kid my dad would take me swimming with Mr. Cunningham and his children. We'd toss around this big, red ball."

Chapter Twenty
Preparations

Bill

After the Reynolds family left, I hardly noticed their absence. I must have sat on the porch for several hours, contemplating what lay ahead and what was in the past. How could I have allowed my family's murderer to enjoy his life all these years without any consequences for his appalling actions? I could've found him and killed him with my bare hands. He left me behind to find justice for my family. To search him out. To see that he paid. I was a fool for waiting all these years. Yes, originally, I was sick physically and mentally. Then I simply had no desire to live. I was a zombie, not knowing if I ate or drank, if I was dead or alive. Then when my brain finally accepted the tragedy, I tried unsuccessfully to kill myself several times. Was I supposed to stay alive for some reason, perhaps predestined to find this maniac? Then why did it take me so long?

I walked to the lake to cleanse my mind. I slowly waded into the cool water until it was up to my waist, then my neck, and then I was totally submerged. Should I stand underwater until my lungs could not escape the murky liquid? Should I end it now in defeat? No! I swiftly jumped up, spraying and splashing as my body broke through the water's surface. I rapidly swam back to shore. I was ready to live again.

For the remainder of the day, I went through the Gunderson House, checking for anything I wanted to keep and placing it in my bedroom. One of the things I found in Mom's closet was her heavy, black metal strongbox. Mom and Dad's important records were kept in it. The key was in Mom's bedroom bureau in the Cunningham House under the fake bottom of her dainties' drawer. I placed the strongbox in my bedroom. Night was approaching, and I was tired. I postponed any further search of the Gunderson House until morning.

The next day, I pulled down the attic stairs in the hallway. Mom had a set of luggage stored there, hopefully in useable condition to hold the meager belongings I planned to take. As I peeked my head above the floor level, shining my lantern around the space, I had both feelings of nostalgia and deja vu. Climbing onto the attic floor and disturbing the thick layer of dust covering the mementos and keepsakes, I remembered the joy in my discarded toys—metal die-cast cars, rusted tin soldiers, worn baseballs, gloves, and bats. My white stallion rocking horse Dad had made. My cradle, also made by Dad. My children had used it as babies too. We were planning to use it for the child Mary carried in her womb.

Looking through the large canvas and metal trunk in the corner of the attic, I found Mom's wedding dress, carefully wrapped in blue tissue paper. Mary had it altered to wear on our wedding day. Betsy Ann had expressed a desire to wear it for her wedding. I'd never be able to walk her down the aisle.

113

In the corner of the attic was Mom's luggage set. I carried each piece down the steep steps, setting them in the corner of the bedroom next to the strongbox.

The next morning, I was not ready to go into the Cunningham House. I started the day by scavenging the woods for some breakfast berries and oranges from the nearby grove. Then I retrieved the luggage to soak in the lake.

Years ago, I had learned to make my own soap. It took me several attempts to get the correct proportion of potash lye and fat, but I had plenty of time to experiment. Since the soap mixture was soft, I kept it in a rain barrel and would ladle it out as needed to bathe or wash my clothes. It probably wasn't until a year or so after the horrid incident I even considered bathing or changing clothes let alone washing them.

I took a scoop of soap from the rain barrel to the lake to scrub the luggage of their dirt, dust, and bugs. Then I placed them fully opened in the hot sun to dry.

My agricultural education in college had helped me tremendously the past forty years. I recalled all the methods of survival available primarily with what nature provided. From the surrounding area, I learned to distinguish the edible wild grains and flowers from those not for human consumption.

I also learned to do without many things during my exile. After my electricity was turned off for lack of payment, I didn't use any form of light. Darkness simply didn't matter. Eventually, I made my own candles with tallow from the fat of the boars I slaughtered. Truthfully, having to live exclusively off my environment helped keep my mind from exploding from the loss of my family.

I took a walk along the banks of the lake: thinking, planning, and reminiscing. After the walk, I had a nap and awakened when the sun was setting. All I had eaten was the fruit at breakfast. I quickly caught a fish and made flat bread. By then, the sounds of the night surrounded me as I sat on the porch. I thought I heard someone calling my name. I leaned forward, cocking my ear toward the sound. Quiet. Alert now, I kept listening. Then I heard it again.

"Mr. Cunningham? It's Frankie and Dani." Carrying a flashlight and coming down the path were the Reynolds children.

"I'm on the porch," I shouted. "I didn't expect to see you this evening. Is something wrong?"

Danielle said, "No, Frankie was worried about you. He bugged Dad and me since Sunday, telling us somebody should be with you this week. Finally, we got tired of hearing him. He says he wants to stay with you and help you prepare for Saturday."

Frankie's face looked concerned. This young man was growing very dear to me. I was a perfect stranger to him until a few weeks ago. Now he had become a very large factor in giving me back my reason to live.

Danielle looked back and forth between Frankie and me. "I told him you wanted to be alone, but he doesn't believe you."

I gazed at Frankie the entire time Danielle explained. Frankie also watched me. How could such a young man of only twelve be so astute, so in tune with the feelings of an old man?

"Nobody should go through that house alone, Mr. Cunningham," Frankie insisted. "Since you haven't been in it for a long time, who knows how you'll feel?

If you don't want me in there, I'll wait outside."

I was touched. This family had taken me under their wings. It wasn't only to find out what happened to their grandfather. They were genuinely concerned about me. "Frankie, these past few days I've been preparing, but also fretting going into the house. I'm glad you're here."

After Danielle left, Frankie said, "I brought my sleeping bag and stuff to last until Saturday. And I also brought a cooler filled with foods.

"Well, there's plenty of food in the area that we can find."

We sat on the porch talking for several hours, getting to know each other quite well. We talked about how I had survived over the years alone on the property. He talked about his friends and family. He confided about his mother. "Just because I was only two when she died doesn't mean I don't miss her."

"I completely understand, son."

Finally, around midnight, I helped him carry his things into Mom's room. I set a candle on the side table while Frankie took off his shoes, laid his sleeping bag on the bed, and climbed into it.

The next morning, I was up around six and put a pot of sassafras tea on the fire. I was drinking a cup when Frankie joined me on the porch. "Did you sleep well, son?"

"Yes. I was surprised I fell asleep right away and didn't wake up until just now. I thought for sure I'd be awake all night."

"Would you like a cup of tea?"

He wrinkled his nose. "Uh, what kind of tea is it? It smells different."

"It's sassafras tea. It's made from the bark or root of the sassafras tree. Actually, that type of flavoring is found in root beer soda. It'll taste like hot root beer without the fizz. Would you like to try it?"

"I guess so."

I filled another mug with the tea, returning and handing it to him. He sipped and smiled. "This tastes pretty good."

"It's a good substitute for coffee, which I ran out of years ago."

As we sat on the porch, drinking our tea, I asked Frankie, "Is today Wednesday?"

"No. This is Tuesday."

I thought for a moment, counting in my head. "Then we have four days until your dad and sister come for us."

"Yes. They'll pick us up on Saturday."

Frankie was quiet for several minutes. "Mr. Cunningham, can I ask you a question?" Then he quickly added, "You can say no if you want. I won't feel bad."

"You can ask me anything."

"Uh, instead of me always calling you *Mr. Cunningham*, can I call you," he paused and looked down into his cup of tea. Then he turned to me. "*Grandpa*?"

It had been a long time since I had felt such warmth in my heart. This young lad wanted me to be his grandfather. I was speechless. Frankie looked at me, not realizing he had woven himself permanently into my life. I put my tea down and grabbed his free hand. "Frankie, I would be so proud if you'd call me grandpa."

After our tea and my blubbering emotions, it was time to rummage for food. "So what did you bring for our breakfast this morning?"

"I brought syrup packets and waffles."

"And I have some dried jerky."

We went into the woods and gathered berries and oranges. I rekindled the fire, and Frankie cooked the waffles on the rack. Then we grabbed our plates, ladled on our food, and strode to the porch to enjoy our meal.

We both ate voraciously. Because of the boy with whom I was sharing the meal, it was the best one I had eaten since my last meal with my family. When I cleaned every crumb, every dribble from my plate, I sat back contentedly, watching Frankie finish his food. When his plate was empty, he set his plate down. "Grandpa, this breakfast was the best I've ever had."

I was too proud to say anything. Smiling, I reached out and patted his knee.

After we cleared everything away, we discussed our plans for the week. "Wednesday we'll go into the Cunningham House. Thursday and Friday, I can focus on my departure."

I gave Frankie a tour of the property. We walked into the garden as I explained how I kept it going each year. We went into the woods, and I pointed out my other food sources. At the sassafras trees and the twisted trunks of the eucalyptus trees, Frankie put his nose to the trunks to smell their aromatic scent. Then, as we stood motionless in the tree stand I had built for hunting, we watched a deer and several rabbits scamper by.

Back at the house, we ate the ham sandwiches Andrew had packed and some of the berries we had picked. Contented after our meal, we sat on the porch and had another long and interesting conversation. Frankie told me about his school, his favorite subjects, and what he enjoyed doing in his free time.

"How are your grades?"

"I mostly get A's and B's. I don't fool around in class, and I always do my homework. Like with American history and social studies, if the teacher asks me what I read, I'm good at that. But if she asks me what somebody was thinking or why he did something, how am I supposed to know what goes on in somebody else's mind? I don't even know why I do some of the stuff I do."

I chuckled at his comparison. He was right—if we only knew why people do what they do. However, if I knew *why* the bastard brutally killed my family, I still wouldn't feel any less vindictive. I didn't say this to Frankie. Instead I said, "Well, Frankie, sometimes I feel the same way."

We spent the rest of the day making soap and candles. Then we went fishing to catch our dinner. Frankie was a natural. I showed him how to clean and prepare the bass he caught. We also gathered some potatoes, okra, and tomatoes from the garden. He washed and peeled the vegetables while I cut them and placed them in a pot over the fire. I had run out of matches and lighters many years ago. I showed Frankie how to use the flint to start the fire. When the food was done, we placed the meal on our plates and sat on the porch to enjoy our labors.

After dinner, I made wild blueberry tea, and we watched the sun vanish into the lake. Frankie was so fascinated with how I had survived over the years I had to go into great detail on many of my experiences.

In a moment of quiet after I had told him a story about running from a crazy, wild boar, he asked, "So are you going into the house tomorrow?"

"Yes."

Frankie put his hand on my knee. "I know it'll be hard, but you're a strong man. Look how you've lived your life. And you're smart too. How many men can say they can do the things you've done? And when you remembered all those names of the people you knew. I thought that was just so cool."

"I do have a good memory. The things I know for survival are things I learned in college."

"Did you get good grades?"

"Yes, I did. I was a very good student. My mind took in knowledge like a sponge takes in water. One thing about my mind that's different from a sponge is it has never dried out. Knowledge always enters it, and what I've learned I rarely forget."

"I wish my mind was like that. Sometimes what I learn on Friday, I forget by Monday. I guess I don't have a sponge for a brain."

He made me smile. "Your mind is just fine. One unique thing you have for a boy your age is your heart. You have such compassion and empathy for others not usually seen by most adults."

"I thought everybody cared about other people."

"Many do care, but many people are so selfish they only think of what is best for themselves no matter how it affects other people. I see in you an innate compassion for others while you're not the least bit concerned about yourself. For example, would you not be frightened going into that house with me

120

tomorrow?"

"I suppose so. I guess I didn't think about it."

"That's exactly what I mean. You didn't even think about yourself. You were only concerned about my feelings. And *that* is what I mean about your heart."

Chapter Twenty-One
Facing the Inevitable

Bill

The next day, I awakened before the sun and sat on the porch with my tea. I hadn't slept well with the anticipation and dread of the inevitable. The orange glow of the sun peeked over the treetops when Frankie walked onto the porch. "Good morning, son. Tea is prepared on the fire. I've decided we'll have a nice breakfast before going into the house. It's entirely up to you whether you want to accompany me."

Around ten o'clock we walked the path to the Cunningham House through Mary's flower garden, now void of flowers and abundant with weeds and wild trees. Our shoes trampled on the broken remnants of the cobblestones leading to the front porch. As we reached the stairs, I stopped to look at the house. It was in such disarray. Mary would be very sad and disappointed. Her stunning, white castle was nothing but abandoned, broken gables, shattered windows, rotting wood, and rusted railings. The only life it held was the intruding rodents and bugs.

We climbed the stairs and crossed the porch to the front door. The regal door was a vestige of its former self, hanging precariously from its corroded hinges. I removed enough boards from across the entranceway to access the door. Its knob was gone, but it was so weak it easily pushed open.

The high walls in the entrance hall were barren, lacking the photographs formerly adorning them and replaced by myriads of cobwebs and aged, smeared dirt. We stepped on the fragmented floor, a trace of the sparkling, white and black tile formerly gracing the hall.

We entered the French doors into the living room. The stains on the carpet and the sofa were as vivid to me as they had been in 1971. I ran my hand tenderly over the blood stains on the frayed sofa. I straightened my body and took a long, examining look around the room at the faded draperies, the tattered curtains, and the splintered furniture. The bleak walls over the fireplace stared back at me minus the family portraits painted so long ago.

With eyes cast down, I walked out of the room, wandering down the hall with Frankie following. We entered the library through another set of badly damaged French doors. Although they were in serious disrepair, many books were still occupying the dusty library shelves. I approached my mahogany desk on the far side of the room. The drawers were broken open, and the papers and documents remaining were brittle and faded. On top of the desk was the paperweight shaped like an orange made by Daisy in art class. I picked it up, turned it over, and read the sentiment she had carved. "I love you, Dad. From Daisy." I stared at the tiny letters before placing the paperweight in my pocket.

As I sat on my worn and cracked leather chair, I felt the leather beneath my buttocks splitting even more. I leaned back and rested my head, closing my eyes. My mind drifted back to a better time. While placing my forearms on the wide chair arms, I touched something on the side table. I looked at the table. There, undisturbed after all these years, was the newspaper I had read that fateful Sunday morning. It had withstood time and the invasion of so many intruders.

The large, framed map of the world formerly shielding the wall safe was lying on the floor with the glass broken and the map ripped. The safe's door was open. I smoothed my hand over the velvety inside surface, pulling out two lone coins. A 1943 steel penny and a buffalo nickel. Mary and Mom's costly jewelry and over one hundred thousand dollars had been in the safe. I put the penny and nickel into my pocket.

We left the library and entered the dining room. As I stood transfixed, I heard my children talking and laughing around the dinner table. Cletus was telling me what he had accomplished while working at the Georgetown Grove. Everyone was complimenting Betsy Ann on her meatloaf and mashed potatoes. Travis was talking about the baseball game the team won. Daisy was excited about the book she was reading on Betsy Ross. My Lily was only concerned that her doll, Charlene, was missing dinner. Little Silas was so busy stuffing the meatloaf in his mouth and listening to others that he was rather quiet. Memories...

I snapped out of my reverie and placed the broken and wobbly chairs upright as I walked around the table.

Next, I went to Mom's bedroom where it was as horrific a sight as it had been over forty years ago. I thought of Mom—how she had been very ill with tuberculosis when she was young, how she ran

Gunderson Groves after Dad died until I was able to take over. Who was so crazed to do such unthinkable things to an old woman?

Looking in Mom's closet, a very large suitcase was stuffed in the corner. I pulled it out and took it into the hallway to see what was inside. The zipper was rusted shut.

Frankie saw me struggling. "Let me open it with my pocket knife." He inserted the blade into the thick fabric. Being careful not to shove the knife in too deeply, he cut around the suitcase directly above the zipper. "There!" he exclaimed when he had made it completely around the suitcase. "You can open it now."

I lifted the flap he had cut away. "Oh, my God. These are my portraits! I can't believe they were saved!" I was too excited to go through the rest of the house. "Frankie, help me drag the suitcase to the Gunderson House. We're taking a break."

We struggled with the suitcase and placed it on the Gunderson porch. I was thrilled to still have a piece of my family. Over the years their faces had grown dim. I couldn't embrace them or see them grow into adulthood, but now I could look at their portraits and never forget how precious they were. I sat on the glider, breathed a deep sigh, and opened the suitcase.

Shortly before their deaths, I had commissioned Mason Whitaker, a talented, local artist, to paint a portrait of each child on eighteen by twenty-four-inch canvases. Mason was able to capture not only their perfect likenesses, but also their essences.

The oil paintings were lying face down in the suitcase. I lifted the first canvas. Turning it over, I saw Daisy holding her red book on Mary Todd Lincoln and wearing a powder blue blouse. Next, I pulled out the painting of Cletus in his starched, blue uniform. I then took out the portrait of Silas, my little man. Mason had captured the mischievousness in those devilish eyes, appearing exceptionally green because of the bright, green jersey he was wearing. The next portrait was Betsy Ann, holding a peach pie looking good enough to eat. Lily was on the next canvas. So perfect, so beautiful, like a little glass doll. I then removed the portrait of Travis in his Baltimore Orioles baseball uniform with the bright orange letters across his chest.

The final portrait displayed Mary and me. Oh, she was so beautiful! It was eerie seeing Mary and my likeness again, side by side. The tears in my eyes were now escaping and rolling down my cheeks. I had to put the portrait down. I cupped my hands over my eyes and sobbed deeply for all those lost years stolen from me.

Frankie wrapped his arm around my back and rested his head on my arm. Finally, convincing myself this type of mourning was doing no good, I took my hands away from my eyes and reached in my pocket for the rag to wipe away the tears.

We sat silently for several minutes, then Frankie suggested, "Why don't we put these away with the stuff you want to take with you Saturday? Then we can have some lunch and go back into the house."

We gathered up the paintings and put them in a couple of Mom's large suitcases. We sat silently on the porch as we ate our lunch. Several minutes after we finished, I said, "Son, I don't want to spoil this jubilation I feel from finding that treasure. Let's wait until tomorrow to return to the house."

****

The next day as we prepared to go to the Cunningham House, I said to Frankie, "I've been selfishly thinking about myself and not realizing I need to look very carefully through that house." I handed him a pad of paper and pencil. "I want to examine those rooms as if I was trying to solve the murders of my family. Who better to do that than me? You told me I have a good mind. For an old man, I have an excellent memory and above average intelligence. I want you to take notes going through the house. I've been thinking of it on too personal of a level."

In the Cunningham living room I spoke aloud, "Any law officer worth his salt would've retrieved all possible evidence from these rooms. I doubt if anything was missed here. Let's go to Mother's room."

In this room, I looked around the space, seeing nothing to warrant specific attention. Upon closer inspection of the bedding, several sections of the bedding and mattress had been removed. My final look into Mom's nightstand revealed nothing. I took the drawer all the way out and checked its bottom and the empty space left by the drawer. Nothing was there either.

I then opened the narrow, top drawer of Mom's bureau to get the key to Mom's strong box. Sliding my fingers along the side, I found the tiny latch to release the false bottom. Pressing the latch, I gently lifted the thin wood and retrieved the miniature key, placing it in my shirt pocket. I then slid my hand on the underside of the top drawer but found nothing. I took out the drawer and felt the space on the back of the bureau. Empty. I did the same to the second and third drawers; not anything there either.

127

I tried to pull out the bottom drawer, but bending my creaky body wouldn't give me enough leverage. I struggled to my feet. "Frankie, will you pull out this drawer and check the underside for anything?"

Frankie knelt on the floor in front of the bureau, pulled the drawer away, and turned it over. Finding only the bare wood, he lowered his upper body enough to reach the back of the bureau. "There's something back here." He struggled to reach it. "I think it's an envelope."

His eyes squinted, his nose wrinkled, and his lips pursed as he stretched to retrieve it undamaged. "Ah! I got it." Maneuvering his arm and the envelope out of the small space, he finally stood, handed it to me, and replaced the drawer.

It was a yellowed, business size envelope. Some of the cellophane tape attaching it to the bureau still clung to it. Why would Mom tape something there? How long had it been there? For some reason, she had wanted to keep it. "Let's go into the dining room to open this."

I sat at the dining table and stared at the envelope. It was addressed to *Ida Gunderson* but with no return address. The postmark over a four-cent postage stamp was indecipherable. "Hmm, I can't see the date on this postmark, but this is a four-cent stamp, which means it was postmarked sometime between 1958 and 1965."

"How do you know that?"

"It's that memory thing." I paused, wondering what could possibly be in this envelope. "I guess I need to open it to satisfy my curiosity."

Carefully slipping my thumb under the corner of the flap and tugging on it with my thumb and forefinger, the dry, brittle glue separated easily from the body of the envelope. Mom must've re-glued it after she had read it.

I stared at this daunting wrapper, wary of removing the letter inside. If Mom had it hidden all those years, it was something she didn't want anyone to see. Had she still been alive, whatever it was would still be a secret. However, she was brutally murdered. Therefore, I *needed* to know what was in it. I pulled out the letter. My hands trembled as I unfolded the tri-fold piece of thin typewriter paper. I took a deep breath.

Dear Ida Gunderson,

I am looking for my mother. I was born on April 14, 1930, in Booneville, Arkansas. My telephone number is FR5-5536. Are you my mother?

Yours truly,
Clay Jackson

Oh, my God. I was an only child. The doctors said she was lucky to birth me because of the tuberculosis she suffered as a teenager. Wait. Booneville, Arkansas. That's where the sanatorium was located where she went for her treatment and recuperation.

Chapter Twenty-Two
Investigation Update

Dani

Dad had come home for lunch and was preparing sandwiches for us when his cellphone rang. "Hey, Frankie, how's it going?"

Looking up from studying at the kitchen table, I watched his eyes open wide as he listened to Frankie. I stopped reading.

"This sure puts a different spin on the case. It's something we need to consider. Joel is coming over tonight. I'll tell him about this. We'll see you Saturday. Love you, son."

When he hung up, I anxiously listened as Dad explained, "When they were looking through the Cunningham House, they found a letter taped to the back of the bureau in Bill's mother's room. This guy named Clay Jackson asked Ida Gunderson if she was his mother. Mr. Cunningham is completely baffled. He doesn't know why his mother would hide the letter—unless it's true."

This was massive! "There's no doubt they'll have to reopen the case now."

Grace and Joel both came to dinner. Dad reiterated his phone conversation with Frankie. Joel agreed with my assumption. "When this discovery is revealed and

Mr. Cunningham comes forward, this becomes a new case. Since your grandfather was murdered instead of him, two new avenues must be investigated. We'll be able to get a warrant to obtain Mrs. Gunderson's medical records."

Grace added, "We should change our appointment with the attorney ASAP to introduce Mr. Cunningham and show Mr. Plimpton this new development. It's imperative we find out what we need to do as soon as possible."

After dinner, Dad and Grace went to the living room while Joel and I went to our usual make-out spot, the back patio. As we were sitting on the love seat looking at the stars, Joel said, "You know, this case is really getting to me. I think I'm becoming as much involved as you. After seeing the evidence and those photos, it just makes me so angry the murderer has gotten away with this for all these years."

"I know exactly what you mean."

Before he replied, he had this tough guy, mug shot look with his chin and closed mouth jutted forward and nose crinkled, and he raised his voice. "You know what I mean? Do you know what I'm thinking right now?"

I was startled. I hadn't seen him act like this before. "Uh, no. Should I?"

Like magic the weird face disappeared. "I'm thinking I want to take you in my arms and kiss those lips until they swell to twice their size."

And he did. We did a little groping too.

****

The next day I changed our appointment with the attorney to Monday at three, texting Dad, Joel, and Grace to inform them. Joel would get Sean Sullivan to

131

talk to his captain about reopening the case. Looks like Mr. Cunningham would only have Saturday and Sunday to acclimate to his new surroundings before we threw him to the wolves.

Chapter Twenty-Three
Indescribable Agony

Bill

I couldn't go back into that house after Frankie's discovery. "We'll wait until morning. This letter has unnerved me. In all my wildest dreams, I never expected to find anything like this hidden in my mother's room."

I had to think why she hid this letter and what the consequences of it were. If she were not this Clay Jackson's mother, why in hell did she hide the letter? What terrible experience did she have that she thought she had to hide the birth of a baby? Did my father know about it? Did she ever call the telephone number on the letter? Did Clay Jackson ever find out if she was his mother? If he had, did he get in touch with her somehow?

"I have so many unanswered questions. I don't feel much like eating dinner either. Can you fix yourself something?"

"Sure, Grandpa. No problem."

I went into my bedroom to think about this unsettling discovery. I lay on the bed for some time with different scenarios attacking my thoughts and eventually concluding: Mom must've given birth to Clay Jackson, and I had a half- brother.

Suddenly, I remembered the strong box I had placed in the corner. Perhaps something in it would shed some light on this finding. I retrieved the box and took the tiny, rusty key from my pocket. I inserted it into the padlock, but the lock was rusted shut. On my way to the tool shed to get some lubricating oil, Frankie asked, "Is something wrong?"

"I'm about to look through my parents' strong box where they kept their important papers. I'm getting some oil for the lock. Would you like to join me in the bedroom?"

Frankie was already sitting on the bed when I returned. I put the box on the desk next to the window and inserted some oil around the lock parts, then squirted some into the keyhole. After rubbing a drop of oil on the small key, I inserted it into the padlock again. Wiggling the key slightly back and forth, the lock finally opened. I removed the lock and set the strong box on the floor next to where Frankie was sitting.

The first packet I removed from the box was a ten-thousand-dollar life insurance policy taken out on me as a child. I laid it aside and retrieved a packet of Gunderson/Cunningham property paperwork. Next, I took out Mom's personal savings account bank book. I then removed a first edition book of poems by Henry Wadsworth Longfellow, Mom's favorite poet. I held the book gently in my hands, rubbing the antique, padded cover and reminiscing of how Mom used to read the poems to me.

I set the book aside and withdrew an unsealed envelope. On the front of the envelope was written in Mom's handwriting, *Milton and Ida Mae's birth certificates*. Dad's birth certificate stated Milton Travis

Cunningham was born on February 4, 1910, in Palatka, Florida, Putnam County, the second son of Gladys and William Cunningham. I laid the birth certificate on my lap as I vaguely recalled meeting Dad's older brother, Uncle Martin many years ago.

I next took Mom's birth certificate from the envelope. She was the only child of Vera and Angus Gunderson, born on July 25, 1913, in Orlando, Florida. I remembered Grandpa Gunderson quite well. He was a cantankerous, old man who seemed to be constantly mad at the world. I was twelve when he died. It always amazed me how Mom could be such a kind, gentle woman while her father was such a tyrant.

The next packet was a copy of Mom's will. Upon her death the groves and all property went to me. Just to guarantee I did remember what the will contained, I glanced through it for any mention of another son. There was none.

When I was growing up, having a child out of wedlock was a sin. Society shunned the mother and baby. A girl might secretly go to a home for unwed mothers until the baby was born. However, most families told their friends the girl was staying with an aunt or a grandparent for the duration of the pregnancy, feigning grandmother was sick or the aunt needed help with her children. Anything to avoid admitting their daughter was unmarried and pregnant. I didn't know how society felt about the issue currently, but if an unwed, pregnant girl was chastised so much when I was young, it had to be worse when Mom was a teenager. If her pregnancy occurred during her stay in the tuberculosis sanatorium, not only was she dealing with her illness, but she was also in a horrible situation of being with child and unmarried. With Grandpa Gunderson being such a strict disciplinarian, her life must've been hell.

I reached into the strong box and pulled out a stack of letters tied with a purple ribbon. These were letters Dad had written to Mom while in the army during the Second World War. I opted not to read them. I doubted if they would help in solving the crimes or finding out anything about Clay Jackson.

On the outside of the next envelope, Mom had written *Billy's Birth Certificate*. I had a copy in my safe deposit box at the bank. Apparently, Mom kept a copy too. I couldn't remember the last time I had looked at it. What occasion would have prompted me to do so? This *was* such an occasion. I opened the unsealed flap and pulled out a faded blue piece of paper:

Department of Health

Certificate of Birth

Place of Birth: *State of Florida. Orange County, City of Orlando, Orange General Hospital*

Full Name Of Child: *William Angus Cunningham*

Sex of Child: *Male* Legitimate: *Yes*

Date of Birth: *July 25, 1935*

Name Father: *Milton Travis Cunningham*

Maiden Name Mother: *Ida Mae Gunderson*

Residence Father: *1001 Gunderson Rd, Nawinah, Fla*

Residence Mother: *1001 Gunderson Rd, Nawinah, Fla*

Father Color or Race: *White* AGE: *25*

Mother Color or Race: *White* AGE: *22*

Father Birthplace: *Palatka, Fla*

Mother Birthplace: *Orlando, Fla*

Father Trade or Profession: *Foreman-Gunderson Orange Groves*

Mother Trade or Profession: *Housewife*
Mother-Number of Children (At time of this birth-including this child):
a. Born alive and now living *2*
b. Born alive but now dead *0*
c. Stillborn *0*

****

Certificate of Attending Physician or Midwife
I hereby certify that I attended the birth of this child, who was born alive at 2:15 P.M. on the date above stated:
(Signed) *Walter O. Malone, M.D.*
Address: *1518 Orange Avenue, Orlando, Fla*
Filed: *July 26, 1935*

I looked at every word on the document and was shocked at what I discovered. Why had I not noticed it before? *Born alive and now living-2*. Obviously, before today I had never paid attention to what it stated. However, there was no doubt in my mind now. Clay Jackson was my half-brother. Mom had a child before me and never told me. I could kick myself for never noticing that statement before, as observant and detailed a person I claim to be.

I reached back into the box to be sure I had retrieved everything. On the bottom was a red satin cloth glued to a piece of heavy cardboard. It didn't seem to fit snuggly against the box's metal edges. I forced my finger under one of the corners of the cardboard. With a little persuasion, I lifted it. Beneath was a tightly sealed, blank envelope. Now was the time to unseal it.

No more secrets, Mom.

I withdrew a cream-colored document:

137

Department of Health
Certificate of Birth

Place of Birth: *State of Arkansas, Logan County, City of Booneville Arkansas*
State Tuberculosis Sanatorium
Full Name Of Child: *Unnamed*
Sex of Child: *Male* Legitimate: *No*
Date Of Birth: *April 14, 1930*
Name Father: _____
Maiden Name Mother: *Ida Mae Gunderson*
Residence Father: _____
Residence Mother: *1001 Gunderson Rd, Nawinah, Fla*
Father Color or Race: _____Age: ____
Mother Color or Race: *White* Age: *16*
Father Birthplace: _____
Mother Birthplace: *Orlando, Fla*
Father Trade or Profession: _____
Mother Trade or Profession: *Unwed-Ark State Tuberculosis San.*
Mother-Number of Children (At time of this birth- including this child):
a. Born alive and now living *1*
b. Born alive but now dead *0*
c. Stillborn 0

****

Certificate of Attending
Physician or Midwife

I hereby certify that I attended the birth of this child, who was born alive at 8:20 p.m. on the date above stated:
(Signed) *Wilma P. Fletcher, Midwife*
Address: *1433 Doan Road, Booneville, Ark*
Filed: _____

138

Absolute proof! Mom had a baby out of wedlock while she was in the sanatorium. Unwed, very young. Mother, why didn't you tell me?

I put all the contents back into the lock box, securing it with the small padlock. I turned to Frankie. "Let's get up early and go through the rest of the house tomorrow. I don't want to go near it in my current state of mind.

****

Throughout the night I tried to make sense of everything. Mom's secret. Why my family was murdered. Why I survived. Why this new family had come to me now, the family of my best friend whose life was lost because of me. *Nothing* made sense. Finally, I drifted off to a restless sleep until I woke up with the sound of Frankie making tea.

The sun had not come up yet while Frankie and I drank tea and discussed the dramatic discovery of the previous day. Frankie had also spent a restless night. I had heard him several times walking out on the porch. Good thing he was going home soon to get a good rest before going back to school.

After a quick breakfast, we trudged to the Cunningham House. Walking down the upstairs hall to the children's rooms, I recalled my same walk after their murders and how I couldn't wrap my brain around the horror. Now, so many years later, I had accepted it, but the dreaded task was not much easier.

We went into each of my children's rooms one final time. It was heart wrenching. It tore at my soul, but I survived with more resolve than ever to find the demon who had done this to me. Enough memories. The sights of their rooms would be imbedded in my

139

mind forever. My family. I have thought of them every day of my life since their deaths, but now is the time to move forward. Before I die, I must avenge their deaths.

After exiting the house, I stared at the decrepit, hollow structure that once was my beautiful home. "Goodbye, Mary, Betsy Ann, Cletus, Daisy, Travis, Lily, Silas, Baby Cunningham, Mom, and Dan. I'll love you forever."

For the remainder of the day we organized the things I planned to take with me. Then we fished and foraged the property for our evening meal. After the sun went down, we retired for the night, the last night I'd spend on this property.

Chapter Twenty-Four
Time to Say Goodbye

Dani

Grace and Joel arrived at the house at eight. Our first stop for the morning was the local superstore to purchase some casual wear and toiletries for Mr. Cunningham. Dad had also made an afternoon appointment for Mr. Cunningham to get a haircut and shave or beard trim. I hoped Mr. Cunningham wouldn't think we were taking over his life, but these things needed to be done. If the attorney and the police were to take us seriously, Mr. Cunningham couldn't look like some homeless drifter.

I had cleaned the spare room, and Dad had taken his office files to the shop. We purchased a bedding set and drapes of gray, maroon, and cream to go with the gray marbleized floor tile. Dad had stocked the desk with paper, pens, pencils, and a calculator. Grace and I removed the tags from the clothes and put everything in the drawers or closet.

About nine-thirty we picked up breakfast at the fast food restaurant and proceeded to the Cunningham property. Not much conversation took place because we were a little apprehensive. This event would change everyone's life.

As we parked at the end of the drive, Frankie and

Mr. Cunningham were walking toward us. I was so proud of Frankie for helping Mr. Cunningham go through these final days. Dad introduced Grace to Mr. Cunningham as we walked to the Gunderson House.

We quickly ate breakfast and got started on our mission. Joel and Frankie retrieved the boxes from the SUV, and we packed all the items that Frankie and Mr. Cunningham had brought to the porch. Everyone grabbed a box or a piece of luggage, and we plodded to the vehicle. Dad and Joel packed everything into the trunk. We took one last glance at the gloomy Cunningham House, looming eerily against the sun as the December wind clanked the loose boards against the outside walls. The shredded curtains and drapes blew in and out of the broken upstairs windows as if they were taking their last breaths. A tear ran down Mr. Cunningham's cheek and was swallowed by his grizzly beard.

On the ride to our house, we made small talk and included Mr. Cunningham in our conversations. I said, "We've prepared a great lunch. Wait until you taste my chocolate chip cookies. They're the best."

Frankie realized what I was doing. "Yeah, every time she makes them, I'd eat them all if she didn't hide them in the washing machine."

"What? You know about that hiding place?" I pretended I didn't already know the answer.

We continued talking, primarily about the many changes in the area. Mr. Cunningham was astonished at all the new restaurants, service stations, and other businesses. When we arrived at our house, he had a slight smile on his face and seemed to be enjoying his new surroundings. Disembarking from the SUV, he gazed at our gray stucco and brick house with the large oak tree in the front yard. "This is a fine house, Andrew."

Frankie excitedly added, "Wait until you see my room. I have different dinosaurs all over the walls. Dani bought me a dinosaur quilt too. And your bedroom is right next to mine. We have to share the same bathroom. Is that okay?"

Frankie and Joel gave Mr. Cunningham a tour of the house while Dad, Grace, and I set out the lunch. The conversations during lunch continued to be light. When everyone had finished their sandwiches, I made a fresh pot of coffee. While it was brewing, Mr. Cunningham said, "I have never smelled such a delicious aroma in all my life. It's been way too long since I've had a good cup of coffee."

I poured everyone's coffee and put the plate of chocolate chip cookies on the table. "Oh, my, this coffee is simply delicious. And these cookies! Amazing! Please don't hide them in the washer," gushed Mr. Cunningham.

After more light banter, Dad got serious. "Bill, we have an appointment with Doug Plimpton on Monday. Since this is a weekend, there's not much we can do as far as finding Clay Jackson. I made an appointment with the barber for you at four today. You might want to take a shower and change into some of the clothes we bought. Frankie, Joel, and I can take you to the barber while Dani and Grace start the spaghetti sauce for dinner. Then you can use the rest of today and tomorrow to somewhat acclimate to our altered world. One of the best ways is to watch television. Granted, it may not be typical of everyday life, but with the news programs and even some of the situation comedies and dramas, you'll be able to see what has changed over the years."

After Mr. Cunningham showered and dressed in his new clothes, he looked like a different person. He had washed his scraggly hair and beard and combed the hair back from his face.

Grace looked at him in amazement. "My, you look like a different man already."

"I definitely feel different. It's been a long time since I've had a hot shower in such luxurious surroundings. I didn't realize how much I missed it."

"Are you ready to finish the transformation at the barber's?" Dad asked.

"I'm as ready as I'll ever be."

Chapter Twenty-Five
A New Beginning

Bill

Andrew's house was warm and cozy. The family went out of their way to be hospitable. I was uncomfortable at first, but because they were so gracious and welcoming, they made the transition easy. The room they prepared was quite suitable, and the clothing they purchased was comfortable. Ah, the shower. It felt magnificent, the hot, steamy water cascading down my wrinkled skin. And the lunch was fantastic. I felt guilty enjoying those chocolate chip cookies so much. I had prepared myself mentally for this drastic change, and the Reynolds were making it easier.

At the barber shop, I was somewhat anxious encountering strangers. I had learned to think of the Reynolds, Joel, and even Grace as my dear friends, and I no longer felt awkward around them. However, it was time to confront the rest of the world.

The barber shop was different from the one I frequented years ago. It was in a corner of a beauty parlor where so many ladies were present. Andrew introduced his barber. "Bill, this is Tiger. He'll do a great job with your beard and hair."

Tiger's name suited him well. He was a large,

muscular man with long, gold hair and black stripes running through it. He also had a pencil thin, black mustache stretching across his cheeks to his ears. His pug nose made him look like a tiger. Andrew noticed my wariness and attempted to put me at ease. "Tiger was a corporal in the army. He served in Afghanistan for two years."

Not only was I surprised by this man's appearance, but to find out he had been in the armed services completely shocked me. I didn't know what was happening in Afghanistan. However, since Tiger used to be a soldier, I was more comfortable being around him. He wasn't at all like my old barber, Charlie Polk. I could see I was in for many changes and revelations.

While looking in the mirror and seeing my transformation, I could hardly believe my eyes. Was this what I really looked like? Tiger did a terrific job of turning a wild hermit into a distinguished, elderly gentleman. Frankie, who had left the shop to get us some sodas, came back and almost dropped the sodas. He stared at me. "Grandpa, is that really you?"

Tiger had neatly cut my hair just above the top of my ears. He had trimmed and shaped my beard to an inch long on the sides and two inches at my chin. As I walked out of the barber shop, I had a hundred percent more confidence in myself. Strange, how small things like a shower, clean clothes, and a haircut could change a man's complete perspective.

When we got back into Andrew's automobile, he asked, "Is there anything you want to do or see? Or do you want to go back to my house?"

I'd been thinking while in the barber chair. "Is there a men's shop nearby? I'd like to purchase a couple of suits and dress shirts. I have no money currently, but I hope to be able to remedy that situation soon. I hate to ask you after all you've done for me, but do you think you could front me the money until Monday?"

"Bill, I have no problem buying the suits for you. However, we have no individual men shops in the area. Stores at the mall sell men's clothing. It may be crowded with people, but if you can handle the crowds, we can go there."

The mall was quite an experience. People were everywhere, people of all kinds, young and old. I was surprised at some of the apparel of the young ones. So much of their bodies were exposed. It truly was a different time and age. At the department store I found two quality suits on the rack. The tailor measured me for alterations and said to return for a fitting in a week.

We left the mall after ordering my suits and went to Andrew's house. When I walked in the door with my new haircut and beard trim, the reception I received was unexpected.

Danielle opened her mouth in admiration. "Oh, Mr. Cunningham, you look so handsome. I never would've recognized you!"

Grace also had a look of shock on her face. "You look incredible."

We had a delicious spaghetti dinner. Both Andrew and Danielle are superb cooks. Then Frankie and I watched the television in his room. As I was forewarned, the programs opened my eyes to the changes over the years from clothes, life styles, and morals. I could only shake my head when Frankie asked me what I thought of these changes. Thinking about life in the sixties and seventies, I guess I could see the trend going toward what life had become. However, the changes had been so subtle, and I was so wrapped up in family, friends, and work I hadn't notice. Now they were bombarding me like a fireman's hose squirting directly into my face.

When the ten o'clock news ended, I said, "I'm going to retire now. We both need to get some sleep."

Frankie was half asleep already. "Okay." Then he slid under his covers. I silently walked out of his room to my new bedroom.

I sat on the edge of the bed, recapping the past week in my head and contemplating what might occur in the coming weeks. Surprisingly, I didn't feel melancholy as I'd expected. I owed that to my new physical appearance and, most of all, to the Reynolds, who made me feel so welcomed. I changed into the pajamas they had purchased for me, crawled into bed, and fell into a deep sleep almost immediately.

The next morning, the smell of bacon awakened me. The clock on the bedside table read seven o'clock. I couldn't believe I'd slept through the night without waking once. I took another set of my new clothes into the bathroom, showered, dressed, and went in search of that delightful aroma.

In the kitchen, Andrew was frying what looked like ten pounds of bacon. "Well, how did you sleep last night?"

"Like a baby. I guess I was worn out. Plus, that bed felt like I was sleeping on a cloud. How different it is from the sixty-year-old mattress in my mother's house."

"Well, I hope you're hungry. The kids will be getting up soon. We go to the nine o'clock mass on

Sunday mornings. Will you be okay here by yourself, or would you like to join us?"

"I need a little more time before confronting another large group of people. The mall was enough for me. I'll watch the television to get some more insight into this new life."

A few minutes later, Danielle and Frankie joined us in the kitchen. I heard the doorbell ring, wondering who would be visiting that early in the morning. Andrew noticed my concern. "That's Emily, Dani's friend. She has Sunday breakfast and goes to mass with us. I hope you don't mind."

"Not at all. I don't want to interrupt your routines or cause any extra burden on you. If there's anything I can do to help, please let me know."

"We have everything covered. You're our very welcomed guest. Just sit back and enjoy the good food."

A pretty, young lady walked into the kitchen, and Danielle introduced us. "Mr. Cunningham, this is my best friend, Emily."

Frankie quickly added, "He's kind of like our grandpa, Emily."

When the family left for church, I switched on the living room television. Frankie had shown me how to use the remote control, which was confusing and a challenge for my aged brain. Of course, I forgot which button was which. Finally, I was able to get a news program on the screen. I was disappointed by all the crime still so prevalent in society. To know so many other victims were also suffering from crimes against them was unsettling. I changed the channel to some light, comedy program, which was a little risqué for my taste.

When the family returned, Grace also joined us. We spent the afternoon playing board games. Joel came for dinner, and Emily went home. We gathered in the living room with our coffee to decide what to discuss at the meeting with Doug Plimpton. Andrew loaned me his spare briefcase for the papers I'd brought from the property. The day had been relaxing and enjoyable. Tomorrow would be the beginning of my fight for justice.

Chapter Twenty-Six
Questions, Answers, More Questions

Bill

Andrew had taken the week off work. We were to meet Grace, Joel, and Danielle at Doug Plimpton's office at three. At breakfast Andrew asked, "Bill, is there anything specific you want to do before our meeting with Doug?"

I did have a few things on my mind. "I need to somehow find out what happened to Gunderson Grove Limited after I was presumed dead."

Andrew added, "Doug will be able to answer most of your questions. I also have the telephone number of Bobby Cooper, your accounting assistant. He's a CPA in Orlando and said he'd help in any way he could."

Ah, yes, Bobby Cooper. "I might give Bobby a call. He was a sharp, young man. If he stayed with the company until the end, I'm sure his knowledge will be helpful."

I thought of another chore I needed to do soon. "I'd also like to get to my banks to see what's necessary to activate my accounts or pay any outstanding debts."

Andrew suggested, "You might want to talk to Doug before you make any financial decisions. He would know what happened to your money.

"Now that I shot down all your plans, is there

anything else you want to do?"

There was something I had been contemplating. "I'd like to go to the Gunderson Groves' office and warehouse. Do you know if the building is still there?"

Andrew tilted his head in thought. "I haven't been over that way for some time. It was leased by a carpet company for a while, but they closed their doors about ten years ago. Since then, I don't know. We can check it out."

Andrew placed my briefcase in the trunk of his vehicle, and we drove across town to the warehouse. I was anxious to see the building where I had spent so much of my time. As we turned the corner on Lowry Road, I saw it standing dark and dilapidated in the distance. I felt a stab to my heart. Had I even thought about it all those years? Had I wondered what had happened to the fine people who worked for me? I was so consumed with grief I was incapable of realizing others were suffering too. Their lives were interrupted. Their jobs were in jeopardy. The Reynolds family and I were not the only ones affected by the actions of that bastard.

Andrew pulled into the rutted, deserted parking lot, which formerly held many employee vehicles and several semi-trucks filled with oranges awaiting shipment to various destinations. Sadness overwhelmed me, seeing the condition of the property. I got out of Andrew's automobile and stared at the decaying building.

"So what's next?" Andrew asked.

"Can you climb the fire escape? On the roof is a door into the warehouse. It's possible it'll be unlocked. If not, on the side of the permanent storage container, I kept a key inside a hidden, metal box glued to the container. If the key isn't there, you can break the window to unlock the door. I'll have the window replaced later. I'll wait near the docks."

While Andrew climbed to the roof, I walked to the warehouse door and waited. Soon he opened it. "The roof door was unlocked. I locked it before coming down the stairs."

Entering the building, I was stunned by the size of the loading area interior, now completely empty. Our footsteps echoed through the vacant space as we walked on the concrete floor. All evidence of this property ever being filled with oranges, people, trucks, forklifts, and packaging was now gone. I walked to the open door of what used to be my office. It was a small room toward the front of the building with doors leading both to the warehouse and to the other office areas. Amazingly, my original desk was still the focal point, though now worn and balanced on only three legs. Everything else had changed. No pictures of family members hanging on the walls or resting on the desk. A hard, plastic chair had replaced my brown, leather chair.

I walked out the door into the other office area and wandered around. I could still visualize Ethel Grumley, my receptionist, with her headphones wrapped around her head, talking to a customer.

After walking through all the offices, I had enough. Nothing was there for me. I'd have to decide what to do with this property. It was now just a big eyesore. I'm sure the orange groves had also gone to seed by now. I'm too old and tired to make this a functioning business again. Besides, I have a more important agenda.

We left the warehouse, and Andrew drove around Nawinah, pointing out the many changes. At one o'clock, he parked his vehicle downtown, and we went to a small restaurant near the police station. A young lady dressed all in black with a long, white apron took our order. When she left our booth, I remarked, "Why are her eyes so black? Do you think someone punched her?"

Andrew laughed. "No, Dani says that's the new smoky eye look. I can't keep up with all these fashion changes. If it's hard on me, I can see the shock you must feel. Wait until summer and you see the skimpy clothes these young girls wear."

To our surprise, Joel walked into the restaurant. Andrew called out, "Hey, Joel! Over here!"

Joel sat at our booth. "I didn't expect to see you two here. I came in for lunch before meeting you at the attorney's office."

I invited him. "So now you've already met us. We'll eat and walk over to Doug's office together."

On our stroll, I enjoyed seeing the town up close and reflecting on all the changes. When we arrived at our destination, Grace and Danielle were already seated. Andrew informed the receptionist everyone was present. About five minutes to three, Mr. Plimpton's assistant led us to the conference room. "Help yourselves to the coffee on the credenza. Mr. Plimpton will be right with you."

Within a few minutes, Doug Plimpton opened the door and strolled toward the chair at the head of the table. He arranged the files he had brought and placed them in their required order before looking at us. "Good afternoon." Then his eyes landed on me.

"Oh, my God! It is you! Bill Cunningham! I can't believe it!"

I stood, walked over to him, and firmly shook his hand. "How have you been, Doug?"

Doug gave me a big hug. "This is unbelievable! It's so wonderful to see you, Bill."

After our happy greeting, I took my seat and Doug spoke, "They told me you were alive, but I didn't believe them. This is so remarkable! To think all these years have gone by believing you were dead. You'll have to excuse my emotions. This has been such a shock."

Doug gained his composure and began to explain about what he found in his files. "As you know, my father was more involved in your affairs than I, but I've read over the paperwork on the disposal of the business and other legal matters. As executor of your estate, my father hired Art Stafford, your accountant, and Charles Taggart, your personal advisor, to assist him in overseeing the business and carrying it to its closing about five years after your, uh, death. Many of the employees saw the writing on the wall and found jobs elsewhere. Art, Charles, and my father found jobs for those who were employed when the business closed. They made sure all outstanding bills were paid and employees received their final paychecks.

"As you know, your properties were paid off completely long before the incident, so there were no issues with mortgage payments. Regarding your bank accounts, the state requires all financial institutions to report intangible property they hold and consider unclaimed or abandoned. The property must be inactive for at least five years. At that time the unclaimed funds are deposited into the State School Fund and used to support our public schools. This did not occur with your accounts with the Nawinah Trust Bank. It is still sitting there and has been accumulating interest. Because you set up in writing the direct withdrawal by the county of your property taxes on all your land holdings, these accounts didn't lay dormant or go to the state. However, your money in the Nawinah National Bank and the Orange Federal Bank was turned over to the state after Gunderson Groves closed and all debts were settled. The state is obligated to return your money when it's made aware you're still alive. I'll start the procedure to get those funds returned to you. It may take a few months.

"I have duplicate copies of all correspondences sent to you from your various banks. For whatever reason, my father never stopped your directive to pay the taxes out of the Nawinah Trust Bank. Perhaps he thought a relative of yours would eventually be found. I only know that after checking with that bank and the county, your taxes have been paid in full on all properties, and you are clear of any debt. Periodically, the city monitored your house to keep the windows and doors boarded up and to chase any squatters away. Other than that, the house and the groves have sat vacant all these years. I'm surprised you never saw any police or workers on your property."

I interrupted, "Oh, I saw them, but they didn't see me. I was aware of most who trespassed on my property, as Danielle and Joel can assure you."

Doug put down the files. "That's basically all I have. Do you have any questions?"

Joel asked, "Since these murders were never

solved, and we now have additional information, we plan to reopen the case. Do you think it would be wise to let it be known Mr. Cunningham is still alive?"

"Frankly, Joel, you'll have no choice. Bill is fundamental to the case. Once he comes forward, it'll blow the case wide open. You'll first need to convince the police that Bill is not the killer. I hope you are prepared. If the police believe Bill is innocent, they may try to keep it quiet as long as possible, but somehow, it'll leak out. The minute Bill goes to his bank to access his accounts, he's exposed to recognition. My suggestion would be to first go to the police to find out how they want to handle the situation. Bill will need documents proving he is who he claims to be. Bill, do you have copies of any personal documents?"

"Yes, I have a copy of my birth certificate with me today. My baptismal record is in my safety deposit box at the Nawinah Trust Bank, which I plan to retrieve ASAP. I also have documents in that box with my signature on them, such as insurance and property records."

"Take those with you when you go to the police. You may also need to show them to the bank."

Doug hesitated while looking around the room. "Is there anything else we need to discuss?"

I reached to the floor for my briefcase. "I have some papers for you to see and give me your advice."

I removed Clay Jackson and my birth certificates and the letter from Jackson. I handed the birth certificates to Doug. "Here is my birth certificate and that of another person who I suspect is my half-brother. Please look them over and tell me what you think."

Surprised, Doug asked, "Your half-brother?"

"Please, just look at the documents. Then I'll explain."

Doug took the creased birth certificates and laid them on the table. He picked up my birth certificate, briefly looking it over. "What am I looking for here, Bill? This looks like a normal birth certificate."

"Look at the number of children born to my mother."

He glanced through the document, searching for the information. I could see in his face the minute he found it. "Oh, Bill, you had a sibling!"

"Now look at the other birth certificate."

He laid my birth certificate aside and picked up the other one. After several minutes of reading the data, he asked, "Apparently, you knew nothing about this child?"

"Let me show you a letter my mother received." I took the letter out of the envelope.

Doug grasped the letter by its corner, laid it on the table, and read its contents. When he was finished, he picked up the other birth certificate and looked back and forth, reading the data on both documents. "I must say, this is truly a shock. Do you know anything about this Clay Jackson?"

"No, I found these documents shortly before I left my property. My mother never talked about her time in the sanatorium let alone any pregnancy or baby. I was mystified when I found the letter and birth certificate. We haven't had time to determine if he's alive or dead. That's my priority. I wanted your advice on how to handle this. Do we first try to locate him, or do we inform the police and let them find him?"

"Bring this up with the police. This is something very important to consider when they review your case. May I make copies of these documents for my files?"

He picked up the phone on the credenza. "Jill, come to the conference room. I have some documents for you to copy. Wear rubber gloves."

After retrieving my originals, we left Doug's office and went back to Andrew's house to plan our next course of action.

Chapter Twenty-Seven
The Big Reveal

Dani

Dad thought it best to wait until morning to contact the police. He had asked Mr. Plimpton to accompany us. Joel also asked Sean Sullivan to join us and make sure his captain would be available. The next morning Dad, Mr. Cunningham, and I arrived at the police station shortly before nine. When Grace and Doug Plimpton arrived, Joel introduced us to Sean. Sean said to the police woman at the desk, "Kristy, this is the group I told you about. Where do you want us to go?"

"Take them to Interrogation Room C. It's large enough to accommodate all of you." Kristy pressed a buzzer, and we followed Sean and Joel through a heavy metal door into a large room with desks and chairs scattered throughout. Several men and women dressed in business suits or police uniforms were sitting at various desks, some on the telephone, some looking through files, and some talking to others. Sean led us around the desks to double metal doors in the back of the room. He punched in a code on a wall keyboard. The doors opened, and we followed him down a wide hallway. When we stopped at the C door, he again punched in a code on a similar keyboard and held the door open as we filed into the room.

Sean asked, "Can I offer you coffee while we wait for the captain?"

We accepted his offer, and he and Joel left the room, returning shortly carrying the coffee in two slotted cardboard containers. Soon the door opened, and a portly, gray haired man entered dressed in a tieless, blue shirt and baggy trousers held up with red suspenders. "Good morning, ladies and gentlemen. I'm Captain Ray Graham."

In unison we greeted him, and Joel introduced us individually. "Captain, this is Andrew Reynolds. He owns Spencer's Body Shop over on Granger Road. This is his daughter Danielle Reynolds. This is Dr. Grace DeMarco, a psychiatrist practicing in Orlando."

The captain looked at Grace. "Are you any relation to Anthony DeMarco, who ran for governor several years ago?"

"He was my father."

"He and I were in the same unit in Vietnam. Small world. I heard he passed away a few years ago."

"Yes. He had a massive heart attack seven years ago."

"My condolences. He was a good man."

Joel continued his introductions. "This is Douglas Plimpton, the attorney for the group."

The captain faced Mr. Plimpton. "I believe we've met before."

"Yes, I was the counsel last year in the embezzlement case involving Bernie Carano. If I'm not mistaken, you were deeply involved in it."

"Ah, yes. What has become of old Bernie?"

"The state won. He was sentenced to fifteen years."

The captain then looked at Mr. Cunningham on his

right.

"Captain, the man to your right is Mr. William Cunningham," Joel said.

The captain stared at Mr. Cunningham as if he was trying to remember if he knew the man. "Have I met you before, Cunningham?"

"I don't believe so, Captain."

"I'm sure I've heard that name before."

"Excuse me, Captain," Dad broke in. "Let me explain. You might want to sit."

Confused, the captain sat and waited for Dad's explanation.

"This William Cunningham is the very same William Cunningham who is the owner of the now defunct Gunderson Groves Limited, and the very same William Cunningham whose family was brutally murdered the night of October 31, 1971."

The captain jumped up. "Nonsense! That William Cunningham was killed in that house. Every law enforcement officer in Orange County knows about those murders and knows William Cunningham's body was found in the same room with his wife's body. This is bullshit!"

Mr. Cunningham slowly rose from his seat and turned to the captain. "It's true. I am that William Cunningham. Only I was not murdered in my house. I was attacked outside the house, shoved in the crawlspace, and left for dead. The deceased found near my wife's body was Daniel Reynolds, my best friend and head foreman, who also was the father of Andrew and the grandfather of Danielle."

The captain sat back down, staring at Mr. Cunningham, who also sat and proceeded to tell how he had spent the last forty plus years. The captain listened attentively while Mr. Cunningham recapped how Joel and I found him on the property and the events leading up to this meeting. When he finished, the captain asked, "Do you have proof you are who you say you are?"

"Oh, yes, I have whatever you need in this briefcase." He lifted the briefcase and placed it on the table. "My birth certificate and my parents' birth certificates. As soon as I access my safety deposit box at the bank, I can show you the deeds to all my properties. Several of those documents contain my signature. You can verify them with my signature today."

Mr. Plimpton interjected, "Captain, I can also vouch for this man's identity. I knew Bill Cunningham forty years ago and know this man sitting beside you is that same Bill Cunningham. My father and I were his attorneys back in the sixties and seventies."

The captain gathered his thoughts, cocked his head to the side, and addressed Mr. Cunningham. "You say you were on that property for over forty years living like a hermit? That's a hell of a long time. Can you prove you didn't kill your own family? If you aren't the killer, why did you wait until now to come forward? Why didn't you get in touch with the police as soon as you realized your family was murdered?"

"Captain Graham, put yourself in my place. I was out of my mind with grief for months, even years. I didn't care if I lived or died. I didn't even care who murdered my family, just that they were gone. Discounting my extreme grief, logically, what reason would I have to kill them and rape my own mother? I had a comfortable life. I had a thriving company; I had more money than I needed. What would be my motive?"

The atmosphere in the room was caustic. Did Captain Graham believe him? Just because we knew he wasn't capable of such heinous acts didn't mean others wouldn't think he was guilty.

Mr. Cunningham reached for his briefcase. "I have something to show you that might add credence to my claim of innocence. Last week, in my mother's bedroom, I found a letter missed by the authorities on the case." He withdrew Clay Jackson's letter. "This was found taped to the back of her bureau."

The captain removed his reading glasses from his shirt pocket, put them on, and took the yellowed letter. With gentle fingers he opened it and read the contents as we waited for his response. "Since I'm not completely familiar with this case, can you tell me what bearing this letter has?"

Mr. Cunningham withdrew the two birth certificates. "Look carefully at these documents. All my life I was under the assumption I was an only child. I believe this Clay Jackson is my sibling."

The captain took the two birth certificates and scrutinized them. Removing his glasses, he put them back in his pocket and handed the three documents to Sean. "Sean, have Sandy make copies of these immediately and give the originals back to Cunningham."

Sean was about to take the documents when the captain stopped him. "Wait! That letter may contain the fingerprints of this Clay Jackson. Have the lab process it." Then he turned to Mr. Cunningham. "Besides yourself, who else has handled that letter?"

Mr. Cunningham patted his cheek with his forefinger as he remembered. "Myself, my mother, Doug Plimpton, and you. Oh, and Frankie Reynolds handled the envelope but not the letter."

"Who is Frankie Reynolds?"

"He's the son of Andrew Reynolds and the boy who found the letter."

"We'll have to get his, yours, and Doug's fingerprints to eliminate them. Hopefully, if there are prints from this Clay Jackson, they haven't been obliterated by any of these others."

Sean put on a pair of rubber gloves from his jacket and took the three documents.

The captain turned to Mr. Cunningham. "Do you know anything about this Clay Jackson?"

Dad interrupted, "Excuse me, Captain. When we found Bill on his property, this group worked to find out who might be a suspect in the murders. At the time we weren't sure what Bill planned to do, but we knew my father, Dan Reynolds, didn't commit those murders since he was also a victim. We wanted to clear his name and find the real killer. Bill gave us a list of all the people he knew at the time of the murders. We are not detectives, but we tried to contact these people, and basically, we came up with nothing. When Bill found these documents, we thought he might have found a very important clue to solving this case."

The captain said, "I'd also like to have that list. You should've come to us when you first found Cunningham."

Dad responded, "You have to understand the delicacy of the situation. Except to frighten away trespassers, Bill hadn't spoken to anyone for over forty years. We didn't want to jeopardize him in any way. Even you questioned his innocence. We had to wait until he was ready to accept whatever consequences developed."

The captain looked at Mr. Cunningham. "I can understand that."

Grace interjected, "Sir, we know this is going to create a media frenzy. Our concern is for Mr. Cunningham's welfare as well as solving these crimes. We need your advice on how to handle that part of the case."

The captain asked Mr. Cunningham, "Are you ready for this?"

"Yes, I am. These friends are concerned for me, and I appreciate that. I may be old, but I'm strong mentally and emotionally. I want to find the bastard who killed my family if it's the last thing I do."

The captain ordered, "This is how we'll handle things. Sean and I will look over the evidence. We'll re-examine the fingerprints and any DNA found at the scene. This Clay Jackson's prints may not have been on file back in the seventies, but they may be today. For now, he's our prime suspect. Cunningham, when Sean returns, you and Plimpton have him get your fingerprints. Also, bring Frankie Reynolds into the precinct to get his taken.

"This has become an entirely different case. It must be reopened. I need some time to look over the cold case files. Sean, I'm assigning you to the case. What are you working on right now?"

"I just wrapped up the Shepherd Street convenience store robbery. Lieutenant Billings planned to assign me a new case today."

"I'll talk to Billings. Since you're somewhat familiar with this case, I want you working on it as soon as we're done here. Bring the files and evidence to me. I'll meet with you and Billings later this afternoon after I've looked at them. I want to be on top of this."

He turned to us, moving his arm around the room. "Give your lists of names to Sean. We'll look into these also. Sean will follow up with the tuberculosis sanatorium to find out as much as possible about Clay Jackson. As far as this causing a sensation with the media? Yes, that will happen. Cunningham, if you're staying with the Reynolds, the media will be at their front door. You all will become unwilling celebrities overnight. Our department doesn't plan to break this news to the public, but you know how that goes. It'll happen. It's just a matter of time. I'll place a patrol at the Cunningham property. We don't need any more intrusions there. But be prepared. You're in for a bumpy ride. Before I leave, does anyone have any questions?"

Mr. Cunningham asked, "I need to access my bank account. Will not this start the media frenzy?"

"It may or may not. It might not be immediate, but anyone at your bank who discovers your identity and puts two and two together will tell everyone they know about you. I'd suggest you only talk to the top official at the bank. Inevitably, someone will discover who you are, and all hell will break loose."

He paused and looked around the room. "If that's it, I'll have Sean keep in touch with you on any developments. In the meantime, if you've any questions, talk to him. He can funnel them to me. If it's urgent, feel free to contact me directly. Cunningham, we'll find this killer."

The captain walked out of the room.

Sean returned with Mr. Cunningham's birth certificates. "Jackson's letter is with the lab for fingerprint analysis. I'll start on your case after we process Plimpton and your fingerprints. Joel, Lieutenant Billings agreed to assign you to this case. You're already familiar with all the details and will be an asset to me."

****

Since Mr. Cunningham had come forward, it was time to put him into my criminology reports. I asked Professor Belinsky to keep his survival secret for now. Sometimes we had to read those reports in class, and I didn't want to cause that media turmoil prematurely.

Chapter Twenty-Eight
Progress

Bill

Doug Plimpton had told me when Gunderson Grove Limited closed, the business bank accounts were also closed. After the final federal tax return was completed, the profit from the business was deposited in my personal savings account at Nawinah Trust Bank, awaiting the eventual settling of my estate. On Tuesday, Andrew accompanied me to the bank to meet with Christine Dwyer, the vice-president. Ms. Dwyer, a handsome woman in her early sixties, welcomed us into her office. "What can I do for you? My secretary stressed this meeting was very important and extremely confidential."

I began, "Ms. Dwyer, your bank has transferred property tax payments on my land holdings for many years with a directive I'd set up in the early sixties. Due to unmitigated circumstances, I've not had any personal contact with your bank since the early seventies. What I'm about to tell you, I'd appreciate if you'd keep in your strictest confidence." I told her an abbreviated version of my situation. "Today I'd like to activate my bank accounts. I've brought any paperwork you'll need to verify my identity. I also have the key to my safe deposit box containing any additional document you may need. Again, a big concern of mine is anonymity. The investigation into the murders of my family has been reopened. You can check with Captain Ray Graham of the Nawinah Police Department on the validity of this."

She looked over my identifying documents. "I see no reason why you can't have full access to your accounts. As for keeping your identity confidential, that's not an issue. I doubt if any of my staff knows your tragic story. I certainly won't bring it to their attention. Now, regarding your accounts, as Mr. Reynolds can tell you, banking has changed since the seventies. One can now do all banking online and paperless."

I was skeptical. "Paperless?"

"Yes, you don't need checks or deposit slips. We give you an ATM card to access your funds, and you rarely need to come into the bank."

"ATM card?"

"We now have Automatic Teller Machines, or ATM's, as well as online, or computer banking. Everything can be done electronically."

"Will I still be able to use checks and a live teller?"

"Of course, that option is also available. You can use all three methods. I'm sure Mr. Reynolds can explain those procedures. For now, we'll set you up with a bank card and a new set of checks. Cheryl, my assistant, will get your current information and give you your bank card and some temporary checks until your personalized checks arrive in a few days. She'll also see you to your safe deposit box."

Cheryl led us to her office. She sat before her computer. "I'll need your social security number or your bank account number."

Since I didn't remember or have the information on the bank account numbers, I recited my social security number. She quickly punched it on her keyboard. When she pulled up my accounts, her eyes widened, and her mouth opened exposing pearly white teeth. "Oh, my God! I'm sorry, sir. I didn't mean to say that out loud."

I smiled at her. "No problem. Can you write down the account number and the balance in my account?"

On a small legal pad, she copied the information and handed it to me. I looked at the slip of paper, and then showed it to Andrew. "Hmm, it's more than I expected."

Andrew had the same shocked look on his face as Cheryl had when she saw the account balance. "Bill, no wonder you kept your money in three banks. The Federal Reserve couldn't insure them!"

I shook my head. "And what has it done for me, Andrew?"

Cheryl asked me several questions while she entered my information into her computer. I used Andrew's address. I did not want to give either the Cunningham House or the Gunderson House. I also accessed my safe deposit box, verifying the contents matched the list I had in my briefcase.

****

At Andrew's house over coffee, we discussed what to do for the remainder of the afternoon. Hesitantly, I said, "Now that I have access to my money, I'd like to buy a vehicle."

Andrew looked surprised. "Sure, do you know what kind of car you want?"

"I like your vehicle. What did you call it? An

171

SUV?"

We went to the auto dealership, and I decided on an SUV in a dark maroon color. I didn't want a vehicle too pretentious or too noticeable. Andrew said plenty SUVs were on the road, so mine would not be conspicuous. Then I remembered I had no valid driver license. The dealership informed me they'd hold the vehicle until the next day. I'd need to return with the license and proof of insurance. So, I left my gorgeous vehicle on their lot.

The next day we went to the Department of Motor Vehicles. What a madhouse! We waited for three hours before they even called my name. I took a written test, a driving test, and a vision test. While taking the eye exam, I decided I should also see an eye doctor soon. With great relief, we walked out of the building about four o'clock, and I had my driver's license with a very unique photo on it.

Andrew called his insurance agent, and I took out a policy on my new vehicle. I arranged to update him with the VIN number and any other needed information. Then we were off to the dealership to pick up my SUV.

The next morning Andrew, Frankie, and I went to the police station. On our way, we bought two dozen donuts. When we entered the station, the eyes of the officer at the desk opened wide as did her mouth. She laid the donuts on a table near her desk. The officers in the room immediately swarmed to the table to help themselves. We heard several "thanks, guys" as Sean came toward us.

"Let me grab one of those donuts before these vultures take all of them." Sean reached for a chocolate delight. "Help yourself to the coffee...and donuts. We'll go back to one of the interrogation rooms. Joel will join us in a couple of minutes." Sean called to one of the other officers, "Hey Mike, will you take this kid to get his fingerprints processed? Then bring him back to D."

Frankie went with Mike while Andrew and I prepared our coffee, passing on the donuts. We followed Sean through the double metal doors to a smaller interrogation room. As we were setting our coffees on the table, Joel arrived.

Sean began, "Let's get started. Joel, you called the Arkansas sanatorium where Mr. Cunningham's mother was hospitalized. Tell them what you discovered."

Joel withdrew a notepad from his shirt pocket. "The facility closed its doors in 1973. Many of the buildings on the grounds are still being used, but not the sanatorium. All the records were transferred to the Arkansas Department of Health in Little Rock. I called them and talked to Mr. Farley Olson, the assistant director. As I suspected, no personal health information, even going back to the twenties, would be released without the permission of the patient. When I informed him your mother was deceased, he said the records would only be released to you personally, showing proof of your identity. Another option would be to send a certified letter requesting the documents along with your original birth certificate and picture ID. The third option is to get a court order. It's your call."

I didn't want to send my original documents, and a court order would be the last resort. I hoped the information we found might lead us to the location of this sibling of mine. "Let's go to Arkansas."

173

Sean also reported on his findings. "I've been reviewing the physical evidence found at the scene. The crime investigators had done a great job of taking samples of all the body fluids. I submitted these samples to the National DNA Database. I also sent a partial fingerprint found on the whiskey glass to see if with today's technology a match could be found. We should get results on the fingerprints tomorrow. The DNA results may take a little more time. I also found an additional set of fingerprints on that letter and envelope from Clay Jackson which didn't match any of the known handlers. I sent that set also.

"I then traced the origin of the telephone number on Clay Jackson's letter. In the fifties and sixties, the FR exchange was Little Rock. FR5-5536 was the number of the Twilight Motel. When I tried to check their guest registers regarding who stayed there when the letter was written, I learned the motel had burned down in the early eighties. All records were destroyed. So, we're at a dead end with the telephone number. That just gives us more reason to go to Little Rock.

"Bill, since you personally want to go to Arkansas, I'll have my department get us tickets on a flight for tomorrow."

"Sean, if Andrew is available, I'd like him to accompany us."

"I'm afraid the department will only pay for your airfare."

"That's no problem. I'll refund you for our tickets; that is, if you're free." I turned to Andrew.

Sean added, "It's about a four-hour flight. We can be there and back in one day."

I considered Sean's statement. "If you don't mind,

I'd like to stay at least overnight to see if we can discover anything else about Clay Jackson while we're there."

"Andrew, do you plan to accompany us?" asked Sean.

"I'm in."

We waited until Monday to make the trip. On Friday, Andrew and I picked up my suits at the mall. I drove my new SUV. I had no trouble on the streets, but the mall parking lot was a little tricky for my ancient driving skills. After getting the suits, we spent the rest of Friday going to my various properties to determine the condition they were in. I had to think about what I planned to do with them.

On Saturday, both Grace and Joel spent the day with us at one of the local theme parks. I wanted to see how much it had changed over the years. I had taken my children when it had first opened, a few weeks before their deaths.

The park brought back so many memories. The children had enjoyed their experience so much, and I had promised to take them every year. I didn't keep that promise.

On Sunday, I went to mass with the family and Emily. Andrew introduced me to the pastor as his *good friend*. Andrew had said the pastor was new to the parish and probably never heard of the Gunderson or the Cunningham families.

We had an early dinner at the house and played board games afterwards. I was beginning to think maybe life was still worth living.

Our flight to Little Rock flew out of Orlando on Monday morning. We had a stop in Atlanta and arrived in Little Rock at one-twenty p.m. Sean's department had arranged a three-thirty appointment with Farley Olson. We checked in at our nearby hotel, dropped off our luggage, and walked to the health department. At the reception desk, we were given ID badges and directions to Olson's office. Exiting the elevator on the fifth floor, we followed the signs to room 520. Olson's door was open as we approached. "Please come in and take a seat."

Sean introduced the four of us. "Mr. Cunningham has the necessary papers allowing access to his mother's hospital records."

I extracted my mother's birth certificate, my birth certificate, and my new driver's license. He asked me for my social security number and verified it on his computer. He looked over the paperwork and called his assistant to make copies of my documents.

Olson reached for a thick file lying on his desk and leafed through the pages. "This is a complete, certified copy of all your mother's files. She was housed in the old Mason Building and attended school on the property."

I retrieved the heavy file and my personal records, thanked him, and we went back to our hotel.

We had rented two rooms. The four of us gathered in Andrew and my room to look at the records. We divided the files among us. If there was anything noteworthy or suspicious, we were to call attention to it and mark it with a sticky note. We had papers spread throughout the room.

Mom's school records were part of my portion. She was fifteen when she entered the sanatorium on September 29, 1928, just starting grade ten. Her records showed her health was too poor in the beginning to participate much in school. However, about six months later, her grades improved, and her attendance increased. According to her report cards, she was a good student able to grasp the subject matter quite easily. As I read further, her grades plummeted when she began grade eleven in 1929, probably coinciding with her pregnancy. According to Clay Jackson's birth certificate, she was impregnated sometime in July of 1929. Thus, her eleventh year of school would be affected. No wonder Mom never wanted to talk about her time in the sanatorium. Not only did she deal with a terrible disease, but she also had the stigma of being an unwed mother. Her entire eleventh grade was probably riddled with doubts, regrets, and shame.

In her twelfth year, her grades improved. She was issued a diploma in June 1931 and was cured and released the following August. The tuberculosis left its effect on her health. Throughout her life, she was susceptible to other contagious diseases and debilitating illnesses. I now also know that the unwanted pregnancy must've had just as devastating effect.

As I finished the paperwork on her schooling, Sean excitedly shouted, "I found something—the attending physician's report on the baby's birth. *'It was a normal delivery on April 14, 1930. The baby boy weighed seven pounds, ten ounces, and was twenty-one inches long. Forceps were used to help remove the baby from the cervix.'* Otherwise, it states it was a normal delivery with no complications. It also states *'the mother was not permitted to see the baby. She was in poor health after the birth, suffering from toxemia and having a very difficult time breathing. Immediately after his birth, the baby boy was taken into the infirmary, cleaned up, and transported to Saint Ignatius Orphanage accompanied by Sister Mary Anthony from the home. The mother was also taken to the infirmary to recuperate and continue her tuberculosis treatments.'* "

I told them of my findings. "That verifies what I found in her school records. In her eleventh year, which was the year of the pregnancy, she did very poorly in school. By her twelfth year, her health and school work improved. She received her diploma and was released from the facility in August 1931."

Sean stated, "At least we have a name where the child was taken. I doubt if this orphanage is still in existence, but it's a starting point. Records still should be available somewhere. Has anyone found anything on the father yet?"

No one had been successful in that area.

We kept searching the documents for two more hours. Our eyes were getting tired and our stomachs were growling. About eight-thirty p.m., Andrew suggested, "I don't know about you guys, but I'm starving. Let's take a break and continue after dinner."

The desk clerk recommended an Italian restaurant within walking distance. The food was delicious, and we were back in the hotel before ten. Sean proposed, "We'll work until midnight. If we don't find anything else tonight, we can go through the rest in the morning. Then we can look into finding the Saint Ignatius' adoption records before we fly out tomorrow night."

We went back to our same positions, reading and leafing through our paperwork, getting more tired as the time passed.

"I've found it!" Joel held up a police report. " *'Ida*

Mae Gunderson was raped by Clement Grooms, an orderly, on July 19, 1929, while being escorted in a wheelchair from her treatment to her ward by said orderly. Clement Grooms took her into a storage closet and sexually assaulted her. She was weak and unable to cry for help or fight him off. Her absence went unnoticed until the nurse entered her ward to administer nightly medications and found her bed empty. A search was made of the building, and she was found unconscious in the storage room. Ida Mae was unable to identify her assailant until the next morning. Two sheriff deputies from the Logan County Sheriff's Department went to the residence of Clement Grooms to arrest him, but his wife said he had gone to Richmond, Virginia, due to the death of his grandmother. The Logan County Sheriff's Department contacted the Richmond Police Department, who went to the home of Grooms' grandmother. His grandmother was very much alive and had not seen Grooms in three years.'

"Logan County made several attempts to find Grooms, but according to this report, they were unsuccessful. We can check with the sheriff's department to see if he was ever apprehended."

Sean added, "Tomorrow we'll search out the adoption of Clay Jackson. We'll see if the whereabouts of Clement Grooms was ever discovered, and if he was ever prosecuted. I'll also call Kristy to change our flight plans. It'll be quicker and more economical to rent a car in Little Rock and drive to Booneville. It's only about a hundred and fifty miles. Then we'll return to Little Rock to fly back to Orlando. I'll get Kristy to have a rental delivered to us."

We retired for the night feeling we had at least accomplished something of substance.

Chapter Twenty-Nine
The Beginning of the End

Bill

The rental car was dropped off at 9:30, Tuesday morning. Kristy also booked us at The Mountain View Motel outside of Booneville and made the changes to our airline tickets. We arrived at the Boonville Police Department shortly before noon. Sean showed the desk sergeant his credentials. "We're working on a cold case with ties to Booneville. Could I speak to whoever is in charge?"

A tall, thin, red-haired gentleman came to greet us. "Good morning, I'm Lieutenant Gary McKinney. What can I do for you?"

Sean asked, "Is there somewhere we can talk? We need to get some information on a cold case from Nawinah, Florida, that has connections to Booneville."

In the interview room, Sean told McKinney the basic information about the murder investigation and the connection with Saint Ignatius Orphanage and Clement Grooms. "Do you know where we could find the records from the orphanage, and if your department has any files on Clement Grooms?"

"Let's start with Saint Ignatius. Since it's a closed facility, all records were transferred to the Vital Records Department of the Arkansas Department of

Health, which is located in Little Rock."

We all looked at one another, realizing that our plans were going to change again. We needed to spend more time in Little Rock.

McKinney continued, "As for Clement Grooms, I can check if he was ever apprehended, incarcerated, or charged with any crime. I'll get one of my detectives started on it. Why don't you gentlemen have lunch and return around three o'clock?"

Thinking about our situation, if Saint Ignatius was located in Booneville, it was likely Clay Jackson was adopted by someone in or around there. If that was the case, we'd be driving back to Little Rock to the health department and then coming back to Booneville to search out Clay Jackson, an unnecessary and time-consuming endeavor. I expressed my concern to the lieutenant. "Is there any way your department can get the adoption records from the health department without us returning to Little Rock?"

McKinney said he'd try to get the records scanned to him. He made copies of Clay Jackson's birth certificate and the police report on Clement Grooms and promised he'd put a rush on getting the information.

The sandwich shop where we ate lunch was not busy, enabling us to hang out a while without taking up valued customer seats. Since we couldn't check into our motel until four o'clock, we had to wait for McKinney to get us some answers. I gave the friendly waitress a big tip for all the coffee refills.

When we returned to the police station, the desk officer buzzed us back to an interview room. McKinney soon entered, laying some paperwork on the table. "I have some good news and some bad news. Good news. We found the criminal records of Clement Lowell Grooms. He was apprehended in Fort Smith about a month after the rape of Ida Mae Gunderson. Detectives spoke to Ms. Gunderson and her parents, but they were unwilling to press charges because they didn't want to subject their daughter to a trial. They felt their daughter had suffered enough with the rape and the tuberculosis. Luckily, Grooms already had a record, and the police connected him to a string of burglaries on the east side of Booneville. Before Ms. Gunderson, Grooms had also raped another female in the Boonville area. Unlike Ms. Gunderson, this young lady did press charges. The case was brought to trial, and Grooms was sentenced to twenty years in the state penitentiary. A year before his release, he was killed by one of the guards in a prison riot. So, I guess that's both good news and bad news. At least he paid for other crimes he committed. Still, that doesn't help you with solving your case."

Sean said, "It *does* eliminate him as a suspect in the murders of the Cunningham family. Gary, what about the adoption? Did you have any success in that area?"

McKinney gave us an apologetic look. "Here again, good and bad news. The captain spoke to the director of Vital Statistics at the health department. After sending him the birth certificate and information on the case, he's willing to release the information on the adoption. However, he won't be able to accumulate it until tomorrow morning."

"Oh, that's okay," Andrew said. "We've arranged to stay overnight in Booneville anyhow."

McKinney picked up the phone on the desk. "Stan, will you tell Harry to join us? He then hung up the phone. "I've assigned Detective Harry Daly to assist you while in Booneville. He knows the area and many families who live here."

Detective Daly was an older, very down-to-earth man dressed in a long-sleeved, plaid shirt, blue jeans, and cowboy boots.

McKinney went to the door to leave. "Detective Sullivan, I'll let you bring Harry up to date on your case. He was the officer who researched the records of Clement Grooms. I gave him a brief rundown of the case, but he needs a more in-depth summary."

We spent the next hour and a half briefing Detective Daly. After we exhausted our knowledge, Detective Daly spoke in his thick, southern drawl, "Well, now, we gonna need this Clay Jackson's adoptive kin afore we can find his whar-bouts. How 'bouts if I meet ya'll here in the mornin' at nine when we git that information?"

When we arrived at the police station the next morning, Detective Daly was already seated with his coffee in hand. He called Vital Statistics in Little Rock shortly after nine. They'd send the records within the hour. At nine-thirty a clerk brought us the scans from Little Rock. Detective Daly briefly looked over them, then handed them to me. I held them in my hands, hesitant to look at them. They might hold the key to all my pain and suffering. I looked around at Andrew, Sean, and Joel. "Here goes."

I read each document and passed each one to the others: Clay Jackson's original birth certificate, which was a duplicate of what was in my mother's lock box; an updated birth certificate with the name of Clay's adoptive parents, Elmer and Bessie Jackson; affidavits from both parents on their intentions and financial status; testimonies from each of them stating the reason for adopting the child; attorney documents confirming it was a legal adoption; character references from friends or relatives of the adopting parents; and a physician's statement on the health of the child, affirming the male child was in good health with no physical maladies. Importantly, the address of the Jackson family was included-13001 Duck Creek Road, Magazine, Arkansas.

In a surprised voice, Detective Daly exclaimed, "I'll be damned. I knowed that address. Beatrice and Billy Bob Willis have lived thar fo' years. I b'lieve Beatrice's given name *was* Jackson. Magazine is jist a stone's throw away."

Sean tilted his head and half-saluted with his left hand. "Then that's where we start. Let's go, guys."

Duck Creek Road was about seven miles away on winding, hilly roads in the middle of nowhere. Eventually, Daly turned onto a long, dirt road, travelling about a mile before coming to a shabby, one-story house with a dilapidated barn in the distance. He pulled onto an uneven driveway and drove up to the house.

The front porch was about ten feet square with two side by side, worn rocking chairs. Daly walked up the narrow steps and rapped on the patched screen door while we stayed on the ground below. For a few moments, no response came from within the house. He rapped again. Then we heard a female voice. "Who is it?"

"Ma'am, this here is Harry Daly from the Booneville Police Department."

The inside door opened about five inches. "What do y'all want?"

"We'd like to ask ya'll a couple questions."

"'Bout what? I ain't done nothin' wrong."

"It ain't 'bout you or Billy Bob. We jist need to talk to you 'bout a kin o' yours."

"What kin you talkin' 'bout?"

"Please, Mrs. Willis, jist let us in, and we'll explain."

Slowly she opened the inside door as Daly opened the screen door. When she saw the group of us walking up the stairs, she backed into the house again. "Hold on here. Who be all these folks? Ya'll can't come in my house."

Sean interjected, "Ma'am, we don't need to come into your home. We can talk on your porch. We don't mean to inconvenience or frighten you. Our questions have nothing to do with you or your husband."

"Aw, okay, but there ain't no husband no more. He be dead now." She cautiously came out the door, closing it behind her.

She was a short, plump woman dressed in a faded, floral-print housedress, white socks, and tattered slippers on her feet. A frayed, brown sweater was draped around her ample shoulders. She went to one of the rocking chairs, squeezing her large buttocks between the arms as she sank onto the seat.

Detective Daly sat in the other chair. The rest of us leaned against the porch railing.

"Now, ma'am, we'all are intrested in Clay Jackson, who used to live here. Do ya'll know anything 'bout this man?" Daly asked.

"I sure do. He be my 'dopted brother."

Sean asked, "Do you know where we might find him?"

"I don't rightly know All that son o' bitch ever want from me was money. He a no-good bum. I tell him I have no money, but son o' bitch knowed I keep some in my music box. He steal it in middle a night and run off again."

Sean continued, "Was he an older brother? Can you tell us anything at all about him?"

"He be eight when Ma birthed me. Ma say he a no-account all the time. Lazy son o' bitch. Ma and Pa didn't think they could have no youngins, so they got him from the orphanage when he jist outta his mama's belly. Pa wanted a boy to help in the fields, but when he growed up, he a lazy bum. I 'member Ma and Pa always a yellin' at him 'bout this an' that. He always runnin' away from home, but always come back, mostly for more money. Ma, she always give him, but not Pa. He tell him he got to work for money. Clay say why should I work when I can git for nothin' from Ma. So he come 'roun' when Pa not home."

Sean continued to ask questions. "Do you know where he lived when he left home?"

"He in Li'l Rock for a spell. He say he shack up with some no-count ho. He say her and him, they rob some stores for money when he run low."

"Is there anywhere else he might have gone?" Sean asked.

"He tole me one time he go to Flarda. He say once he go to somewheres in Pennavania. Clay say he stay with Pa's kin up thar for a spell."

"Mrs. Willis, did your brother finish school?" I asked.

"He quit agoin' when he run away from home. I heerd tell he finish learnin' somewheres. Sometime when he come back, he dress real nice and fancy like a rich man. I ax him whar he git the fancy duds. He say he have money now. He even buy Ma and me purdy new dress."

"Do you recall when he came back with the nice clothes?" I asked.

"Oh my! Long, long time. Maybe thirdy, fordy years."

"Did he ever tell you where he got the money for the new clothes?" asked Joel.

"He say he have rich kin in Flarda who gave him lots o' money. I tole him he be crazy. We have no rich kin in Flarda. He say he do, but I din't. It jist his kin, not mine or Ma or Pa."

My heart began beating so fast. All four men looked at me, then each other without speaking. Was I hearing correctly? Could this be the clue we've been looking for? I then asked, "Did he mention what sort of kin this was?"

"Naw. Jist that they be rich. He show me lotsa money in his pocket. I think he rob bank or somethin'. He say no. It from his kin. He not have to rob stores no more."

Excitedly, I asked, "Is there anything else you can tell us about him? Anything at all, even if you don't think it's important?"

She hesitated and gave me a strange look. "Why you want to know 'bout Clay so much? What he do? He start robbin' agin?"

After looking at me, Daly answered, "Ma'am we think your brother might be involved in a crime in

Flarda."

"What kind a crime?"

Sean replied, "We aren't at liberty to discuss it at this time, but it's a very serious offense."

"I done knowed he git in big trouble someday! He a bad man, even if he be my kin."

Sean pleaded, "That's why it is so important we learn everything about him we can. If there's anything at all you can tell us, we'd greatly appreciate it."

"Well now, lemme think. He brung that ho back here one time. Her name be Gypsy Rose Lepard, but I heerd Clay call her Sylvia sometime. She weared these lepard skin, skimpy, li'l clothes alla time. She weared so much paint on her face she look like a Kewpie doll."

"Do you remember how long ago he brought Sylvia to your home?" Sean asked.

"It be afore he git rich, maybe ten, fifteen years, 'cause he be askin' Ma for mo money."

She paused and wrinkled her nose, squinting her eyes partially closed. "I 'member he tellin' me he got some book learnin' from some mail order books. He tell me it gonna make him a honest man."

"Do you know what kind of learning he received?" I asked.

"Naw. Jist that he say he be impotant afterward."

"Do you happen to have any pictures of him?" asked Sean.

"I only gots baby an li'l boy pitchers. He gone so much Ma didn't take no pitchers when he growed up."

"How about any birthmarks or anything that would help us identify him?" Sean questioned.

Her eyes opened wide, as if she were visualizing Jackson. "Well, one time he come home, he done have this here tattatoo on his shoulder. It be this here skull with a big knife stuck in da eyeball, and blood a drippin' all da way down da skull. I ax him why he do dat to his body. He say 'cause he tough."

"Thanks, Mrs. Willis. This information could prove very important. We appreciate talking to you," Sean remarked.

Both Detective Daly and Sean gave her their business cards and told her if she remembered anything, whether she thought it was important or not, to give one of them a call.

Beatrice Willis was still standing on her porch waving as we drove away.

Chapter Thirty
One Step at a Time

Dani

Dad and Mr. Cunningham returned home late Thursday night from their trip to Arkansas. At breakfast on Friday, they told Frankie and me the details of their trip.

Joel and Grace joined us for dinner that night. Joel updated us on what he and Sean had learned. "Sylvia Leopard had an extensive criminal record. She was incarcerated for the robbery of several grocery stores in Little Rock in the early sixties as well as prostitution charges. Ms. Leopard died of a drug overdose in the late seventies.

I didn't care about this woman. I wanted to know about Jackson. "Joel, what does she have to do with Clay Jackson besides being his girlfriend?"

"Here's the clincher. The clerks at each grocery store she robbed said she was accompanied by a tall, thin male with light brown hair, beard, and mustache who wore leather gloves. Ms. Leopard would confiscate the money putting it in a leopard print handbag while her male accomplice held a gun on the clerks. I called Beatrice Willis to get a description of Jackson. Her description fit that given by all the store clerks."

Frankie asked, "How about fingerprints? Has

anything come back on those?"

Joel took a sip of his coffee. "Well, the partial print found on that whiskey glass hasn't been identified yet. However, it's surprising how little a print is needed to get a full identification. We're hoping Jackson's prints might be in the national database. Maybe we'll also be able to identify or match the fingerprint on the letter Jackson sent Bill's mother. I know this is sensitive, Bill, but as for the semen left on the sheets in your mother's room, hopefully it can still give us the DNA of the killer.'

Mr. Cunningham let out a deep breath. "Joel, it's okay. I'm trying to think of all these findings from an observer's point of view."

Frankie patted Mr. Cunningham on his shoulder. "That's hard to do, and sometimes it doesn't always work, does it?"

"You're right son. You're right."

After a few moments of silence, Grace thought it best to move on to another topic. "What about the bullet found in the boy's room?"

Joel gave us the latest information he had. "The bullet and the bullet casing found in the kids' rooms were both .380 millimeter. With all the time that has passed, the gun may have been used in another crime, and the new technology on weapons and ammunition enables us to search prior crimes in the database for matches. So this is another avenue where we're still looking."

****

Joel and I hadn't had much quality time alone since he began working with Sean. After he finished his update, I grabbed a light jacket, and we went out to the back patio. Grace and Dad got comfortable on the living room couch. Frankie and Mr. Cunningham went to play computer games.

We were getting serious about each other. He was so different from most of the guys I'd dated who were only interested in partying, drinking, sex, and drugs. Joel wasn't like that. He was more mature and knew what he wanted out of life. We seemed to have so much in common, at least with important things, like politics, religion, and family. Sure, we didn't agree on everything, but that also made the relationship more interesting. I had this game I'd secretly play with him. We'd talk about something controversial, and I'd take the opposite side from what I really believed. Every time, he'd try to convince me of his views, which were my views too. Someday he'd catch on to my game.

That night on the patio, we kissed and made out, wanting more, but knowing it wasn't the time and place. We both were having difficulty pulling away from each other. I wanted him so badly, but I have the Reynolds stubborn willpower. I had to use every ounce of it when I was with him in these compromising situations.

We heard Grace leaving about eleven. Joel said he probably should go too. He gave me a long, passionate kiss before walking through the patio doors. I stood there, my body still trembling with desire.

****

I needed to catch up on my homework, especially for the criminology report. I had brought out Mr. Cunningham's identity in my last reports. Late that night, I added the information learned from the men's trip to Arkansas and from the investigation by Sean and

Joel. Shortly after I emailed my report to Professor Belinsky, he texted me saying how pleased he was with the report and how he'd never had a student take such a direction as long as he'd been teaching. I was proud of myself. Granted, I wasn't the one who discovered Clay Jackson or the one looking into all the evidence. But what if I never had all those terrible nightmares, and my grandfather never reached out to me beyond the grave? It's strange how one seemingly unrelated and personal event can lead to something so gigantic and so important that it affects many lives.

I went to bed after reading Mr. Belinsky's text. I hadn't had a dream I could remember in quite some time. I'd usually fall asleep quickly, but this night was different. I tossed and turned for a couple of hours. Maybe I had too much coffee after dinner. Maybe I worked too late on my report. Or maybe I was still worked up from Joel's fantastic kisses. I don't know. When I finally got to sleep, I found myself on Mr. Cunningham's bench near the Gunderson House passively looking out at Lake Gossette, throwing stale bread into the lake.

Fish would come to the surface to grab the morsels and plop back into the water. My mind was clear of all thoughts. Soon my grandfather sat on the bench beside me. I knew immediately it was he, not Mr. Cunningham, not Clay Jackson, not a monster, but my grandfather. He took a handful of the bread crumbs from the plastic bag and also tossed them into the lake. Then he put his arm around my shoulders. Oh, my gosh! I had the most comforting, most protective feeling I've ever had. He turned his head to my ear and whispered, "Thank you." Then he was gone and the dream ended. When I awakened in the morning, I still had that peaceful feeling enveloping me.

****

On Saturday, we gathered in the living room after dinner for additional information from Sean and Joel.

Sean began, "First, we checked the .380 caliber bullet and bullet casing. As we suspected, they were shot from the same gun. We also found a match with another bullet on file fired from a Walther PPK pistol."

Mr. Cunningham shouted, "Amen! This is a huge breakthrough."

"Hold on, hold on." Sean quickly interrupted. "Here's the thing making this case even weirder. That weapon was used in a home invasion in 1965. The perpetrator was not apprehended at that time. He shot the homeowner, but in a struggle with the homeowner, he dropped the gun and escaped. The fingerprints left on the gun were from the homeowner and a perp named Lemont White, who'd been previously charged with crimes in the same area. The gun has been in the possession of the Orange County Sheriff's Department ever since that incident."

This didn't make sense. Dad asked, "What are you saying, Sean?"

"I'm saying the county has that gun in their possession, and it was used in a crime *before* the Cunningham murders. The sheriff in 1971 didn't look specifically at that gun as the weapon used to kill the Cunningham children because it already had been confiscated."

"How can that be?" asked Grace.

"Every law enforcement agency has strict procedures regarding the handling of evidence from a

195

crime scene. It does *not* leave the evidence room, especially a weapon, unless an officer of the law removes it. Officers will oftentimes re-examine evidence, just as Joel and I are doing now, but the whereabouts of that evidence should be known at all times."

"Did they ever catch this guy, Lemont White?" I asked.

Sean retrieved his notepad. "Yes, they arrested him in March 1971, when he committed another home invasion. Fingerprints at the scene were enough to convict him. He then confessed to several home invasions going back to 1963, one being the crime when the Walther PPK was collected in 1965."

Frankie wrinkled his forehead. "So, he was in jail when Grandpa's family was killed?"

"That's correct. Even if it was the gun White used in a prior home invasion, he could not be guilty of the Cunningham murders."

I guess I wasn't the only one not understanding what Sean was telling us. Grace asked, "If that gun never left the evidence room, and if Lemont White was in jail at the time of the Cunningham murders, how did the bullet and casing from it get into Mr. Cunningham's house?"

Sean said nothing at first. Then he looked around the room and shook his head. "I don't know."

Everyone started talking at once, trying to make sense of this Catch-22.

Frankie asked, "Do they keep a record who takes evidence from the room?"

Joel answered, "Yes, every officer must sign it out with their signature, their department, and the date and time the evidence is removed. They also need to show valid ID to the officer manning the evidence room. When it's returned, they must sign and date when they return it. The officer on duty verifies it has been returned and is in the same condition as when it left the room. If it's a gun, it has to be noted if, when, and why it was fired by a police officer for testing. Sean and I checked all guns shooting .380 caliber bullets we had in evidence, including this Walther PPK. According to the records, this gun was signed out several times between August 1965 and March 1971. The last time was by my grandfather, Scott Adams, when he was a deputy with the sheriff's department."

"Did it say why he was looking at the gun?" I asked.

Joel turned toward me. "Yes, he was comparing the fingerprints on the gun, trying to link Lemont White with the 1965 home invasion. So, the gun was removed several times before March 1971, but we were the first to access it since then."

Thinking out loud, I said, "In other words that gun supposedly stayed in that evidence room even though the bullet and casing were shot from it seven months after it was last accessed."

"That's the way it appears," responded Joel.

Mr. Cunningham finally spoke, loud and indignantly, "That's impossible!"

"I know, sir," said Sean. "It *is* impossible, but we also discovered something unique about that gun. Portions of Lemont's fingerprints had been partially blotted out or smeared compared to the copies of the fingerprints on file. If an officer handles an evidence gun, he wears special gloves and handles the gun in a manner to avoid damage to any markings or fingerprints. Someone must've accessed *and* fired that gun possibly using gloves, which would result in the smearing of the original prints. He must've removed the gun illegally after March of 1971."

No one spoke. Our minds were trying to process this enigma.

Joel urged, "Let's leave that area of investigation for a while and focus on the fingerprints found at the scene. We compared the partial print on the one whiskey glass with the National FBI Database. There was no match. We got in touch with Beatrice Willis to see if she had anything with Clay Jackson's fingerprints on it. To our delight, she possessed a large belt buckle Jackson had left at the house. Detective Daly of the Booneville Police Department, who had worked with us in Arkansas, retrieved the belt from Mrs. Willis, took the fingerprints, and sent the result to us. They match the partial that was found on the whiskey glass."

Mr. Cunningham quickly stood, throwing his arms in the air. "I knew it! Ever since I found that letter to my mother, I knew he was the one. That dirty, rotten bastard. Brother, humph. He's no brother to me, nor son to my mother. He is the devil himself."

"That's not all, Bill," continued Joel. "Not only did that partial print match those on the belt buckle but also those on that letter you found."

Sean took out his notebook. "I'd like to tell you what we learned about this Clay Jackson. He had quite an extensive criminal career as a youth, mostly petty theft. What was most disturbing are the incidents of extreme cruelty to animals, cutting off appendages of cats, tying bricks to dogs and drowning them, horrible acts like that, indicating his violent nature. We also learned he's gone by many aliases. First, they were similar to his real name, like Carl Jepson. Later, he chose aliases completely different, such as Wilbur Cummings, names like yours, Bill. However, we were unable to find any the same as someone you knew. We also found no death notices for his name or any of the aliases, so we think he's still alive. We can't even be sure of that since we might not have the correct alias he used when and if he died."

Mr. Cunningham sighed, "That doesn't give us very much, does it?"

"I'm afraid not, sir, but we're still working on it."

Before we called it a night, we concluded whoever removed the Walther PPK from the evidence room had to be familiar with the procedures of the department and able to circumvent the process. So, who had access to the evidence room? Anyone who worked at the sheriff's department including Sheriff Albert Bailey; Chief Deputy Edgar Fitzsimmons; Deputy Scott Adams; Deputy Phil Drummond; Deputy Glen Myers; Dr. Wade Perkins, the coroner; Trudy Prout, the desk clerk, and Maureen Sturgis, the part-time receptionist.

Sean said, "Joel and I will investigate these individuals. Maybe we'll get a lead on Clay Jackson from one of them."

Chapter Thirty-One
Merry Christmas!

Dani

Monday was Christmas Eve. I bought a tree during the week, and we decorated it Monday morning. As Dad put Mom's angel on the top, Mr. Cunningham had a melancholy look on his face. Christmas had to be a horrible time for him, remembering the many others he'd spent with his family. I retrieved my gifts and placed them under the tree while Dad fixed breakfast. Frankie also placed his there, all looking like they'd been wrapped by a monkey. Dad was the procrastinator. He always waited until Christmas Eve to shop. After breakfast, he and Mr. Cunningham went to the mall. Frankie and I went to the grocery store to get the last-minute food items for Christmas Eve and Christmas dinners. We were eating lunch when Dad and Mr. Cunningham returned. Dad rushed into his bedroom immediately without acknowledging us, and Mr. Cunningham came into the kitchen with a big smile on his face.

I tilted my head and grinned. "What are you smiling about?"

"Am I smiling? You must be mistaken."

"Oh, yes. You were smiling all right. Wasn't he, Frankie?"

"Yes, he was. I saw it too."

"I was smiling because I wanted you to fix me one of those delicious looking sandwiches you're eating."

"No, that isn't the reason, but I'll fix you one anyhow. Roast beef or ham? I guess we'll have to wait until you're ready to tell us about that silly grin."

His smile turned into a chuckle as I stood to fix his sandwich.

Dad came out of his room several minutes later with his wrapped packages, placing them under the tree and joining us for lunch.

****

Joel had asked if I'd go to midnight mass with him and his family. I was apprehensive about meeting his parents but pleased he'd asked me. This was a big step in our relationship. I wanted to look good but not as if I were trying too hard to impress them. After our Christmas Eve dinner, Dad and Frankie cleaned up the kitchen while I got ready. I decided to wear my royal blue dress with sheer, lace, three-quarter sleeves and a scooped neckline. The bodice had a lace overlay, and the modified A-line skirt just touched the top of my knees. Dad and Mr. Cunningham said I looked beautiful. Of course, they're both prejudiced. When I answered the door for Joel, he whistled. I guess he approved.

I was nervous as he drove to his house. "What if your family doesn't like me? What if they think I'm not good enough for you? What if I say stupid stuff when they ask me questions?"

"Dani, calm down. How could they *not* like you? I talk about you all the time. They already suspect you're something special to me. Just relax and act yourself."

"You talk to them about me?"

The evening was perfect. We had coffee and dessert at his house before going to mass. Joel's parents, Paul and Angie Adams, were very nice, and I felt at ease with them. We talked about Joel's grandfather and my grandfather and the irony of both Joel and my involvement in the same case. We had a very pleasant evening topped off with the emotional midnight mass.

****

Everyone slept in on Christmas morning except Mr. Cunningham. The coffee was brewing when I wandered into the kitchen. "Merry Christmas, Danielle." He greeted me as I walked sleepily over to grab a coffee cup.

"Merry Christmas to you also. You're up very early, sir." I poured my coffee.

"Force of habit. Old people have a difficult time changing their ways."

"Well, I think you've done a terrific job in that department."

Our plan for the day was to open our presents. Then I'd stop over Emily's to exchange our gifts, and Frankie would go to Dylan's and give him his gift. We were having an early dinner at three with Grace and Joel joining us. Dad, Frankie, and Mr. Cunningham would go to Grace's mother's house for a light, late supper. I was going with Joel to his family's house for coffee and snacks.

After breakfast and still in our robes and slippers, the four of us gathered in the living room to open the presents. Frankie passed out his gifts first. Dad opened a set of baking pans to make hot pockets. "Frankie, these are great. I can't wait to try them."

I opened mine next, a sturdy, purple book bag. "Oh, Frankie, now I can throw the old one away. Thanks."

Mr. Cunningham opened his gift, a wallet. "Frankie, this is perfect."

Frankie smiled with pride. "Since you look so good in all your new clothes, I thought you needed a new wallet too."

Next Frankie passed out the gifts I had bought, opening his first. I had purchased a new Xbox sports game for him. Dad's gift was an Xbox game system, but since Frankie had opened mine first, he was a little confused. "Dani, I can't play this game. I don't have an Xbox."

Grinning, I glanced at Dad. "Oh, I guess I'll have to exchange it."

"That's okay. I know you don't know much about games. Maybe I can go with you and choose one."

Dad then opened his gift from me, a new, black work hoodie.

Mr. Cunningham opened my gift next. I had the hardest time finding something for him. What do you get a man who has more money than he knows what to do with? Or a man who has gone through what he has? On a twelve by eighteen piece of sky blue material, I had embroidered a tree with each of his children's names in vibrant colors on a different branch. On the very base of the tree, I had put his mom and dad's names. And on the trunk was his and Mary's names. I framed it in a handsome, walnut frame. When the wrapping paper fell away, Mr. Cunningham's eyes opened wide as he stared at the tree. I held my breath waiting for him to speak. He held the frame at arm's length. "Danielle, this is beautiful."

Frankie then unwrapped what Dad had bought him, hurriedly tearing at the paper. When he saw the Xbox, his mouth and eyes opened in complete surprise. "Oh gosh! An Xbox. Thank you. Thank you. This is what I really wanted. Dani, now you don't have to return the game."

A knowing smile etched across my face. "I knew I wouldn't. I'm surprised you didn't catch on when you opened it."

"I just never thought. Oh boy. An Xbox. Wait until I tell Dylan."

After Frankie gained his composure, he handed me a small box. "Here Dani. It's from Dad."

When I unwrapped my gift, my eyes opened wider than Frankie's had with his Xbox. It was a gold heart locket with tiny diamonds encircling the edges. I opened the locket and saw a picture of a young woman about twenty years old. She looked like me, but I never wore my hair like the girl in the picture.

Dad noticed the confusion on my face. "It's your mother when she was your age. You look so much like her."

I stared at the picture. I *did* look like her.

"Let me see." Frankie came over to look. "You look just like her, Dani."

I showed the locket to Mr. Cunningham. "Such a resemblance. It's uncanny."

Frankie gave Mr. Cunningham his gift from Dad. Mr. Cunningham unwrapped the small box. He carefully removed the lid. "Andrew, it's your dad's pocket watch. He didn't wear it the day of the fire because he didn't want it to get damaged. Thank you so much."

We were quiet, filled with emotions and thoughts. No Christmas could ever top this one.

Then Mr. Cunningham asked Frankie, "Son, can you get the envelopes on my nightstand?"

When Frankie returned, Mr. Cunningham said, "Please give your father the one marked for him and Danielle the one for her. The third one is yours."

The three of us opened the envelopes.

"Oh, my gosh!" I opened my mouth in complete shock and looked toward Mr. Cunningham. "I can't accept this."

Frankie was speechless. "Wow!"

Dad exclaimed, "Bill, what have you done? This is not necessary."

Mr. Cunningham had given Frankie and me the paperwork on trust funds, each with two hundred thousand dollars in them. Dad's folder contained a bank book and a deposit slip for a bank account in his name at the Nawinah Trust Bank for the same amount.

We argued with Mr. Cunningham until our mouths were dry and our faces turned blue. We couldn't accept his gifts, but he refused to listen. He said we were his family now, and he could do whatever he wanted with his money. No matter what we said, he wouldn't listen. At one point he even covered both his ears and sang some crazy song about a lovely bunch of coconuts. He'd made a decision, and we couldn't change his stubborn mind.

For the rest of the afternoon, Frankie and I were giddy with excitement. Who would think befriending a sad, old man would lead to this? Who would think all those terrible nightmares I had would culminate like this?

Joel and Grace arrived shortly before three for dinner. I planned to give Joel his gift, a new watch, before we went to his house.

All through dinner, Joel and Dad kept looking at each other as if they were conspiring about something. Mr. Cunningham also glanced at them with an odd grin on his face. Something was up. I couldn't take it any longer. Finally, I laid my fork on my plate. "Okay, what's going on? The three of you keep smirking at each other. What do you know that we don't know?"

Grace put her fork down too. "I've also noticed some strange male behavior around here. Frankie seems to be the only one acting normal."

Frankie was about to take a large bite of mashed potatoes. His fork stopped just short of his open mouth as he looked around at us.

Dad took something out of his pocket, got out of his chair, and knelt on one knee next to Grace. Grace covered her mouth and gasped, "Oh, my God!"

Dad opened a tiny, red velvet box containing a beautiful diamond engagement ring. "Grace, I haven't known you for very long, but you have come to mean so much to me. Grace DeMarco, I love you with all my heart. Will you marry me?"

I hadn't seen that coming. I guess I was just too wrapped up in my own life I was oblivious to what was going on with Dad and Grace.

Grace was beside herself. This woman who always had a composed, demure manner was completely flustered and out of control. "Oh, my God! Yes! Yes! I'll marry you, Andy."

Dad slid the ring on Grace's finger, and they stood and hugged each other so hard I thought they'd break each other's ribs.

Eventually, Dad and Grace broke apart and sat down. However, they continued to look tenderly into each other's eyes.

Mr. Cunningham cleared his throat and picked up his fork. "Ahem. Can we get back to eating this delicious meal?"

Frankie had since dropped his fork full of potatoes onto his plate. He picked it up and had the same fork of potatoes near his open mouth when Joel spoke, "No, not yet."

Frankie, again, held his fork full of potatoes poised to enter his open mouth.

Joel got out of his seat, took something out of his pocket, and knelt on his knee beside my chair! He opened a tiny, black velvet box, holding it up to me. I saw the most beautiful diamond engagement ring I've ever seen. His hands shook and his voice cracked. "Danielle Anna Reynolds, I have loved you since the moment I saw you outside the police station. I loved your spunky, unpretentious attitude when we first met. I knew even then you were the one for me. Will you marry me and spend the rest of your life with me?"

If I thought Grace was out of control with her reaction, hers was nothing compared to my behavior. I screamed. You would think someone was murdering me instead of proposing. Frankie dropped his fork full of potatoes on the floor. And what did I say? Nothing romantic like Joel had said. Nothing sweet like Dad had said to Grace. Not even like Grace had said to Dad. "You're crazy. What's wrong with you? You're nuts."

Joel, still on his knees holding the ring out to me, wrinkled his face and turned his head to the side. "Does that mean you won't marry me?"

"No. You dope. That's not what I mean." I punched him in the shoulder. "I mean you're crazy. I'm crazy too. Yes. I'll marry you. You've just added to the most insane day of my entire life." I jumped out of my chair, grabbed Joel, and almost broke his ribs too.

That night Dad, Frankie, and I had a long talk. Dad apologized for not telling us in advance about his plan to propose to Grace. "I'm not trying to replace your mother. You both must know that."

I took Dad's hand. "I don't think that at all. You've a right to happiness, and Mom would be glad you finally found someone like Grace."

"I'm glad you feel that way. You know, you're an incredible daughter."

Dad put his hand on Frankie's shoulder. "And you are an amazing son. Are you okay with this?"

"Uh, I guess so. But I have a question."

"What is it?"

"Where is everybody going to sleep? Do I have to give up my bedroom?"

A big smile reached across Dad's face. "Of course not. That room is yours for as long as you want it."

Still smiling, Dad turned to me. "Oh, by the way, Joel had asked me last week if I would give my blessing. Of course, I told him yes."

Chapter Thirty-Two
So Much Pain and Sorrow

Bill

Christmas was quite unique from the many Christmases I'd spent throughout the years. It gave me such pleasure to watch the reactions as the proposals took place. And the dinner with Grace and her mother, Evelyn DeMarco, was also very entertaining. Evelyn seemed like a lovely woman with an infectious sense of humor. I'm looking forward to other gatherings where she might be included.

On the day after Christmas, Andrew gave me Bobby Cooper's telephone number. I called him with the hope of getting some insight into what happened to Gunderson Groves during those years before it closed. I also wanted to hear about his life and career. He had been such a bright, responsible, young man and an asset to the company. "Hello, is this Bobby Cooper?"

"Yes, it is. Who is this?"

"This is Bill Cunningham."

At first there was silence. "Who is this, really? No joking around."

"Really, Bobby, this *is* Bill Cunningham. I know it's hard to believe, but I'm not dead. I've been living like a hermit and just recently came out of my exile."

"You're shittin' me. This can't be Bill

Cunningham. I'm in no mood for this crap!"

"Bobby, I'm telling you the truth. I'd like to explain everything. Is it possible to meet for lunch?"

"Uh, you sure you aren't shittin' me? Is this some kind of prank? Whoever you are, will you even show up if I agree to meet you?"

"Oh, yes, I'll be there. Just tell me where and what time."

"Uh, where are you now, Bill Cunningham, if it's really you? Uh, I'll meet you on my way home from work about one-thirty."

"One-thirty is fine. I'm in Nawinah. Where would be a good place to meet?"

"There's a restaurant called the Hot Spot on the corner of West Colonial and Maguire in Ocoee. Meet me there. If I find out this is a sick joke, I have this phone number, and I'll hunt you down."

"There's no need for threats, Bobby. I'm staying at Andrew Reynolds' house. This is his phone. He's Dan Reynolds' son. You remember him."

"*What*? Okay, mister, I'm going to check this out before I meet you. If you're lying to me, I'm getting in touch with Reynolds and telling him some psycho is stalking him. How's that?"

"You can do that, but please don't forget to meet me. I really want to talk to you. I'll be at the restaurant at one-thirty."

I hung up with a smile on my face. Same old Bobby. He's still as feisty as ever. He must be in his sixties now. All I have missed.

One of the things I did before meeting Bobby was to buy a cellular phone like everyone carried. They either talked on them constantly, or what Frankie told me, they did this thing called "texting." The clerk at the mall showed me various types of telephones, but I chose a simple, flip-open one with a camera. He connected it for me and taught me the basics. There was a way to use it as a telephone book too. I'd ask Frankie to teach me that capability.

After lunch, I called Doug Plimpton, hoping he could tell me what happened to my family's remains. Mary, Mom, and I had cemetery plots at the Oakmont Gardens Cemetery where Dad was buried. I needed to know if my children had been buried there also. Doug was with a client, but the receptionist said he'd call me back. I gave her the number of my cellular telephone, then I left the mall and drove to meet Bobby. The telephone rang while I was driving. Since I didn't know how to answer it and drive at the same time, I let it ring. The clerk at the cellular phone store had told me there was a way to find calls I didn't answer. I'd get Frankie to help me locate it later.

I ordered a pot of coffee at the restaurant, hoping Bobby would show up. I sat in a booth facing the entrance, wondering if I'd even recognize him. A man and woman entered and were seated at a booth. Not Bobby. Then a man wearing a plaid shirt and blue jeans arrived. That couldn't be Bobby. Too young. Several more minutes passed. A few other couples of various ages entered. Then a white, bushy haired, burly gentleman wearing a navy-blue suit entered. He was looking around the restaurant. I stood. "Bobby! Bobby! Over here!"

Bobby stopped and focused on me. At first he stared in complete astonishment. Then he strode toward me. He firmly grabbed my hand and put his other arm around my shoulder. "Bill Cunningham? It is you. Well, I'll be damned."

He kept shaking my hand and patting me on the back as if he were killing a bunch of ants. When he dropped my hand, he backed up slightly and looked at me as he held my shoulders at arms' length. "In a million years, I never would've believed this. I really thought you were some crackpot when you called."

He slid into his seat at the booth as I slid into mine. "Let me explain, Bobby. I know this is a complete shock to you."

"Shock. That's putting it mildly. Bill, you don't know. I can't believe it's really you. And I even recognized you as soon as you called my name."

I looked down into my coffee cup. Visions were racing through my mind. Bobby was bringing back so many memories. "Bobby, it's good to see you again."

"Hell, you can't even begin to know how we missed you. Everyone at Gunderson Groves. It was so hard to go on after your death."

"Let me brief you on why and where I've spent the last forty years." I told Bobby what had happened to me on that tragic day and how I survived afterward. I told him about the Reynolds family and how they brought me back to reality and gave me the will to live again.

"Oh, I'm so sorry. You must've lived in hell for all those years."

I then told him of the discovery of my half-brother and how we were almost certain he was the murderer.

"Bill, is there anything, *anything* at all I can do?"

"As far as the crime, no. The police are working on the case and updating me on a regular basis. I wanted to talk to you about the closing of the company. I've talked to Doug Plimpton, the attorney who took over the law firm after his father died. I know Matt, Art, and Chuck handled the closing of the business, but I wanted to get your take on it."

"Those three men did as good a job as possible under the circumstances. Your secretary, Marion Taylor, worked until the company closed five years after what we thought was your death. Chuck found a position in his firm for her. As for Jennifer Weber, the accounts payable clerk, we got married. She quit when she got pregnant with our first child, William."

"William? That's what you named your first child?"

"Yes, we named Billy after you. You'd be proud of your namesake. He's an attorney in Atlanta and has given me three beautiful grandchildren."

"Bobby, I'm honored."

"Hey, I'm so grateful to have worked with you. No one could've asked for a better employer. By the way, Jenny is a great girl. I never would've met her if she hadn't worked at Gunderson Groves."

Bobby explained how he'd become a partner at his CPA firm. Then he told me what had happened to the rest of my employees. He put my mind at ease, knowing that everyone was taken care of. "So you don't need to feel bad about any of us. We were better people because of you and Gunderson Groves."

Bobby and I talked about many of the other changes over the years. Then I asked him if he knew what had become of my family's remains. "They were all buried at Oakmont Gardens. Almost everyone at Gunderson Groves attended the mass funeral. I don't want to bring up bad images for you, but it was heart-wrenching. There wasn't a vacant seat or a dry eye in the church. I'm so sorry, Bill."

"Thanks, Bobby." I didn't know what else to say.

Since Bobby had taken off work early, I knew he had other plans. We said our goodbyes, and he gave me a big bear hug before leaving the restaurant.

I returned Doug Plimpton's call while I was still seated at the booth. "Doug, I just got done talking to Bobby Cooper. He informed me all my children are buried at Oakmont Gardens Cemetery."

"Yes, and Mary is buried in the plot reserved for her in the Tranquility section. Dan is buried next to her because of the mistaken identity. Your mother is buried next to your dad. Enough plots weren't available in Tranquility for all the children to be near each other, so they are buried in the Beloved section, specifically reserved for children."

"Thanks, Doug. I appreciate it."

I left the restaurant and drove to the cemetery, entering through the large archway to the grounds. The bright floral bouquets on the gravesites spotted the green blanket of lush grass, extending for several acres. The office was off to the right. Doug had given me the plot numbers of the children's graves. I'd be able to locate Mary, Dan, and Mom since they were near Dad, but I had to ask about the children.

As I entered the office, the scent of gardenia permeated the room, causing me to immediately picture images of my poor children rotting in their graves. It was so overwhelming I had to steady myself on a side table before I could continue.

The door had sounded a soft bell upon my entrance. The woman in front of me was looking in a

214

file cabinet behind her desk. When she heard the bell, she turned, seeing me leaning on the table. "Are you okay, sir?"

The dizziness diminished, and I released my hold on the table. "Yes, I'm fine, just a momentary bout of vertigo."

She was a thin woman in her fifties. "Please sit down. I'll get you a glass of water."

I sat on a chair against the wall while she retrieved the water. I was surprised at my reaction to the smell of the gardenias, for the vertigo was not completely gone. Apparently, I didn't have as much control over my emotions as I thought. The woman returned with a paper cup of cool water. "Thank you. I'm okay now."

"Are you sure? Do you need me to call someone?"

"No, I'm fine. I just came to ask the location of some graves."

I gave her the plot numbers. She took out a map of the Beloved section and marked where I'd find the children. I thanked her for the map and the water and got up to leave, still a little unsteady.

"Sir, are you sure you're all right?"

"Yes, ma'am. I'll be fine. This just has been a very emotional day. Thanks for the water." I felt her eyes watching me as I walked out the door.

The air was brisk and chilly when I exited my vehicle at the Beloved section. The children were located toward the back near a high, cement wall. Off to the left was a small outdoor chapel. I found them without any difficulty. Individual bronze markers identified each child's grave. Betsy Ann, Cletus, and Daisy were next to each other and close to the wall. Travis, Lily, and Silas were in a row directly below them. My heart was breaking into a million pieces. I was so close to them and yet so far. Kneeling at each marker, I kissed the name of each child. Then I stood, went to the foot of the six graves, and said a prayer aloud. "God, if you're truly there, and if you're truly good, you must've had a damn good reason for allowing the deaths of these innocent children. They suffered so severely in their last moments. I've been told countless times you're a merciful God, you know best, and we should not question your judgment. But, God, help me to understand why the slaughter of these children was something you condoned. I'm having a very hard time here. They were children. *Damn it, Children*!"

At that point I realized I was no longer praying but screaming at God. Eventually, I stopped rebuking him and said goodbye to each of my children.

Seated in my vehicle, I had to compose myself before driving to the Tranquility section, anticipating, yet dreading finding Mary's grave. I remembered Dad was buried near a large oak tree at the north end of Tranquility. It took me a while, but I found Mom and Dad's graves and its double bronze marker.

I don't think I've ever felt so emotionally drained. First, seeing my children's graves, then my mother, and seeing that date of their deaths, *October 31, 1971*, over and over again! This wasn't due to some epidemic or illness or even a tragic accident. No. *God damn it!* It was that demon!

I knelt at the bronze marker and kissed their names.

Sluggishly, I stood, searching and thinking. I remembered the plots I had purchased for Mary and me were east of Dad's. Mary had selected plots next to a flower garden. I walked unhurriedly as I searched for Mary. Thankfully, the flower garden was still there. Since no one had been around to put flowers on her grave, at least she had the bright hues of their petals so close to her. I read the double bronze marker:

CUNNINGHAM
William Russell
Loving husband and father
March 20, 1935-October 31, 1971
Mary Eileen
Loving wife and mother
July 18, 1937-October 31, 1971

There's nothing like being slapped in the face with reality. There, beneath that ground laid the bodies of my wife and my best friend. Poor Daniel, lying in someone else's grave. My grave! Yet I stood looking down at the veracity of this terrible travesty. I knelt and gently rubbed my hand back and forth over Mary's name. Then the tears came—deep, throaty sobs. For Mary. For Mom. For all my children. And for Dan.

I don't know how long I sat beside Mary's grave. I completely lost track of time. I reminisced about our lives together. I thought about Dan, his friendship, his loving family. I said aloud while looking down at the grave, "When all this is over, we'll take you home, Dan. You'll be with Anna again."

Before I realized it, the sun was setting. The winter air was getting cooler. I kissed Mary's name and struggled to my feet. A little dizzy, I gained my equilibrium. "Goodbye, Mary, my love. I'll be back."

Chapter Thirty-Three
At Last!

Dani

It was almost seven-thirty, and we were extremely worried. Dad was waiting dinner. Where could Mr. Cunningham be? Everyone had left in the morning, not even asking him what his plans were for the day. Now that he had a car and was finally getting familiar with his new surroundings, I doubt if he wanted to sit in the house watching TV. At last, we heard a car pull into the drive. He walked in the house, looking extremely tired and sad.

"Bill, where have you been?" asked Dad. "We were worried about you."

Mr. Cunningham looked confused, gazing at the three of us. "Oh, I'm sorry. I didn't know I'd be so late. Can we sit down?"

"Let's eat dinner, and you can tell us what happened." Dad began to put the food on the table.

"The first thing I did was buy one of those cellular telephones. I'll give you my telephone number. Frankie, will you put everyone's number into the telephone directory and show me how to use it?"

We hadn't even thought about a cellphone for him. Dad apologized, "I'm so sorry. I should've suggested that days ago."

"Andrew, I thought today was a good day for me to stop depending on everyone and do things for myself. You have your lives and shouldn't be catering to me."

"Listen, Mr. Cunningham," I vehemently responded. "Don't you think for one minute we don't want to help you? Like it or not, you're now part of this family."

His smile looked more sad than happy. "I feel the same way about all of you, but just the same, I need to become more independent and let your family get back to living your normal lives."

Frankie interjected, "Grandpa, you *are* part of our normal life."

He reached over and took Frankie's hand. "Thank you." Then turning to Dad and me. "All of you."

Next, he told us about meeting Bobby Cooper and his trip to the cemetery. I could not even imagine how emotional that experience had been. I felt so sorry for him.

****

Joel had called saying he and Sean had some new information for us. A new person joined our weekend get-together—Evelyn DeMarco. Mr. Cunningham sat next to her on the sofa.

Sean began, "With Captain Graham's approval, we immediately eliminated Sheriff Bailey, Scott Adams, and Dr. Perkins from the suspect list. Sheriff Bailey was so consumed with the case that many thought his inability to find the murderer contributed to his death. As for Scott Adams, Joel knows his grandfather also spent many days trying to solve the crimes. And Dr. Perkins, the coroner never had access to the evidence room.

"So, we began by talking to the others employed by the sheriff's department at the time of the crime. Phil Drummond was very cooperative and said he'd talked to Dan Reynolds' son recently. When I informed him William Cunningham was still alive, he was shocked. I asked if he'd seen any unusual activity or actions from his fellow officers and staff during the crime investigation. According to him, everyone had put forth extreme effort to find the assassin. We looked into Drummond's lifestyle and found no inconsistencies or extravagant activities. He now lives in an assisted living facility in Clermont. Frankly, I don't see him being involved.

"We next talked to Glen Myers and checked his background. He too lived a modest lifestyle with his wife and family. He lives in an unassisted home, has taken no extravagant vacations, and has purchased no large ticket items that might indicate having come into significant wealth."

I asked Sean, "Just because a criminal hasn't spent two hundred thousand dollars at one time, should we exclude him from being guilty?"

"You may be right, Dani. However, when we look at Myers and Drummond's overall lifestyles, what they've done with their lives, whether they've committed any crimes, the people with whom they associate, we can get a good picture of their guilt or innocence. Both Myers and Drummond have led lives indicative of good people not capable of such a horrendous crime. They had no motive. Nothing has shown up in either of their backgrounds to convince Joel, Captain Graham, or myself they could be guilty. Therefore, at this time we won't look any further into these two individuals.

"Next, Joel and I went to The Villages to speak with Maureen Sturgis and her husband. According to Maureen, she never had access to the evidence room. As far as the Sturgis' lifestyle, they too lived a typical, blue collar life. She only worked part time and her husband worked at the auto parts warehouse. It's doubtful she had either the opportunity or means to aid and abet in this crime. For now, she too can be eliminated as a suspect.

"That leaves three others: Trudy Prout, Edgar Fitzsimmons, and Horace McIntire, because of his relationship with Prout.

Let's start with Prout. She had moved to an exclusive area of Miami Beach and married a stockbroker named Herbert Worthington. We went to their residence to talk to them. They have a beautiful Spanish style home. When we talked to Prout, she said she remembered the Cunningham murders. She was surprised that the case had been reopened. I asked her if she had any idea who might have been the murderer. As far as she knew, it was Reynolds. I mentioned her leaving the sheriff's department shortly after the crimes. She said she had received approximately three million dollars from her grandmother's estate, which was the reason she left her job. When I asked her about her husband, she became suspicious. I told her we were checking on everyone involved in the case since the gun used in the murders had come from the evidence room. She was shocked at this revelation and claimed she had no idea who in the department would be capable of such a crime.

"You want to take it from here, Joel?"

Joel stood. "We next went to Herbert Worthington's office, which was as plush as their home. The building was a high-rise in Miami with a frontage made almost entirely of glass. His brokerage firm occupied the top two floors. He's a trim, distinctive-looking gentlemen, very cordial and accommodating. He told us he had met Trudy a few months before the murders. He had been in town on a business trip when his rental car was stolen. When he went to the sheriff's department to report the crime, Prout was on duty, and they connected immediately. At the time she didn't tell him of her relationship with Horace McIntire. We asked him if he knew about her inheritance. He said she informed him of it several months after they met. He was independently wealthy, and the inheritance made no difference to him. When I asked him if he knew anything about the Cunningham murders, he said even in Miami the crime had been in all the media. However, he knew nothing of any details other than what the media conveyed. He was cooperative, but it could be just a façade. What do you think, Sean?"

"I agree. We still need to check his background. I'll research his investment firm to see how financially sound they were in the seventies. According to the building and Worthington's office, it is definitely doing well today."

"Did you get any more information on Edgar Fitzsimmons?" I asked.

Sean looked at his notes. "We were unable to locate him. He's not in Huntsville, Alabama anymore, where he went to run his father's hardware store. An Edgar Fitzsimmons in Georgia passed away in 1990.

Judging from Fitzsimmons' application with the Orange County Sheriff's Department, this man could be the Fitzsimmons we're looking for. His widow still lives in Atlanta. We may also be making a trip to visit her."

Sean paused, then shook his head and pursed his lips in displeasure. "Then there's Mr. Horace McIntire. Joel and I went to his place on a Sunday afternoon. We figured he'd probably be home watching football on TV, like all red blooded American men except Joel and me. As we drove to his property, his dog was chained to a tree, barking incessantly. All types of trash filled the yard. McIntire met us at the door before we had a chance to knock. We showed him our badges and told him we had a few questions. At first he was hostile, but we assured him it wasn't about his prior dealings with the law. He finally let us into his house.

"I asked him about Trudy Prout. He was surprised we were focusing on her. He said they were getting serious when Prout cheated on him. I asked if she had ever asked him to do anything illegal or involve him in any criminal activity. He told us even if she had, he'd never have done it. I got the feeling he wanted to blame Prout for something but didn't know what.

"When I asked him if he remembered the Cunningham murders from 1971 and where he was that night, he became defensive and ranted about how he'd committed no crimes. All those accusations about child molesting were false; the law was always out to get him. He immediately refused to answer any more questions without an attorney. Since we couldn't charge him, our questioning stopped."

Dad asked, "Does that mean you're done with him?"

223

Sean responded, "Not at all. However, before we can force him into the station for questioning, we need more evidence. We plan to get samples of his DNA. I don't see him volunteering this, so unless we find some other evidence against him, we'll try to get the DNA on the sly. That's our next step with McIntire.

"So that's it for now. We have a lot of legwork to do this week on these three persons of interest."

"Good work, guys," said Dad. "Sounds like you're making progress."

I had to agree. "What would we have done without you? We wouldn't know the first thing about tracking down these people."

Mr. Cunningham arose from his seat and approached Sean and Joel. He shook Sean's hand. "Thanks, Sean." Then he shook Joel's hand. "Thanks, Joel. I'm beholden to you both."

Sean responded, "It's a job, guys, and we love our jobs."

****

The next Monday was New Year's Eve. We had a small gathering at our house; Joel and his parents, Grace and her mother, Emily and her family, and *my* family, including Mr. Cunningham. Dad even let Frankie and I have a little champagne. I was almost twenty-one, and Frankie had just a taste. Joel joked with Dad. "Hey, Andrew, you know I could arrest you for serving alcohol to minors."

"Well, Joel, I could say *you* gave them the champagne. How would that go over with Captain Graham?"

Mr. Cunningham spent considerable time talking to Evelyn DeMarco. I was glad he was relaxing and making friends.

That night after all our guests had gone home, Dad, Mr. Cunningham, Frankie, and I sat on the patio watching the fireworks still lighting up the darkness. For some reason, thoughts of my grandfather were occupying my mind. "Dad, Mr. Cunningham, can you tell me about my grandfather? I know so little about him."

Dad admitted, "I was young. I've told you all I remember. He was a good man. That I know for sure."

I looked at Mr. Cunningham. "He was your best friend. What was he like?"

Mr. Cunningham looked up at the sparkling explosions in the sky. After several seconds he sat back in his chair, glancing between Frankie and me. "Yes, he was my best friend, the best friend a man could ever have. A smart man too. He knew all there was to know about oranges—planting, harvesting, packing, and shipping. Any day I could've walked away from Gunderson Groves, leaving it in his capable hands, and it would've prospered.

"But I don't think you're interested in his business sense, although it does give you some insight into his character. You need to know he was a proud, compassionate man. A family man. He loved you dearly, Andrew. Every single day he'd praise you in some way. And my children? He treated them like they were his own. I'll never forget seeing him get on the floor to play with little Silas. He loved your mother too. It's such a shame she didn't get the chance to know he hadn't betrayed her."

We probably sat outside for another couple of hours listening and asking questions about my grandfather. Dad even remembered some of the things he'd completely forgotten. When I went to bed that night, I felt I knew my grandfather so much more. But I was sad I never got to see him in person. One thing was certain—I was thankful for all those horrible nightmares. They opened my eyes to a kind and gentle man.

****

When Joel came over Sunday night, we were able to spend a little 'alone' time. On the patio I said, "You realize I haven't seen you all week. I had *Joel* withdrawal."

He chuckled. "What is *Joel* withdrawal?"

"Well, if you don't have *Dani* withdrawal, I guess you'll never know."

He pulled me close as we sat on the swing. It was a chilly evening. Drowning in his blue eyes, I shivered. Not quite sure if it was from the cold or from the exploding passion.

"Hey, you're shaking."

"You need to keep me warm."

"I have no problem with that."

The first kiss was sweet and tender, but the rest of them set me on fire. I was plenty warm enough.

Chapter Thirty-Four
So Close It Bites

Bill

During the week, the Reynolds went their separate ways with their work and school obligations. They had asked me if I wanted anything, but I told them not to worry about me. It was just a waiting game. I'd find something to keep me busy. I called Evelyn DeMarco on Monday morning to take her to lunch. Instead, she invited me to her house.

It was very easy to talk to Evelyn. She told me about her husband Anthony and how his sudden death had devastated Grace and her. He had been the picture of health before the deadly attack. She told me she completely understood how I couldn't cope with life after the deaths of my family.

Evelyn and I got together several times during the week. We went riding a few days; we saw a few movies; and we walked around the mall. It helped pass the time. Besides, I sincerely enjoyed her company.

I had also made a "private" appointment with Doug Plimpton to discuss some personal business I didn't want the Reynolds to know about. I made out a new will, making them the beneficiaries of my estate.

When Saturday arrived, the group gathered in the living room to hear what Sean and Joel had discovered.

Sean started with Trudy Prout. "It's possible Prout knew nothing about her inheritance at the time of the murders, still leaving a question about her innocence. I'm not sure she would've been physically able to commit the crimes on her own, like dragging Bill's unconscious body into that crawlspace. Or how can the rape of Mrs. Gunderson be explained? So, if she were involved, she couldn't have done it alone.

"As for Herbert Worthington, nothing in his past indicates he had anything to do with the crime. His firm has been successful since the early sixties, and he comes from a prominent family in the Miami area. There is no reason to look any further into him.

"Next, Horace McIntire. One of our attractive, female detectives followed him to a fast-food restaurant. She talked to him and gave him a fake telephone number. When he left the restaurant, she grabbed the disposable cup and utensils from his table, putting them in a bag concealed in her purse. We've submitted them to the lab for DNA and fingerprints. So we're still looking at McIntire and perhaps Prout as his accomplice. If his DNA and fingerprints are matches to what we have on file, we'll charge him with the murders and look further into Prout's involvement.

"Now for Edgar Fitzsimmons. We went to Atlanta to talk to his widow. Cora Fitzsimmons told us her Edgar, originally from Cleveland, Ohio, had never even been to Florida. He had no other relatives with the same name as he, so she couldn't see how anyone in Edgar's family could be involved. When I asked her if her husband had ever been away from the family for long periods, she said they always took vacations together. His job never required any travel. When I got back to

Nawinah, I checked out her information. That Edgar Fitzsimmons couldn't be our suspect. It was discouraging, but we didn't give up.

"Joel, do you want to tell them what happened next?"

Joel cleared his throat. "We talked with Phil Drummond and Glen Myers again to see if they either socialized with Fitzsimmons or knew somebody who did. Drummond and Myers both said they remembered Fitzsimmons talking about hanging out at a bar outside of town called the Dirty Dungeon."

"Yes, I know that place," I interrupted. "Dan and I stopped there once in a while. I remember seeing Fitzsimmons on occasion."

Joel continued. "The owner of the Dirty Dungeon, Jimmy Caldwell, died several years ago, but his son, Jimmy Junior, ran the business until the property was sold. As a college student, he had also helped when his dad owned the place. When we talked to him about Fitzsimmons, he remembered him. He said Fitzsimmons was a friendly guy, never getting drunk or causing any issues. Fitzsimmons often talked to that weirdo who lived out on the edge of town. Jimmy knew his first name was Horace but didn't remember his last name.

"Then we did an extensive search for Edgar Fitzsimmons, again coming up empty-handed. It was as if he'd vanished from the face of the earth. No death notices, marriage applications, or real estate purchases, nothing at all. We found no record of any Edgar or Dorothy Fitzsimmons living in Huntsville at that time. We also found no record of Fitzsimmons working for the Limestone County Sheriff's Department as he had claimed on his Orange County application. Therefore, we came to the conclusion Edgar Fitzsimmons must've changed his name and lied or forged documents to get the job with the Nawinah Sheriff Department."

My mind started spinning. Could Edgar Fitzsimmons be Clay Jackson, the assassin who killed my family? Then I put the facts together. Clay Jackson had contacted Mom. She didn't answer his letter. Somehow, he must've found out she was also *my* mother, and I was his half-brother. He must've found all of this out before he decided to move to Nawinah. How could he have become a deputy? He had worked in the department for several years, keeping a low profile. I had come in contact with him so often during that time on personal and professional occasions totally unaware of who he really was. He must've planned his evil crime for years, waiting for the perfect opportunity.

This was too much for me. I was getting short of breath and sweating profusely. I felt like I was going to pass out! My chest felt very heavy, like a vise was squeezing it from both sides!

Chapter Thirty-Five
Emergency

Dani

The entire room was in an uproar. None of us could believe what we heard. Then I looked over at Mr. Cunningham. He was clutching at his chest and his eyes were rolling back into his head. "Dad, something is wrong with Mr. Cunningham!"

Dad and Joel rushed to him. "Bill! Bill!" But Mr. Cunningham was unresponsive. Dad shouted, "Dani, call 911!"

I fumbled with my cell phone, finally pressing 911.

"911. What is your emergency?"

With my hands and my voice shaking, I yelled into the phone. "I think a man is having a heart attack. He passed out and is unresponsive."

"Is he still breathing?"

"Dad, is he breathing?"

"Yes, but very shallow."

The emergency operator then asked me for our address. "The ambulance is on its way. Stay on the line with me. Is this individual conscious?"

"No, he isn't."

"Does he have any heart medication prescribed for him?"

"No. He doesn't have a history of a heart condition.

He just found out some very disturbing news."

"Is anyone there to administer CPR?"

"Uh, I think so. Joel, do you know CPR?"

Joel had already started the procedure by loosening Mr. Cunningham's shirt and unbuckling his pants.

"There's an off-duty policeman doing the CPR."

"Is the person still unresponsive?"

"Yes."

"Have the policeman keep up the CPR until the EMTs arrive. They should be there in less than five minutes. Stay on the line."

"Okay."

"Tell me again what pre-empted this attack."

I talked very fast and had a hard time forming my words. I was short of breath and even thought I had pains in my chest. "He heard some very distressing news. Then he started to sweat and grab at his chest, and his eyes rolled back into his head. Is that ambulance almost here? Can you please get them to hurry?"

"They should be there very shortly. Is he responding to the CPR?"

"I think so. I don't know."

"Have you contacted the person's physician?"

"No, I don't think he has a physician he sees regularly."

"How old is the gentlemen?"

"I'm not sure, probably in his seventies."

"Okay, an emergency physician will be on hand at the hospital. Stay calm. Keep giving him CPR until the EMTs arrive. Is he still unconscious?"

"Oh, I hear the sirens. They must be close."

"Is there anyone else with you beside the

policeman?"

"Yes, several people?"

"Have someone open the door to allow the EMTs to enter."

"Frankie, open the front door. Open the screen door too. Set the stopper so the door stays open."

Frankie ran to the front door and did as I asked. Within minutes the EMTs entered the house with a stretcher and all kinds of elaborate medical equipment.

"They're here now. They're in the house. I'm hanging up now."

"Good luck." She hung up, and I stood there helplessly watching as the EMTs worked on Mr. Cunningham.

"Is he going to be okay?" Frankie asked.

One of the EMTs responded, "We'll do all we can, son. He's breathing now."

They placed his pale body on the stretcher, connected all their equipment to him, and took him out the door, swiftly lifting him into the ambulance.

"Can I go in the ambulance with him?" Dad asked.

"Yes. The rest of you can follow in your own vehicles. We'll be transporting him to Nawinah General Hospital."

Dad tossed his car keys to Joel as he climbed into the back of the ambulance. "Joel, take the SUV. There's room for everyone in it."

The ambulance took off with sirens blaring and lights flashing.

As I climbed into Dad's SUV, Grace said, "I'm taking Mom home. Mr. Cunningham doesn't need all of us at the hospital. Call or text as soon as you find out anything."

"I'm taking off too," said Sean. "Joel, keep me posted."

Joel drove as quickly but as safely as possible to the hospital. Arriving minutes after the ambulance, we hurried through the emergency entrance. Mr. Cunningham had already been transported into an ER cubicle. We approached the nurse at the reception area. Joel said, "We're here with the patient who just arrived by ambulance."

"Please be seated in the waiting area. The doctor will speak to you as soon as possible."

Dad was already in the waiting area, filling out the paperwork. "How do I fill this out? What do I put for his family? What about a doctor? What about insurance?"

"Dad, he doesn't need insurance. He can pay cash for whatever they do to him. I guess just leave those parts blank. There isn't much to fill out. His name and *our* address. That's where he lives now. You don't know anything about his health history, so you can't fill that out either. We'll have to explain this after they look at all the blank lines."

Frankie had sat next to me. I saw the frightened look on his face. He tapped me on the shoulder. "Dani, can I hold your hand?"

I felt his trembling hand as I grabbed it. Frankie had gotten very close to Mr. Cunningham. Not knowing his real grandfathers, he had adopted Mr. Cunningham as a surrogate. We had assumed Mr. Cunningham, even though old, was strong emotionally and physically. However, finding out the possible identity of his family's murderer was just too much for him. And to learn that murderer might be his half-brother and a person of the law. Who could accept all that without some type of explosion?

Dad and I took the paperwork to the nurse at the desk. We waited while she looked it over, knowing she'd have questions. "I see you haven't completed the form. Do you know the man who was brought in?"

Dad answered, "Yes, we do, but we don't know very much about the questions on that form. He's been living with us for a few months. We know he currently has no physician."

"What about an insurance card? Do you know where that might be?"

"I'm certain he doesn't currently have any health insurance, but I also know he'll take care of any charges he incurs at the hospital or with any of the physicians."

The nurse looked at Dad as if she were saying, *What planet do you think I'm from if you think I believe that crap?* Instead, she sternly but politely said, "Sir, you do realize I can't just take your word for his ability to pay."

Dad recognized the dichotomy of the situation. "Yes, I know, but because this is a Saturday night and any place capable of verifying this is closed until Monday, I don't know how I can prove it to you. How about if I sign some type of document stating I'll be responsible for any financial obligations he incurs at your facility if he doesn't pay?"

"Yes, I can accept that. Let me call the finance department. They'll have the necessary paperwork to fill out."

About fifteen minutes later, a pleasant, gray-haired woman came into the waiting area. She first talked briefly to the nurse and then turned to us. She was smiling as she approached Dad. "I'm Miriam Simpson. Are you the gentleman who accompanied," then looking down at her clipboard, "Mr. William Cunningham to our hospital?"

"Yes, I'm Andrew Reynolds."

"Mr. Reynolds, please come with me. We'll get the required documents filled out to allow Mr. Cunningham to get the fine treatment he deserves." She smiled again and turned away.

Dad got up to follow her. "Dani, in case I'm not back in time, wait here for the doctor to update us."

About a half hour after Dad returned from filling out the paperwork, the doctor came out to talk to us. "I'm Dr. Shapiro. Mr. Cunningham has been sedated, and we have controlled his heart rate. Are you his family?"

Quickly, Frankie spoke, "He's my grandpa!"

"Well, we don't know how much damage was done to his heart. We're transferring him to ICU to monitor him and run some tests. I'd like to get in touch with his personal physician and cardiologist."

With a worried look on his face, Dad said, "He has no personal physician or cardiologist. I'll call my doctor to see if he'll take him on as a patient. As for a cardiologist, could you recommend someone? "

Dr. Shapiro agreed and said we could see Mr. Cunningham, but he was heavily sedated and might not be able to communicate. They were preparing a bed for him in the ICU, and he'd be taken there as soon as they were ready. Dad called the answering service for Dr. Nichols, our family physician, and left a message to call at his earliest convenience. He also texted Grace to let her know Mr. Cunningham was now responding and was being transferred to the ICU. Joel texted Sean the same message.

Frankie was again tightly grasping my hand as we walked to Mr. Cunningham's cubicle. Dad gently pulled the sliding, pale green drape aside as we entered and surrounded him. He looked like a robot with wires, tubes, and machines attached to almost every part of his body. So ashen, he surely didn't look like the monster I'd seen on his property months ago.

Frankie dropped my hand and rushed to Mr. Cunningham, placing his hand on Mr. Cunningham's shoulder. "Grandpa, are you okay?"

Mr. Cunningham opened his watery, red eyes. "Hello, son. I'm fine. No need to worry. I'll be out of here soon. Now I'm tired. I hope you don't mind if I rest my eyes."

Dad went closer to the bed. "Bill, they're taking you to ICU shortly. The cardiologist will see you in the morning. I'm also getting in touch with our family doctor. Don't worry about anything. You just rest and get better."

As Dad was talking, two orderlies came into the cubicle to transport Mr. Cunningham.

"We'll see you upstairs, Grandpa," Frankie said as we left the cubicle to let the orderlies do their job.

When we got to the ICU, Mr. Cunningham was not settled in his bed. The nurses were still hooking up machines. Dad said, "One of us should stay the night, and keep an eye on him."

I volunteered. "I'll stay. I don't have work or class tomorrow."

Joel added, "I'll keep Dani company. You and

Frankie come in the morning to relieve us."

When Mr. Cunningham was settled, Dad and Frankie went to see him. Since Mr. Cunningham was sleeping, they only stayed a few minutes. Frankie gave him a gentle hug before he left. Joel and I found comfortable seats in the ICU waiting area. We didn't bother Mr. Cunningham while he was sleeping, but we took two-hour intervals to check on him every fifteen minutes.

****

Sean and Joel were still working on solving the case. When Joel came to dinner on Saturday, he told us they had gone back to Horace McIntire's house to bring him in for questioning. "At first, he refused to go with us, but we told him he could contact his attorney and have him meet at the police station. Otherwise, we'd get a court order, and he'd be forced to accompany us or go to jail. At the police station, we outright asked him if he had anything to do with the murders of the Cunningham family. He vehemently denied any involvement and even agreed to a polygraph test. We eventually questioned him about Edgar Fitzsimmons. McIntire admitted he was an acquaintance of Fitzsimmons, and they often drank socially together. Once in a while they got together to watch a football game. When we asked if he knew anything about Fitzsimmons' background, he said he only knew Fitzsimmons was from Alabama, nothing else.

"The more we questioned McIntire, the more relaxed he became. I asked him if Fitzsimmons acted strangely around the time of the Cunningham murders or if he said anything out of the ordinary. I think McIntire then got the connection why he was in for interrogation. He figured the pressure was off him, and he was merely at the police station because of his friendship with Fitzsimmons.

"McIntire remembered Fitzsimmons once asked him if he wanted to make some money. Since Fitzsimmons was a law officer, McIntire never suspected anything illegal. When Fitzsimmons told McIntire he'd pay him five thousand dollars to start a fire in an orange grove, McIntire was shocked and refused any part of it. At that time, he had already been suspected of child molesting, and he didn't want to get into more trouble. He said Fitzsimmons dropped the subject and never mentioned it again."

Dad asked Joel, "Do you know if McIntire had any contact with Fitzsimmons after he moved away?"

"That was our next line of questioning. McIntire remembered he had received a letter from Fitzsimmons two or three years later stating how he enjoyed overseeing his father's hardware store in Huntsville and had married a nice woman named Arla, Alma or Arna, some strange 'A' name. She was pregnant with their first child. When Sean asked McIntire if anything else was in the letter, he remembered the envelope had no return address on it. He happened to notice this because he normally didn't receive personal letters, just bills or junk mail. This made him curious about who'd be sending him a letter. When he checked the postmark, it read from Ocala, Florida. He was confused to find the letter was from Fitzsimmons living in Alabama. However, that mix-up meant nothing to him, and he never thought about it again until we questioned him about Fitzsimmons."

"That's terrific," said Dad. "Granted, it isn't a huge

239

lead, but it has to mean something."

"Yeah, that's our next challenge, to search Ocala, Florida. Wish us luck."

Chapter Thirty-Six
Rest and Recuperation

Bill

I had never felt such pain before! Not even when I woke in the crawlspace after that horrible day. I thought my heart had cracked my ribs open and leaped out of my chest, pulling every organ in my body with it. When I finally became conscious, I was in the ER at the hospital. I don't even remember the ambulance ride. I awakened to see Frankie's cherubic face with eyes filled with tears and asking me if I was okay. He looked so worried, but I was too weak to say much. Then Andrew said something about being moved. The next thing I remembered was waking in the Intensive Care Unit with my own private nurse constantly monitoring the machines to which I was connected. I raised my head a few times and saw Danielle or Joel staring at me. It wasn't until I saw this strange man looking over me and holding what I assumed was my medical chart that I was somewhat aware of reality.

"Billy, looks like you tried to leave this world for some other place."

I didn't quite understand what he was talking about. My brain was still foggy.

"I'm Dr. Louis Frasier. You needed a cardiologist, and guess what? I'm the lucky guy. I see you're not a young man. I also see we have no medical history on you. I expect you'll give us that information soon. In the meantime, we've stabilized your condition and are looking into what treatment you'll need. One thing I know without a doubt. Your heart won't stand another episode like it just experienced. You must modify your lifestyle. No more running marathons or having a heavy sex life, no matter if you're a Casanova or on Viagra."

This man was very strange! At least he was direct.

"I've ordered several tests while you're here. Don't think you'll escape this place tomorrow. As much as I know the food here is atrocious, the nurses are hot and sexy, and they're good at their jobs. So enjoy the scenery and choke down the food. Lay back and let them fondle that old body of yours. Just don't get too aroused in the process."

I guess I was staring at this doctor.

"So are you there yet, or are you still in LaLa Land? Speak, man, speak! Nobody took your tongue."

I didn't realize I was required to respond to this madman. "I must say you have a unique bedside manner, Louis."

"Hey, we're almost friends. You can call me Louie, and I'll call you Billy. Glad to see you're still alive and kicking, Billy."

"I'm alive, but I'm not sure how much I can kick right now."

Louie chuckled and put his hand on my shoulder. "Since you're coherent, I'm sending in the nurse to get your medical history. Don't participate in any hanky-panky with the pretty young thing."

As he walked away, I saw him smiling and talking to the nurses. They seemed to enjoy whatever he was saying. Apparently, he had a good rapport with the staff. When Andrew comes in, I'll ask him how I ended up with this kook.

The "pretty young thing" came with a form to fill in my medical history. Yes, as a child, I had chicken pox, measles, and mumps. I think I had pneumonia once. No, I never had any major surgeries or major illnesses. I didn't tell her about almost being murdered by my half-brother and the trauma taking place afterward. Nor did I mention how I tried to kill myself several times. Those incidents were so long ago and not significant currently. She seemed to be satisfied with my responses, although she looked strangely at the huge scar on my abdomen. I told her a bunch of malarkey about accidently falling on a knife.

Andrew arrived while she was finishing the report. I wanted to know what Sean and Joel had found out about Ed Fitzsimmons.

"Sorry, Bill, I was given strict orders from the cardiologist not to approach that subject for at least a week."

"Well, I don't agree. After all, this is my life and these are things I deserve to know."

"Hey, I sympathize with you, but I'm not going against the doctor's orders. You realize it was the emotional stress that sent your heart in a tailspin."

So, in the end, I didn't badger Andrew or anyone else about the case.

****

I recovered slowly from this very serious heart attack. I saw Dr. Louie and Dr. Nickols regularly during my hospital stay. I went back to Andrew's house on Friday after almost two weeks, getting to know the pretty nurses and Louie quite well. I took his advice and enjoyed the scenery, but not the food. He had put me on a low cholesterol, low salt diet and warned me to stick to it. I made an appointment to see him in two weeks.

In the meantime, I was given four powerful prescriptions whose names sounded like a one-year-old child trying to talk. Eventually, I might not need all of them. I was also given strict orders to avoid any strenuous physical exertion and traumatic events, a task quite difficult for me with my entire life being an emotional roller-coaster.

So I was a good, ol' boy for the next two weeks, never exerting myself, doing the simple exercises Louie ordered, sticking to my low taste diet, and being bored out of my wits. I couldn't drive for at least two weeks. Thus, I was stuck in the house unless I was driven by someone. I read several books, watched television, learning so much more about how the world had changed. I even played some combat games on Frankie's Xbox. During the second week of my recuperation, I took short walks around the neighborhood, enjoying the mild weather. Evelyn came over several times while I was recuperating. Sometimes I'd fix a light lunch for us. We had many pleasant conversations. Joel came over some of the evenings to see Danielle, but we didn't discuss the investigation.

On Friday, Andrew drove me to my appointment with Louie.

"Good job, Billy. I'm pleased with the progress you've made. I'm reducing your medications. You can also start driving—no long trips, just around town. But you must still take it easy on the physical activity. You can even resume your moderate sex life with partners of you own age—no pretty young things. And stay away from too much drama in your life. Stress is a big cause of heart issues."

At that point I explained what had precipitated the heart attack.

The doctor hesitated before he spoke. "That creates a bit of a problem, doesn't it? You can resume discussing the progress of your case. However, if you have any sign of trouble or agitation, stop immediately, and take appropriate action, whether it be taking a break and continuing at a later date or calling 911. And don't ever forget to take your medications."

"Yes, Boss Louie, I will obey. Seriously, I know how vulnerable my heart is now. I'll definitely be very careful."

"I'll keep a close watch on him," Andrew assured. "I'll make sure his diet and lifestyle are modified, and I'll chase all the 'pretty young things' away."

Andrew invited everyone to dinner the next evening. He forewarned them we'd be having a healthy meal of garden salad, baked perch with lemon and dill, and a side of grilled vegetables with herb-infused chicken broth. Lime gelatin would be the dessert. With that menu for enticement, he'd be lucky if anyone came.

He then told me of Horace McIntire's knowledge on Ed Fitzsimmons. I took the news calmly. However, it did take my mind some extensive acceptance to come to terms with Ed Fitzsimmons conceivably being Clay Jackson. Recalling the man from years ago, I couldn't fathom him the murderer of my family *or* my half-brother. He didn't resemble me in the least. Most ironic, he'd been the chief deputy sheriff, an upstanding law officer. Sheriff Bailey would've gotten rid of him if he'd the slightest suspicion he was not who he claimed. So how could a law man be such a monster when his very job was saving lives? How could he fool an entire town? Even more difficult to accept was how he could be my brother, born of my quiet, loving mother.

Chapter Thirty-Seven
It Was Inevitable

Dani

The dinner guests gushed extensively over the fish dinner. After all the praises and accolades, Dad finally said, "It's okay, guys. I know it isn't prime rib, but we can all eat a little healthier, not just Bill. So I'll accept your commendations as if you really meant them."

It was such a nice evening we decided to sit on the back patio. Sean began telling us what they had learned. "In our research to see if Fitzsimmons was in Ocala instead of Huntsville, we found no one with the name of Edgar Fitzsimmons or Clay Jackson living in that area. We knew Jackson, I'll call him by his real name, changed his name many times, so it was no surprise we couldn't find either of those names. Our next step was to figure out where to go from there. Thanks to Horace McIntire's letter from Jackson, we were optimistic. Maybe Jackson really did get married and had a child. Maybe he used his wife's real first name, which was an unusual name. And we hit pay dirt."

We were all anxious to hear what they discovered. Dad kept looking at Mr. Cunningham, who smiled back at Dad. "I'm all right, Andrew. I can take this." He looked around the yard and gazed up at the stars. "It was a good idea to come out here."

Evelyn took Mr. Cunningham's hand and snuggled closer to him.

Mr. Cunningham nodded at Sean. "Please continue. I'm ready to hear this."

"Okay, Bill. Here goes... In our search for odd female names beginning with 'A' in the Ocala area, we found an Arna Marika Kozloski Jordan living on SW Eighth Street with her husband Claude Hiram Jordan. This street is a very exclusive area with homes worth millions of dollars. Arna Jordan is in her seventies and her husband is in his eighties. They have two children, Craig Jordan, born in 1976; and Marcella Jordan Hinkle, born in 1980. We're certain Claude Jordan is Clay Jackson. However, we couldn't simply arrest him without further proof. First, we knew he had access to the gun that killed the Cunningham children. We also knew the fingerprints of law enforcement officers are kept on file as part of their permanent records. Therefore, we checked the partial print on that glass found at the scene of the murders with the prints on file for Fitzsimmons. We found they were a possible match, but it wasn't conclusive. Not enough of a print was available. However, the prints on Jackson's letter were positively identified as belonging to Fitzsimmons."

"Great work, guys," declared Grace.

"Thanks," said Sean. "We knew you'd be pleased with this news. Finally, something concrete. But the fingerprints were not the only evidence we had from the crime scene. After all these years, we were still able to obtain the DNA of Mrs. Ida Mae Cunningham's rapist from the semen on the bedding. This coming week we plan to collect Claude Jordan's DNA. Joel and I are going to Ocala on Monday to inform the local police of our suspicions. No death certificates have been filed for either Claude or Arna Jordan, so we're certain Jordan is still alive. We need to get a warrant and obtain Jordan's DNA before charging him. We'll determine how to do this after we stake out his pattern of behavior."

"I want to go with you to Ocala, Sean," Mr. Cunningham said.

"Bill, do you think that's wise so soon after your heart attack?" asked Dad.

"I don't know if it's wise, but I *deserve* to be there when that bastard is arrested."

Sean disclosed, "We don't plan to arrest him until we have solidly identified he is Jackson through his DNA. It'll take a few weeks to confirm this even after we obtain it. Joel and I will go to Ocala, secure the DNA, then when we go back to arrest Jordan, you can accompany us. You'll then have a few more weeks to recuperate and check with your doctor if your heart will be strong enough for the personal encounter with Jackson."

"I'll wait until you arrest him, but I'm going with or without the doctor's approval. I *need* to be there to see that demon's face when he is captured."

****

I'd been handing in regular reports to Dr. Belinsky for my criminology class assignment. He texted me, "Danielle, your reports are like reading a suspense novel, and I can't wait until the next chapter."

I had something to add this week. I wrote about the discovery of Claude Jordan and how Edgar Fitzsimmons was Clay Jackson who was Claude Jordan. After Monday's class, Dr. Belinsky called me to his desk. "I can't believe the turn of events unfolding

249

in this case. Do you know when you might be able to present it to the class? I know you don't want to jeopardize the case in any way, but the class would truly benefit from your determination and progress."

"Sir, I really don't think it's time yet. If it's okay with you, I'd like to still keep it confidential."

Dr. Belinsky understood my position.

Chapter Thirty-Eight
Bastard!

Bill

Sean called me Wednesday night. He and Joel had met with the Ocala Police Chief, Captain Richard Thompson, who told us Claude Jordan had been a model citizen of the community for many years. He had served on the city council and the board of education. Jordan's son, Craig, was currently a member of the city council. The captain was surprised at the allegations. Sean told him they'd verify the evidence before arresting Jordan.

Here's how the sting went down: Sean and Joel had arranged to obtain Jordan's DNA at the monthly city council meeting. Captain Thompson had told them Jordan usually attended the meeting even though he was no longer a councilman. The captain, who also attended the meeting, identified Jordan for them. At a table in the back of the meeting room, coffee was served in paper cups. Before the meeting, Jordan got his coffee and talked to various people. When the mayor called the meeting to order, Jordan left his coffee cup on the serving table. After the meeting ended and everyone had exited the room, Joel picked up the cup with an ink pen and put it in a paper bag. It'll take forensic about a week to get the DNA results. As soon as they're in, they think Captain Graham will want to formally charge Clay Jackson for the murders of my family.

After Sean's phone call, I was in an edgy state of mind. Sean and Joel had seen the devil! They had been in the same room with him, mere feet away. They said he was a pompous ass. Even though he was no longer a councilman, he had something to say about every topic discussed. But here lies the clincher. They said everyone else had the courtesy to throw their used paper coffee cup in the trash. Not Jackson. He left his on the serving table. It was a minor transgression, but it showed his arrogance, too good to throw his own cup in the trash. Well, that selfish action would be his ruination.

Sean had described Jackson. "He was trim and well dressed, but even the expensive tailored suit, the silk shirt, and the Italian leather shoes couldn't hide his true character. I personally think it was the pure evilness showing through. He was tall like you, Bill, but there the resemblance ended. He had wide nostrils at the end of a narrow, long nose. His beady, round eyes were deeply set in a clean shaven, angular face. His hair was thin but trimmed neatly and probably tinted a light brown. His Southern drawl was very prominent."

That wasn't a surprise. I remember his accent from when he was still Edgar Fitzsimmons.

When Joel came over that evening, he commented, "Bill, what really surprised me at that meeting was how much Craig Jordan, Jackson's son, looked like you. He was tall, like both you and Jackson, with dark brown hair, deep brown eyes, and facial features very similar to yours. If I had a picture of you when you were his age, the two of you would look like brothers. What impressed me about him was he didn't seem at all like his father. In fact, a few times I noticed him rolling his eyes when the man interrupted one of the speakers for some inconsequential comment. Craig Jordon seemed to be a bit annoyed with Claude Jordan."

****

On the following Tuesday afternoon, Sean called me again. "The DNA is a positive match. We've got him, Bill."

The euphoria I felt at that moment was indescribable. At last! The monster who killed my family, who destroyed my life had been found. No, he wouldn't have enough years left of his life to suffer as much as he should for his despicable acts, but at least he'll be brought to justice.

Sean told me Captain Graham had contacted the Ocala police captain to arrange a joint arrest. Sean, Joel, and two other Nawinah detectives would drive to Ocala in two official police vehicles. Andrew and I would follow in Andrew's SUV.

Early Friday morning, Andrew and I drove to the Nawinah Police Headquarters to meet up with Sean, Joel, and the other two detectives, Brian Headley and Rick Gomez. The captain briefly described his plan and gave Sean the warrant for the arrest. Andrew and I were to stay at a safe distance until the situation was completely under control.

We arrived at the Ocala Police Headquarters at eight a.m. They had been monitoring Jackson's movements since Tuesday. He didn't leave his house until at least nine a.m. each morning. The plan was to arrest him in his home, keeping any endangerment to

253

innocent bystanders to a minimum. They didn't know if Jackson would be carrying a weapon. However, since he'd be unaware of their presence until they knocked on his door, it was doubtful he'd even think to grab one.

Our caravan of five vehicles drove to Jackson's quiet, tree lined street, first the two Ocala police cars, then the two Nawinah police cars, then Andrew's vehicle. A few cars were pulling out of their long driveways heading for their morning destinations. Otherwise, no activity occurred outside nearby houses. No one doing yardwork. No pedestrians walking the street.

Jackson's spacious, two story home, similar to others on the street, was in the middle of the block set back about forty yards. It was the typical architecture of a Florida home—sand colored exterior and terra-cotta tile roof. The shrubbery was clipped to perfection, and the Saint Augustine lawn was pristine and well maintained. A large bay window covered with closed, dark drapery faced the cement walkway leading to the rustic, oak front door. Andrew would park on the street until Sean called him from inside the house. The other four vehicles pulled into the long driveway minus sirens and lights. The two Ocala detectives from the second automobile walked around the house to station themselves outside the back door. The chief detective from Ocala, the other officer in his vehicle, Sean, and Joel walked up the walkway two abreast to the front door. Headley and Gomez waited at the bottom of the stairs. Ocala's chief detective lifted the brass door knocker and let it bang against its brass plate three times. Like soldiers, they stood upright and rigid, awaiting the door to open.

Soon a gray-haired woman dressed in a crisp, blue uniform appeared in the doorway. I couldn't hear what was said, but I saw the woman's facial features change to one of surprise when she noticed the four men standing before her. The chief detective said something to cause her to open the door wider, allowing the men entrance into the house. Then the door was closed.

Andrew and I sat quietly in his vehicle, awaiting the telephone call from Sean. My insides were turning somersaults. My heart was fluttering a mile a minute despite my medication. I had to pull in my emotions.

"Are you okay, Bill?"

"Yes. I'm just so worried about this whole situation. After all these years…"

They were in the house a total of fourteen minutes when Andrew's telephone rang. He put it on speaker, and Sean's voice roared, "We're coming out. He's in handcuffs."

I exited Andrew's automobile faster than a ten-year-old kid running to first base and rushed up the driveway.

"Bill, I'll drive us."

I was already halfway up the drive when Andrew parked his car behind the others. I suddenly stopped at the beginning of the walkway as Sean and Joel exited the house followed by the two Ocala detectives. The devil was between them, his hands cuffed behind his back and the detectives firmly grasping his upper arms on each side. He had his head down as he descended the stairs, focusing on the walkway and shuffling between the two detectives.

Since I blocked the area where the walkway met the driveway, Sean and Joel walked around me.

However, the Ocala detectives abruptly stopped in front of me. Jackson, still looking at the ground, was unaware of the reason for the sudden halt. He raised his head coming face to face with me no more than a foot away. I said nothing. My entire body shook with rage and hostility. My eyes felt on fire as I stared at this vile creature. I didn't know I could feel so much hatred for one human being. He looked back at me with bewildered and vacant eyes. He had no idea who I was.

Within a few seconds his empty eyes seemed to change from confusion to recognition. Then the fear and dread in his stare appeared to take over his entire face. His mouth gaped open in complete surprise. He backed away from me, causing the detectives to grasp him more firmly. He let out a strange whimper like an injured, trapped animal. He tried to free himself, but the detectives held more tightly to his arms. Those not gripping him pulled their weapons and pointed them at him.

Someone yelled, "Jackson, stop resisting! Now!" He looked around like a frightened deer surrounded by wolves. All the while I sneered at him as I felt the venom fill my eyes. His body trembled when he tried to avoid coming any closer to me, but it was not his decision to make.

At the house's doorway, an elderly woman dressed in a soft, pink robe wiped her tears away with a lace handkerchief, her wispy, white hair uncombed and escaping like feathers from her scalp. The woman in the blue uniform had an arm around the other woman's shoulders, comforting her. For a moment I felt compassion for that sad, crying woman. But then I looked again at the devil and all thoughts of any type of empathy left me immediately.

His voice frantic, Jackson called out to the woman, "Arna, git in touch with Gary Palmer. Tell'm what's happenin' and to git to the Nawinah Poleece Station right away."

As the detectives dragged him forward again, I moved to let them pass. Jackson wouldn't look my way while they dragged him mere inches from me. They walked him to the first Ocala patrol car. I followed closely behind. When they assisted him into the back seat of the vehicle, pushing his head down, I yelled his name, "Clay Jackson!"

The sound of my gruff voice startled him, and he jerked his head around. I propped myself a few inches from his face, and I spat on him. I watched the surprised look in his eyes as the spittle ran down his cheek unable to be wiped away.

Our cavalcade returned to the Ocala Police Headquarters. Sean presented the extradition paperwork to transfer Jackson to Orange County, where he'd be charged. Still securely handcuffed, he was moved to Sean and Joel's vehicle. Headley and Gomez's car pulled out of the parking lot immediately after Sean's vehicle. Andrew followed.

After the drive to Nawinah, our vehicles pulled into the police parking lot. Sean, Joel, Headley, and Gomez exited their vehicles while Jackson remained in the confined back seat of Sean's cruiser. Then Headley and Gomez assisted Jackson out of his seat. I stood very close by, staring at him. He sheepishly avoided looking at me.

Much to my surprise, reporters and cameras were waiting in the parking lot. Somehow, the press had become aware of a newsworthy event. Sean told everyone not to speak to any of the reporters. Captain Graham would give a statement in time for the nightly news. I wouldn't have talked to them, anyhow. My focus was completely on the monster being led into the station.

I watched as Jackson was fingerprinted and asked a series of questions, including his name and his birth date. He gave his name as Claude Hiram Jordan, born on June 15, 1931, and currently living on SW Eighth Street in Ocala, Florida. The only truth in his statements was his current address.

Jackson had been searched for weapons and read his Miranda rights at his home. All his personal property was now confiscated, including his rich leather wallet containing hundreds of dollars in cash and several credit cards, his Rolex watch, and his sleek clothing. He was ordered to take off his tailored pants and crisp, white shirt and to put on the orange jail jumpsuit. He was then photographed, both a front view and a profile with his criminal number plaque in front of him. Joel remarked, "He no longer looks like the arrogant bastard we had seen at the council meeting. In his jail cell garb and his hair no longer neatly coiffed, but wild and uncontrolled, he looks like a broken, old man."

Later that night in front of several television cameras and radio and newspaper reporters, Captain Graham gave a press conference. "Ladies and gentlemen, Claude Hiram Jordan, an Ocala businessman, has been arrested for the 1971 murders of the Cunningham family. Jordan will have his first appearance before the judge tomorrow morning. You'll be made aware of any further developments as they unfold. I'll take no questions at this time."

On Saturday morning, Andrew drove us to the Orange County Court House for Jackson's first appearance. I planned to be in the courtroom every time he was brought before a judge or a jury. He'd see my face in his nightmares before I was through with him. When the bailiff called his case, the guards brought a handcuffed Jackson into the courtroom. He still had that frightened, wrongly accused look on his face. He wasn't fooling anybody. The bastard!

He was led in front of the judge and joined by his attorney. Andrew whispered, "I don't want to scare you, Bill, but Gary Palmer is a well-known defense attorney who has represented many high profile criminals and won most of his cases."

"That may be, Andrew, but he will lose this time. Mark my word." Was I trying to convince Andrew or myself?

The judge called Sean and asked for the affidavit on the case. After looking it over, the judge spoke, "Claude Jordan, I find probable cause for the crime of murder in the first degree. Because this is a capital offense, I am holding you at no bond. Do you have an attorney or does one need to be appointed for you?"

Gary Palmer interjected, "Your Honor. I am representing Mr. Jordan."

"Then, Claude Hiram Jordan, you are remanded to the Orange County Jail to await your arraignment, where you will present your plea regarding these charges."

The judge banged his gavel. "Next case."

As Jackson was led from the courtroom, his eyes

darted around the room. Our eyes locked when he saw me. I'm sure my hatred for him was spewing from my eyes. His eyes only showed defeat. We watched each other for several seconds before he was led away.

Jackson was incarcerated in the county jail while the district attorney set the wheels rolling for the grand jury to file a capital murder charge against him. We had to wait patiently for the grand jury to convene. Captain Graham arranged for me to see Jackson in the county jail every day. A deputy would bring a handcuffed Jackson into a secured interrogation room and stand directly behind him. I sat across from him and stared for at least an hour, not speaking, just staring. Each day Jackson appeared more unnerved, sweating profusely, his body jerking involuntarily as I stared. He tried to have conversations with me. "I'm a sick, ol' man. You know I got diabetes. My ticker ain't so good no more either, and I got high blood pressure."

Blah, blah, blah. I said nothing in return. Just the sound of his voice made me cringe. His attorney tried to put a stop to my visits. However, whatever arrangement Captain Graham had with the county sheriff, I was still permitted to see Jackson until his arraignment.

Chapter Thirty-Nine
The Circus Begins

Dani

After Clay Jackson was booked and put into his cell, Sean, Joel, Dad, and Mr. Cunningham returned to our house. Sean gave us an account of the take down.

"Jackson was completely surprised when we arrived at his house. He had been reading the newspaper in the kitchen with his wife. His housekeeper directed us into the living room while she informed Jackson of our presence. We waited about ten minutes before Jackson walked into the room. Still holding his coffee, he looked at us with irritation, like we had no business in his house. His reaction showed he was totally unaware of why we were there."

"Gentlemen, what's this all about? You're interruptin' my private time with my lovely wife. Git this done with and be on your way."

Without hesitation, Sean ordered, "Claude Jordan, you are under arrest for the murders of the Cunningham family: Mary, Elizabeth Ann, Cletus, Daisy, Travis, Lily, and Silas, and the murder of Daniel Reynolds. You are also under arrest for the rape, sodomizing, and murder of Ida Mae Cunningham. Oh, yes, and the murder of Unborn Baby Cunningham.

"We surprised him, all right. He dropped his cup

261

filled with coffee right on the ivory carpet. His eyes opened so wide they looked like they were coming out of his skull. His body stiffened and started to shake.

"Then at the doorway of the dining room, his wife screamed and covered her open mouth with her hands.

"After I read the allegations, Jackson was silent. His wife, however, kept sobbing, saying in broken English, 'No! No! Claude, what do they talk about? There must be mistake. Tell them this is mistake.'

"Jackson looked at her in defeat. I read him his Miranda rights as Joel handcuffed him. And now, at last he's in the Orange County Jail."

****

I knew the publicity would be inevitable, but I never expected its enormity or how it would disrupt our lives. The murders had been committed so long ago I didn't think people would remember or care anymore. We were bombarded with reporters, cameras, and microphones. If we turned on the radio or television, the case was constantly in the news, local and national. They knew our names but not how or why we were involved. One station dug up our relationship to my grandfather. They referred to him as the "alleged" killer of the Cunningham family, assuming Claude Jordan was my grandfather. That was revolting. I wanted to scream at them, but as instructed, I said nothing.

What did we know about the case? How were we involved? Who was the elderly gentleman seen at our house? Was Daniel Reynolds being held in the county jail? Captain Graham told us he'd take care of any statements made to the press. Easy for him to say. He wasn't accosted every day. They even camped out on our street. Police patrolled the end of our block to maintain crowd control. The press followed Frankie to school and had pictures of him going in and out of the building. Luckily, the school officials didn't allow them inside. They followed me to campus too. When they started confronting me at work, Dad told me to take a leave of absence. He also heavily relied on Carl at the body shop to handle most of his managerial duties.

To relieve some of Mr. Cunningham's stress, Dad drove him back and forth to Orlando to harass Clay Jackson in the county jail. I would've loved to be a fly on the wall and watch Jackson's face while Mr. Cunningham stared at him for an hour.

My first day back to criminology class after Jackson's arrest was a fiasco. Somehow, the class was aware my project was the Cunningham case. Probably because my face was plastered all over the television. Talk about being noticed. I'd walk down the halls getting stares and fingers pointed at me. When I got to class, everyone waylaid me with questions, especially on how I was personally involved. I told them the police ordered me not to discuss the case. I also told Dr. Belinsky that Captain Graham said I was no longer to report to him on any more developments. Since the actual trial would be public knowledge, I could then report on the court proceedings. However, I was to refrain from mentioning anything I might learn outside of the courtroom. Dr. Belinsky and the class were elated they'd be getting firsthand information on such a high-profile case. I'm sure my name was mentioned at many dinner table conversations.

Chapter Forty
Arraignment

Bill

A few weeks after Jackson's first appearance, I read the following article in the *Orlando Sun* newspaper, dated March 11:

*Grand Jury Returns Murder Indictment
in 1971 Cold-Case*

By Alex Trexler,
DNA evidence led to the first-degree murder indictment on Monday in the cold-case killings of the Cunningham family more than four decades ago. New evidence was presented to the grand jury, and Claude H. Jordan was indicted on the murder charges. Jordan had been arrested by both Ocala and Nawinah police officers in February at his residence in Ocala. The State Attorney's Office stated a DNA database matched Jordan's DNA with evidence recovered over forty years ago at the scene of the Cunningham murders in Nawinah. Jordan is also charged with statutory rape, sodomy, and incest, and seven counts of aggravated child abuse. He is being held at the Orange County Jail without bail.

Jackson's arraignment was set for ten a.m., Wednesday. When we arrived at the courthouse, we were assaulted by the press. Since I had kept on my medical regiment and had even been back to see Louie and Dr. Nichols, my heart was healing fine, and I was able to withstand the stress and emotion.

Doug Plimpton met us and told me he'd be assisting the prosecution team when the trial began. The courtroom was extremely crowded. Doug had found out Jackson's arraignment was the second on the docket. The bailiff called, "All rise for the Honorable Judge Irwin Prescott." The judge took his seat, and the bailiff handed him paperwork on the first case. The bailiff looked out into the audience. "The court calls Elena Diego to the bench."

We waited as the judge read the drug, prostitution, and soliciting charges against Elena Diego and she pled not guilty. The judge set a trial date for Diego and released her on bail.

The bailiff handed the judge paperwork on Jackson's case. "The court calls Claude Hiram Jordan."

From the side of the courtroom, Jackson was led in by two guards. All eyes in the room turned to look at this broken, old man dressed in his orange jumpsuit as he labored to stand before the judge. Gary Palmer came forward to join him.

The judge addressed Jackson, "State your name to the court."

"Claude Hiram Jordan."

"Claude Hiram Jordan, you have been indicted on ten counts of murder in the first degree on Mary Louise Cunningham, Ida Mae Cunningham, and the Cunningham children: Elizabeth Ann, Cletus Isaac, Daisy Estelle, Travis Angus, Lily Diane, Silas Milton, and the unborn baby. In addition, you are charged with the murder of Daniel Joseph Reynolds. These crimes took place in the late hours of October 31, 1971, in the home of the Cunningham family, Nawinah, Orange County, Florida. How do you plead to these counts?"

Jackson hesitantly looked at his attorney, then at the judge. "Not guilty."

The judge read the additional charges. "You are also indicted on seven counts of aggravated child abuse." The judge read the children's names again. "How do you plead?"

"Not guilty."

"In addition, you have been indicted on one count of statutory rape, sodomy, and incest against Ida Mae Cunningham. How do you plead?"

"Not guilty."

"The capital crimes of murder in the first degree in the state of Florida are punishable by death by lethal injection. Your pretrial status conference is set for Wednesday, April 9."

Jackson was taken away by his two guards.

As we turned to leave the courtroom, I noticed three people approaching Gary Palmer. The older woman was Jackson's wife, who I remembered from his arrest. A younger woman, who looked very much like the older woman, stood next to her. I watched the young man standing near Palmer. Something was familiar about him. I asked Joel, "Who is that man talking to Gary Palmer?"

"That's Jackson's son, Craig Jordan."

Surprised, I stopped in the aisle and stared at the man, realizing why he looked familiar. "Ah, no wonder his looks caught my eye. He bears a very strong resemblance to my son Travis."

"Bill, remember I told you he looked very much

like you as you probably looked at that age? Did your son Travis look like you?"

"Yes, he did."

Exiting the courtroom, we were aggressively met with cameras and reporters. Microphones were shoved in front of my face.

"Are you William Cunningham?"

"Where have you been all these years?"

"Why would Claude Jordan kill your family?"

Some questions were very personal and accusing.

"Why have you waited so long to come forward?"

"Did you see the mutilated bodies of your family?"

"How did you escape being killed while your entire family was murdered?"

"Did you hide while they were murdered?"

On the way to Andrew's house, I continued to think about those hurtful, accusing questions. It was their job, but did they have to be so cruel without even knowing the facts? Did they only care about their story? This was not a story. This was my *life* and my *family* who had been brutally murdered.

I also thought about Craig Jordan since the resemblance was so similar. Why did he have to look so much like Travis? If he had looked like his demon father, I never would've given him a second thought. But I kept reminding myself that his father murdered my family. Why should I care about his son? However, when I thought rationally, I realized this man was *not* his father. Truth be told, besides the evil half-brother Clay Jackson, the others, Craig Jordan, his sister, and their children, were my only living blood relatives. How did I feel about that? It would be different if I didn't know they existed, but now I knew. Now I knew.

267

The next day, Andrew again drove me to the Orange County Jail to harass Jackson. He refused my visit. Apparently, he'd complained to the judge, who ordered the guards to abstain from forcing him into the visitation area. I guess Captain Graham only had so much clout. He couldn't override a judge's order. So we left the building without confronting Jackson.

As we were leaving the jail, climbing up the stairs was Craig Jordan and his mother. When I looked at him, he also caught sight of me. He quickly touched his mother's shoulder, said something briefly to her, and approached me. "Mr. Cunningham, I know you have no reason to speak to me, but may I have a word with you?"

I did want to talk to him, but not on the steps of the jail surrounded by reporters. Andrew quickly recognized my dilemma. "Meet us at the coffee shop around the corner in an hour." Then we walked to the parking lot, leaving Jordan standing on the steps to deal with the reporters.

At the coffee shop, Andrew said, "Bill, I hope I wasn't out of line telling Craig Jordan to meet us. It seems ever since you saw him in court, you've been thinking about him."

"You weren't out of line. You're correct. He looks so much like Travis."

"I recognized that yesterday also. Remember, Travis was my best friend. I also noticed throughout the court proceedings, Craig Jordan kept looking your way. You were so focused on what the judge was saying you weren't aware until Craig Jordan walked up to Gary Palmer."

"I didn't notice him until then. Do you think he

knows what a monster his father is?"

"No, I really don't, but since he wants to talk to you, it makes me curious."

When Craig Jordan walked into the restaurant, Andrew signaled him in our direction. He didn't reach out to shake my hand, and I made no such jester either. I wasn't his friend, nor did I want to be. I did want to hear what he had to say.

"Mr. Cunningham, I'm Craig Jordan."

"I know who you are," I curtly responded.

"This probably means nothing to you, but I sincerely want to apologize, not for my father, but for what he did to your family and to you. His crimes are incomprehensible to my mother, my sister, and me. Please believe me. We knew nothing of this part of him. That's not to say I didn't think he had something evil about him. I recognized that trait even as a child, but I never expected he was capable of such atrocities."

I was staring at Jordan when Andrew asked, "Then do you think your father is guilty of these crimes?"

"Yes."

He surprised me with that brusque, single comment.

Andrew continued, "That's quite unusual for a son to have those feelings about his own father, especially when he hasn't even been convicted."

"Believe me, I've wrestled with this since Mom called me about his arrest. Originally, I thought he was caught for some of his fraudulent business deals. When I learned what the accusations were, my heart told me no way, but my mind and gut told me he may have committed those murders. My father is a very evil man. As a youth, I lived in terror, never knowing where his temper would lead. I have scars on my back from beatings with whatever he could get his hands on. If I did anything he was displeased about, I'd first be lectured for days what a terrible person I was. Then he'd schedule what he called an 'organized beating.' Those were worse than the almost daily spur of the moment thrashings because I'd worry about them for days. And they were horrible. Several times I passed out from the pain."

Andrew asked, "What about your mother? Surely she knew this was going on?"

"She did to some extent. Poor woman. She's terrified of him. She was an immigrant from Poland coming to this country to escape the violence of the Polish uprising in the seventies. She had been working sixteen hours a day cleaning houses when my father met her. One day, she was assigned to clean his house, and he took a liking to her and married her. This man promised to love, honor, and protect her, but his evil nature is not capable of those deeds."

Craig Jordan pleadingly looked at me. Finally, I asked, "Why are you telling me these things?"

"As I said, I know it doesn't mean much to you, but I'm truly sorry for what my father has done to you. My mother, my sister, and I are in no way like my father. Mom is a kind, sensitive woman. She just didn't have the means or the knowledge to get free of him. As for my sister, she was an adult before she admitted the kind of a person he is. For whatever reason, he didn't beat her. She got the lectures like I did and oftentimes was slapped when he didn't like her attitude, but no beatings. She knew he was cruel but thought all fathers were like him. I think she blocked out much of the violence. When he'd beat me, she'd hide in her room under her blankets, covering her ears to avoid hearing my screams. She never talked to me about what she heard. She feared if we discussed it, she'd have to admit what he did. By ignoring it, she could pretend the beatings never happened. She was just a kid. That's how she was able to cope.

"We're a very dysfunctional family. To the public, Dad is a great community leader, businessman, and family man. But in the dark, recesses of our own home, that monster showed its evil face."

I said nothing for a while, then I asked, "What do you want from me?"

He looked surprised at my question. "I want nothing from you."

He arose from his seat and pushed his chair under the table. "Thank you for your time." And he walked out of the restaurant without looking back.

After several minutes, Andrew asked, "What do you think, Bill?"

This man didn't have to talk to me. He wasn't asking me for anything. He didn't even ask me to forgive his father. "I don't know what to think."

Chapter Forty-One
The Waiting Game

Dani

The pretrial conference was almost a month away. The Assistant State Attorney, Dean Baldwin, was appointed as prosecutor to present the state's case. I looked up the credentials of Gary Palmer to add to my criminology report as well as finding out more about him. Palmer had been successful as the defense attorney in several murder trials in Florida. I was impressed with his credentials. Did we have reason to worry?

Not much happened while we awaited the pretrial. Sean and Joel were under a gag order not to release any information about the case. I presented to my criminology class whatever I could, which wasn't much. The rest of the class had already finished their reports, and we had moved on to other projects. My case project would continue until the trial ended. Dr. Belinsky assured me my grade for the course wouldn't be affected if the trial was still in process when the semester ended.

Mr. Cunningham continued to visit the county jail every morning to harass Jackson, who'd never agree to see him. Mr. Cunningham would simply drive back home. I asked him why he kept going even though he knew Jackson refused to see him.

"He doesn't have to see me, but they tell him every time I'm there. I'm not going to let him forget what he did."

Dad and Mr. Cunningham spent a good deal of time with Grace and Evelyn. Frankie hung out with his friends. He'd sneak over to Dylan's house through the back woods so he wouldn't be confronted by any reporters. A few of them were still stationed outside our house. We learned to deal with them and realized they'd be around for a while.

When Joel was busy on the case, I got together with Emily for movies, bowling, or just girls' nights out. I also met her new boyfriend, Troy. They made a cute couple. He had a cool sense of humor.

With the case taking up much of Joel's time, he needed to step away from it and relax. We tried to find ways to get away together. We took day trips around Central Florida, sometimes with Troy and Emily: a helicopter ride, kayaking on Lake Louisa, a water park, even skydiving. With so much entertainment facilities in the Orlando area, we had something different to do every weekend. However, I refused to go on the ghost tour. I had experienced enough paranormal activity; I didn't need to purposefully look for it.

Speaking of the paranormal, since Jackson's capture, my nightly dreams were filled with the usual, crazy stuff, like seeing people I knew in strange situations. In one of them, Dr. Belinsky was Grace's brother. Things like that. But the night before the pretrial, my grandfather visited me again. I'm not sure if it was just a dream or him communicating with me. He was standing before me in what seemed like empty space. He had his hands on the shoulders of a naked, shriveling Clay Jackson. As I watched in horror, Jackson turned a flaming red and melted before my eyes. My grandfather saw my distress. He stepped over the red liquid and put his arms around me. "Do not be afraid."

I wasn't even going to attempt to figure this one out.

Chapter Forty-Two
The Pretrial Conference

Bill

During the pretrial proceedings, Dean Baldwin gave Palmer the names and addresses of all the relevant lay and expert witnesses who'd be making statements at the trial. Andrew, Danielle, and I were on that list. Palmer also provided his list of witnesses. Baldwin then presented a list of the physical evidence and exhibits to be introduced.

In addition, Baldwin added a new charge of complicity to commit arson to the list of Jackson's crimes. Sean and Joel must've found direct evidence linking Jackson to the burning of my orange grove on the night of the murders. Palmer tried to get the charge dismissed, but the presiding judge refused.

After both Baldwin and Palmer presented their requirements, the judge informed the courtroom he was setting the trial date as timely as possible because of the age of Claude Jordan. Thus, both the prosecution and the defense would have to work diligently to prepare their cases. The trial would begin on July 16.

Preceding us from the courthouse was Craig Jordan, his mother, his sister, and another young woman who had her arm locked in Craig's elbow. At the bottom of the stairs, they met another young man who was holding a little, blonde child in his arms. Three young boys stood nearby. As our group passed them, Craig Jordan turned to me and nodded. I returned the nod.

Walking toward our vehicles, Frankie asked, "Grandpa, who are those people?"

"The one man is Clay Jackson's son. The older woman is Jackson's wife, and the younger woman is his daughter. I'm assuming the young woman with her arm in Craig Jordan's is his wife. I'm not sure who the people are at the bottom of the stairs."

"I saw you nod to him. Do you know him?"

"Your dad and I met him outside the county jail. He wanted to talk to me."

"What did he want?"

"He wanted to apologize for what his father had done."

"Wow! Does that mean he thinks his father really killed your family and my grandpa?"

"Yes. He thought his father was capable of those crimes. According to him, his father is a violent man. Craig had a very abusive childhood."

"That's really weird! His own son thinks he's guilty!"

At dinner that evening Danielle asked me, "Sir, I know this has been an emotional time for you. Probably most of your speculations are about Clay Jackson and what will become of him. But I noticed you looking at his family. How do you feel about them?"

"It's a conundrum, Danielle. On the one hand I despise everything remotely connected with Jackson. Yet I know his family is *not* him. Even though at times I look at them in disgust, knowing that despicable being is their father, their husband, their grandfather, who am I to judge them? I don't know what their lives were like. I don't know what pain and agony they've endured. When your dad and I met Jackson's son a few weeks ago, he informed us of his terrible childhood and of his mother being terrified in her marriage. So I'm tormented. Then as we were exiting the courthouse, and I saw that beautiful little child in the arms of, I assume, her father, how could I have any hatred for her? She is as innocent as my children were. She, like them, doesn't deserve any ill will from anyone, especially me, because of her grandfather. I can't feel hatred for Jackson's family as he did mine."

Frankie once again surprised me with his astuteness. "They're your real family, aren't they? That Craig Jordan is your real nephew and his sister is your real niece. You *do* still have a family."

"Frankie, you and your family are my *real* family. Yes, they are blood related to me, but that doesn't make them my family. I don't know them."

"Do you want to know them?"

"I don't know."

That evening when Joel joined us, he said Jackson was complaining of chest pains. They called in a cardiologist to examine him.

That son of a bitch better not die on me.

Chapter Forty-Three
Surprises While We Wait

Dani

The college semester ended in May. I had completed two semesters of Criminology I. As Dr. Belinsky promised, I got an "A." I had enrolled for the summer semester, taking the first half of Criminology II with Professor Belinsky so I could continue with updates on Clay Jackson's trial. Dad told me to keep my work schedule at Sand and Surf to just a few evening hours a week because of everything going on.

Joel was still involved in helping Sean and the prosecuting attorney accumulate and verify all the evidence and reports on the case against Jackson. We saw each other every weekend and enjoyed each other's company more and more on the back patio. It was difficult seeing him so little, but it made those weekends fantastic. I guess the old saying, *absence makes the heart grow fonder,* is true. I loved him a lot on that patio.

At the beginning of May, a letter arrived for Mr. Cunningham from a Casey Jordan of Ocala. Mr. Cunningham immediately opened the letter.

Dear Mr. William Cunningham,

My name is Casey Jordan. I'm the sixteen-year-old son of Craig and Linda Jordan. My father told me you're my uncle. I'm writing this letter because I'd like to meet you. Dad told me I shouldn't contact you, but I told him I wanted to anyhow. So in case you wanted to know, he didn't put me up to this.

I want to tell you about myself, so maybe you'll want to meet me too. I'm a junior in high school. I don't smoke, drink, or do drugs. I'm on the varsity baseball team and get pretty good grades. I have a girlfriend, Kayla, who's smart, pretty, and wants to be a doctor. I'd like to get a scholarship to play college baseball and maybe try to play professional baseball someday. I mostly play first base. My favorite baseball team is the Baltimore Orioles. All my friends like the Tampa Bay Rays. Since we live in Florida, they think I should like that team too. I'd like to play for the Orioles someday.

I don't have any brothers or sisters. I have three cousins who are Aunt Marcie's kids. Jason is 12, Justin is 10, and little Nikki (Nicole) is 4. Even though they're my cousins, they're like brothers and sister to me. We get along with each other pretty well, and we hang out sometimes. They like to play baseball too.

Jason, Justin, and I would really like to meet you. Nikki is too little to understand. My dad told me all about my grandfather and what he did to your family. If you don't want to meet us, that's okay too. I just hope you don't hold what my grandfather did against us. My address is 1529 Cassidy Lane, Ocala, Florida 34471. In case you want to call me, my cellphone number is 352-555-9336.

Your great nephew,
Casey Jerome Jordan

Mr. Cunningham's face was noncommittal as he read the letter. When he finished, he handed it to me. It was computer generated, but hand signed. I don't know if Mr. Cunningham was surprised with its contents, but I was. It seemed like it came from the heart of this kid, Casey. After reading the letter, I asked, "Do you plan to get in touch with this kid?"

"I have to think about it."

Joel, Grace, and her mom came to dinner that night. Mr. Cunningham showed everyone the letter. He asked Joel, "Is there any legal reason I shouldn't contact this young man?"

"As far as I know, there isn't, but you might want to check with Doug Plimpton, just in case."

The next day Mr. Cunningham called Doug Plimpton and asked what his opinion was regarding the letter. Mr. Plimpton told him he saw no legal reason he couldn't contact the boy. However, he did advise not to discuss anything about the case with either Casey Jordan or any other family member of Clay Jackson.

That afternoon Mr. Cunningham answered Casey Jordan's letter. He read the letter to us before mailing it.
Dear Casey,

I received your letter and would also like to meet you and your cousins. I'm pleased that you are doing well in school. Keep up the good work. It's important if you want to get into the college of your choice.

You'll be surprised to know that my son, Travis, was a good baseball player too. What is more surprising is that his favorite team was also the Baltimore Orioles.

I saw you outside the courthouse a few weeks ago with your family. You and your cousins are fine looking, young men. Your little cousin, Nikki, is beautiful. She reminds me so much of my daughter,

Lily, who also had very blonde, curly hair.

Please let me know the next time you plan to be in the Orlando area. We'll arrange to meet. If you'd like to call me, my cellular telephone number is 407-555-5168.

Thank you for the very nice letter.

Yours truly,

William Cunningham

I thought the letter was just right, not too personal, but just enough to give this Casey kid a little glimpse of Mr. Cunningham and his family.

A week after Mr. Cunningham had mailed the letter to Casey Jordan, he received a phone call from Casey. We heard his side of the conversation.

"Yes. This is William Cunningham." He looked at us as we sat around the kitchen table. "Ah, yes, I remember you, Casey. It's good to hear from you." Mr. Cunningham sat down at the table. "No, you didn't interrupt anything. How are you?" He smiled at Casey's response. "I'm glad to hear that." Then there was a long pause. "This coming Saturday?" Mr. Cunningham looked surprised. "Yes, I'd like that very much. Then a short pause. "I'd like to meet them too. Let me check with my family, and I'll call you back shortly. Thank you for calling, Casey. Goodbye."

Mr. Cunningham hung up. "Casey and his two cousins will be in Orlando on Saturday and want to meet me. I do want to see them, but I didn't know the best place. I'd also feel more comfortable if some of you were with me. The boy said they'll be here early in the morning. His father has some business in Orlando. What do you think?"

Dad suggested, "Let's meet them for breakfast. I

can join you, but afterwards, I have to get to the shop and help Carl. Frankie and Dani should go too. Frankie, you're about these boys' ages, and you might have things in common with them to help them feel more at ease."

Mr. Cunningham wanted to meet in a public place. Dad suggested a breakfast gathering at Sammy's, the restaurant across from the Citrus Tower in Clermont. Mr. Cunningham called Casey back to make arrangements with his father.

"Hello, Casey, this is Bill Cunningam. Is your dad available? I'd like to talk to him regarding our plans."

"Yes, Craig, this is Bill Cunningham. I wanted to verify it's okay if your son meets up with me." Mr. Cunningham's voice sounded more serious when talking to Craig Jordan. 'Yes, I thought when he called you were probably aware, but I'm just making sure. I also wanted to know how long you planned to be in the area." He was nodding his head as he listened. "Oh, I see. Then how about if we meet the boys for breakfast?" Apparently, Craig Jordan agreed. "Okay, I'll let Andrew explain where the restaurant is located."

Dad took the phone and gave Craig Jordan directions. After hanging up he said, "Craig's dropping the boys off at the restaurant at eight o'clock. He has to be in Orlando by nine."

Mr. Cunningham added, "He'll be done with his business at noon. Does anyone have any idea what we can do with the boys after breakfast?"

Frankie had a plan. "Dylan is playing a Little League baseball game at Brady Field. It starts about ten. Since those boys like baseball, maybe they'd like to see a game."

"That's a good idea, son," agreed Mr. Cunningham. "His dad will call us when his meeting is over to find out where to pick them up."

So, our plans were made for the following Saturday. I don't know who was more excited about meeting the boys, Frankie or Mr. Cunningham. They talked about the coming breakfast for the rest of the week.

Chapter Forty-Four
Strangers When We Meet

Bill

We took two vehicles to the restaurant and informed the hostess we'd be having three more in our party. She sat us in a large, corner booth. Andrew ordered coffee while we waited for the boys. Five minutes after eight, the boys arrived with Craig Jordan and his wife. Since Andrew and I were sitting at the ends of the booth, we stood to greet them.

"Good morning, Craig," I began. "How are you this morning?" Small talk when we all felt awkward.

"I'm fine, sir. This is my wife Linda."

I gently shook her hand. "I'm pleased to meet you, Linda."

Craig continued, "This is my son, Casey, and my sister's sons Jason and Justin."

I shook each of their hands. "Please to meet you."

Each of the boys responded politely.

I then introduced my party. Andrew shook everyone's hand. Since Danielle and Frankie were too far into the booth, they both nodded, smiled, and said, "Hi."

Craig then said, "I'll give you a call around noon to see where I can pick up the boys. I'll also give you my phone number in case you need to get in touch with us."

When I reached in my pocket for my cellular phone, Frankie immediately said, "Here, Grandpa, I'll put it in for you."

I handed the telephone to Frankie as Craig repeated his number.

"Okay, then," murmured Craig, uncomfortably. "We're taking off." He and his wife hugged each boy and walked away, waving as they went out the door.

The boys were timid after Craig and Linda left. Andrew said, "Bill, how about if I sit next to Frankie and you sit next to me. The boys can all sit on the other side together. Dani, you're in the middle."

While our breakfasts were being prepared, we tried to get acquainted with the boys. Frankie was very good at making conversations. He asked them about their schools, their interests, and their favorite movies and computer games, keeping the dialogue going quite well. The boys were relaxing and talking more freely. Frankie mentioned we were going to a Little League baseball game after breakfast. The boys were excited about that prospect.

Our breakfast came, and the conversations were limited while we ate. When we finished and began our dialogs again, the youngest boy, Justin, who seemed to be the most outgoing of the three, asked, "Frankie, can I ask you a question?"

"Sure, Justin."

"If our Uncle Bill is your grandpa, does that mean we're cousins, like Casey and us?"

Frankie smiled. "Your Uncle Bill is sort of my adopted grandpa. Both of my grandpas died a long time ago. I never knew them, so your Uncle Bill said he'd be my adopted grandpa."

Justin frowned and looked down at his plate. "You're lucky. I wish I had an adopted grandpa. My grandpa is real mean."

Almost before Justin was able to finish his sentence, Casey taped him on the shoulder. "Justin, you know you're not supposed to talk about Grandpa."

"Oh, yeah, I forgot."

The atmosphere was a little tense for a while, then Frankie broke the silence. "Casey, Grandpa says you play baseball at your school. Maybe next time you guys come to town, we can get up a game with some of my friends."

Casey, still upset with Justin, said, "That sounds like fun. We'll ask our parents tonight."

When we finished eating, Andrew went to work while everyone else got situated in my SUV. Danielle sat in front to direct me to the baseball field.

At the game, Frankie introduced Dylan to the boys. Dylan's team, the Nawinah Nationals, beat the Gotha Gorillas four to three in a very exciting game. Craig Jordan called a few minutes before the game ended, asking where to pick up the boys. Danielle gave him directions to the field. When the game ended, I treated everyone to ice cream. The boys from Ocala began to mingle with some of the players on the team, discussing baseball and whatever else boys discuss. Danielle and I, enjoying the camaraderie between the kids, were surprised at how well the Ocala boys got along with everyone.

Craig Jordon pulled into the parking lot just as we were finishing our ice cream. "Did everything work out okay?"

"Oh yes. The boys seemed to have a good time," I

told him.

Justin excitedly asked, "Uncle Craig, can we come back again? Frankie said we could play baseball with him and his friends. Please! Please!"

Jordan looked at me warily. "Is this okay with you, or was this the boys' idea?"

"Frankie and your boys planned this. It's fine with me as long as the parents agree."

Frankie quickly added, "Maybe they could spend the night. I have a big tent, and we could camp out in the backyard."

"Yeah!" Justin cried. "Can we Uncle Craig? Please."

Craig looked at me to see if I had any objections to this sudden arrangement. I nodded to signal my agreement. Then he asked his wife, "Mom, what do you think?"

"I suppose it's okay." She turned to Jason and Justin. "We'll need to check with your mom and dad."

Craig agreed to call me after he discussed the plans with his sister. Everyone shook hands before getting into our vehicles. Frankie remarked as I drove away, "I like those guys."

Danielle agreed, "They seem like nice kids. Although, you never know about people. I think we should still be a little cautious. When you meet somebody for the first time, they want to give a good impression, so they're on their best behavior. You'll have to get to know them a little better to really know if they can be your friends."

I added, "Remember, I socially knew Clay Jackson as Edgar Fitzsimmons for many years never realizing what a monster he was. Some people are very good with hiding their true nature. I also thought the boys seemed nice, but like Danielle says, we have to be cautious."

I didn't want Frankie starting off a friendship with these boys always waiting for them to show some unpleasant personality traits. "Frankie, you're a very perceptive young man. I have no doubt if these boys are not what you think they are, you'll detect it early in your friendship. Then we'll pull back on any future dealings with them. In the meantime, give them a chance."

On Wednesday a few weeks later, Casey called and asked if the boys could come the following Friday night and stay until Saturday evening. I told Casey I'd check with Frankie and have him call.

Frankie had another idea. "Grandpa, if it's okay with you, since we're going to camp outside this weekend, do you think we could go into the woods behind us and find some of the stuff you used to use when you were living on your property? Maybe we could catch fish at Lake Charlotte."

I thought they should come on Saturday morning and stay until Sunday evening to allow more time for the planned activities. Thus, Frankie called Casey, and I called Craig. Before the evening was over, it was finalized. Craig would drive the boys to Andrew's house on Saturday morning. We told the boys to each bring a sleeping bag, a swim suit, and long sleeve clothing for foraging in the woods.

I was pleased with the conversation I had with Craig. We discussed the boys going to church with us on Sunday morning. It sounded like they attended church on a regular basis. Of course, that was no guarantee they were of good character simply because they went to church. I used to see Ed Fitzsimmons in church every Sunday morning dressed in his Sunday best, sitting in the same pew each week. Look what kind of a man he turned out to be.

Frankie had invited Dylan to the foraging and campout also. On Friday the three of us gathered or purchased our supplies. We made a dry run through the woods to see exactly what was available to collect for our meals. We set up Frankie's tent near the back of the yard. Andrew had a cooler the boys could use to store their drinks and food items. By dinner time we were thoroughly prepared for the weekend.

Craig, Linda, and the boys arrived about nine on Saturday morning. Frankie and the boys took off immediately to get Dylan. After they walked away, I asked Craig, "Would you and Linda like to come in for a cup of coffee?"

"No, thanks. We're on our way to visit friends. Maybe next time."

I wasn't sure whether he was avoiding any personal social contact with me, or if he was truly busy with other engagements. But then, I also hadn't been very forthcoming with friendliness toward him either.

Craig said, "We'll pick the boys up tomorrow night about seven, if that's okay with you."

I thought I'd make one last gesture toward an amicable rapport. "Would you like to come about six tomorrow and stay for dinner?"

Craig and his wife exchanged knowing glances with one another. "Uh, I don't know. Are you sure?"

I wanted to clear the hostility between us. "Craig, let's get this out into the open. I know you've been concerned about how I might feel about you. That compassion shows me you are *not* like your father. I hold no animosity toward you, your sister, or your mother. I sincerely would like to get to know you and your family. Do you think we might have that opportunity tomorrow night?"

I could tell by the expression on Craig's face he was not expecting my little speech. "I didn't want you to think my family was trying to invade your space, what with my dad and all." Then he raised his shoulders and spoke with conviction. "You're absolutely right. I'm *not* my father in any way. I can't deny I'm his son. I thought I loved him simply because a son is supposed to love his father, but I literally hate him for what he's done to you and our families. I'm only attending the trial for my mother's sake. She needs my support more than ever. After the trial, I never want to see him again.

I heard him take a deep breath. "Yes, we'd like to come to dinner tomorrow night."

"Then it's settled. We'll not mention your father in any more of our conversations. He will not be part of this relationship. Is that okay with you?"

"That is absolutely my sentiments also."

After Craig and Linda left, I told Andrew and Danielle of our conversation.

Andrew remarked, "Bill, that's great. I sincerely think they want to have an amicable rapport with you."

"Thankfully, since not one of them even looks like Jackson, it'll make that friendship a hell of a lot easier for me."

Andrew chuckled as we went into the kitchen to have another cup of coffee before the boys returned and the chaos ensued.

****

The day was quite an adventure. After the boys laid their sleeping bags in the tent, which almost covered the entire floor, we set out to gather our food for our meals. We each grabbed a bottle of water and a basket for our findings and headed into the woods. We gathered chickweed, dollar weed, and purslane for our salad. We found some Jerusalem artichokes, picking off the tubers for our potato substitute. We picked persimmon leaves, passion flowers, and blackberry leaves to make tea. For dessert we picked various wild berries. Those chores took the rest of the morning and part of the afternoon. Though tired and hungry, the boys had a great time. Then we came back to the house and cheated by having hot dogs, potato chips, and soda pop for lunch.

After a brief rest, we collected our fishing supplies. Andrew drove us to the lake and helped the boys set up their fishing poles before we waded into the water prepared to catch a twenty-pound bass. After a couple of hours, we caught five fish. None of them weighed over a pound, but they would be sufficient for our supper. We gathered our belongings, packed up the vehicle, and headed back to the house.

I didn't know if the boys had enough energy to help prepare dinner, but after some rest, a short swim, and some cold drinks, they regained their stamina. I barked orders to my kitchen staff.

"Frankie, you and Justin wash and dry the salad ingredients. Dylan and Casey, you boys wash, scrape, and slice the artichoke tubers. I'll show you how it's done. Jason, you can help Andrew wash and boil the leaves for the tea. Anyone who finishes their chore can wash the berries."

We "modernized" our fire pit by using a small grill from the hardware store. We had gathered dried branches from the nearby woods. I showed the boys how to start a fire with friction. Each of them tried but were unsuccessful. "We'll try some other day when we have more time and are not so anxious to taste the delicious, new cuisine."

The boys finished their chores while Andrew and I cleaned the fish. Then the fish and the artichoke tubers went on the grill to cook to a golden brown.

It was late when we sat on the patio to eat our meal. The food had mixed reviews from the dinner guests.

Casey said, "I liked everything."

Justin didn't agree. "I only liked the fish. That salad was pretty gross."

We also cheated with the dessert berries and put them over vanilla ice cream. Justin remarked, "Now this is really good."

By eleven o'clock we had eaten and cleaned up after our meal. The boys were very tired when they took their flashlights to the tent. Whether they'd sleep, regardless of how exhausted they were, was anyone's guess.

Chapter Forty-Five
Meet and Greet

Dani

Dad had said we'd go to the noon mass on Sunday, allowing the boys to sleep late. I was up at eight to find Dad and Mr. Cunningham in the kitchen drinking coffee. The boys were still asleep in the tent.

"So, did the kids have a good time yesterday?" I had been to the movies with Joel the night before.

Dad remarked, "They sure did. They'll probably be very tired this morning. Bill worked their butts off. It was educational, yet still fun. None of the boys complained. Well, maybe Justin, a little, mainly about the food."

Dad quickly changed the subject. "Oh, by the way, Craig and his wife are coming to dinner tonight. He called Bill early this morning to see if his sister, Marcella, and her family could join us. I guess we'll have a house full."

The boys wandered into the kitchen about ten o'clock, sleepy-eyed and tired. Dad was at the stove. "How about some good old pancakes for breakfast, gentlemen? Or should we go into the woods again to find our food?"

Pancakes was their definitive choice.

At mass that morning the homily was about

forgiveness. I wanted to go onto the podium and ask the priest how it was possible to forgive somebody for brutally killing your grandfather. Maybe Mr. Cunningham should ask how he could forgive a man who viciously killed innocent children. Neither he nor I left our seats. Maybe someday we'd understand and be capable of forgiving Clay Jackson.

After mass, the boys' choice for lunch was peanut butter and jelly sandwiches. They changed out of their dress clothes, disassembled the tent, and packed up their sleeping bags. While Dad and I cleaned the kitchen and started dinner, everyone else took off with baseball gear for the ball field. Dinner was in the oven by the time the group returned from the ball game. They were all sweaty, dusty, and exhausted. The boys went swimming in the pool to cool off and relax before they took showers.

When our adult guests arrived, the greetings were rather awkward at first. However, as soon as the boys came bounding into the room talking all at once about their adventures, their excitement relaxed everyone. We sat at dinner, conversing about everything and anything. The only subject that wasn't discussed was Clay Jackson.

Overall, it was a pleasant evening. Little Nicole was not at all shy and sat on Mr. Cunningham's lap for most of the visit. He had a contented smile on his face as he looked at the little girl. I wondered what was going on in his mind. Since he was smiling, it must've been pleasing thoughts.

After dinner the boys took their desserts into Frankie's room to play on his Xbox. While we were in the living room having our desserts, Craig spoke, "Mr.

Cunningham, I'd like to ask you something." When he made that statement, I was aware of a slight tension in the room. Mr. Cunningham had the hint of a frown on his face. Since they had made an agreement on Friday not to discuss Clay Jackson, I was curious about his request.

Craig Jordan quickly added, "It's about my mother. She's an old woman now and would like to put the past behind her. She was wondering if she could speak to you sometime to offer her condolences and apologies."

Mr. Cunningham looked at little Nicole, caressing her soft, blonde curls as she sat quietly on his lap, her eyes wandering around the room watching the adults. Then he looked at Craig, dropping his hand from Nicole's head. "Craig, I hold no ill-will toward your mother. Please tell her it's not necessary for her to apologize. As for meeting her, how about the next time we get together, because I want there to be a next time, she join the rest of us."

"Mr. Cunningham, you have to be the most understanding individual I've ever met."

"Well, Craig, there's one contention that I have…" Mr. Cunningham looked very serious. Before he could tell Craig what that contention was, Casey and Jason came vaulting into the living room with Jason shouting, "Uncle Bill, Uncle Bill, Frankie says you know how to play Fruit Ninja better than him. Will you come show us?"

The serious look on Mr. Cunningham's face was replaced with a large smile. "I sure will, son."

As he placed little Nikki gently onto the floor, still smiling, he turned to Craig. "That contention is that you stop calling me Mr. Cunningham. That goes for you also, Danielle. How about if everyone takes Jason's lead and calls me Uncle Bill?"

Uncle Bill followed Jason and Casey into Frankie's room to beat them at Fruit Ninja.

After that initial get-together, we had several more with the Ocala group. For the next meeting, we went to Craig and Linda's house. Uncle Bill would never go to Clay Jackson's house, so Mrs. Arna Jordan met us at Craig's. She was a very slight woman with beautiful white hair that looked like a wafting cloud atop her head. At first she was timid and shy. I think she was afraid we might bring up her husband even though Craig told her no one would discuss him. She seemed to love her children and grandchildren very much, and the feeling seemed to be mutual.

Thus, we got to know the Jordan and Hinkle families quite well over the time before the trial. Uncle Bill appeared happier and more content. We took the kids to the theme parks during the interval. Money was no object for Uncle Bill. He'd buy all our tickets. Dad and I would object each time, but he'd shut us down immediately.

The time passed rather quickly. Joel, Grace, and Mrs. DeMarco were included in most of our activities also. Our entourage was growing by leaps and bounds.

Chapter Forty-Six
The Trial

On the day Claude Jordan's trial began, the temperature in the courtroom was cool as Frankie, Grace, and Evelyn entered, passing the armed guard next to the heavy door who reminded them to turn off all cellphones. Since Danielle, Andrew, and Bill had been subpoenaed as witnesses for the prosecution, they were seated in an adjoining room, unable to attend the trial to avoid being prejudiced by the testimonies of witnesses before them. Frankie, Grace, and Evelyn took their seats directly behind the prosecution. Craig and Linda Jordan, Marcella and David Hinkle, and Mrs. Claude Jordan were already seated behind the defense. Jackson was escorted into the courtroom by two guards and seated between Gary Palmer and his assistant, Sheldon Goldberg. Jackson was dressed in a dark brown suit, cream colored shirt, and a muted striped beige tie. His hair was neatly trimmed, and his face was cleanly shaven.

Assistant State Attorney, Dean Baldwin, sat at the prosecution table. Joining him were Doug Plimpton and Mark Novotny, both part of the prosecution team.

In the front of the courtroom was the judge's polished, mahogany desk elevated above the main court floor with a wide, plush, leather chair behind it. In the gallery off to the right was the jury box with sixteen empty chairs, two rows of eight each. Two court reporters hustled to place documents on the prosecution and defense tables and the judge's bench.

The courtroom was filled to capacity. Many were without seats and lined against the wood paneled walls. The members of the jury filed in at precisely ten a.m. The bailiff addressed the audience. "All rise. The Court of the State of Florida, Orange County, is now in session, the Honorable Thomas J. Marchese presiding."

The judge, a tall, thin man in his long, black robe, entered and took his seat. His dark rimmed glasses solidly rested against his tapered nose.

The bailiff announced, "Your Honor, today's case #9946 is the State of Florida, Orange County versus Claude Hiram Jordan." Then he turned to the jury and swore them in.

The judge looked at Dean Baldwin. "Is the prosecution ready to begin this trial?"

"Yes, Your Honor, the prosecution is ready."

Then the judge looked at those seated behind the defense table. "Is the defense ready to begin this trial?"

Gary Palmer arose from his seat. "Yes, Your Honor, the defense is ready."

Dean Baldwin began his opening statements, mentioning by name all the murdered victims, describing the fire on the night of the murders, and pointing out the raping and sodomizing of an old woman. With this statement, the courtroom filled with chatter and commotion. The judge had to call for order.

Baldwin read from a piece of paper every one of Jordan's many aliases. He ended his statement by saying, "I intend to prove to the court that Claude Jordan was Baby Boy Gunderson, the half-brother of

William Cunningham, the father, husband, son, and friend of Claude Jordan's victims brutally murdered on October 31, 1971."

With that statement, there was such an uproar in the courtroom Judge Marchese had a difficult time restoring order. Several members of the press rushed out of the courtroom to relay this development to their newspaper editors, radio stations, or television networks.

When the courtroom was quiet, Gary Palmer addressed the jury. "I will prove Claude Jordan is innocent of all the charges." He portrayed Jordan as a loving family man, a city councilman, a Vietnam War hero, and a respected businessman.

When Palmer completed his opening statements, the prosecution began the presentation of the evidence against Jackson. The first witness called to the stand was former deputy, Phil Drummond. Although physically handicapped, he was alert and articulate. His descriptive delivery of what he remembered created horrible visions of the tragic scenes in the minds of everyone in the courtroom. "I still have nightmares from the visions."

Baldwin asked, "Was Fitzsimmons in charge of any ongoing part of the investigation?"

"He headed up the search for Daniel Reynolds, the prime suspect in the murders."

When Baldwin finished his questioning, Gary Palmer cross examined Drummond, focusing mainly on the reliability of the evidence collected and Drummond's own statements. "Mr. Drummond, I understand you currently reside in an assisted living facility. Is that correct?"

"Yes, that's correct."

"Do you currently take any medication for dementia or Alzheimer's?"

Baldwin quickly jumped up. "Objection!"

Judge Marchese addressed Baldwin. "Overruled. Witness please answer the question."

Drummond's annoyance with the question was evident on his face. "No, I do not."

"Then what is the reason for your current living situation?"

Drummond snickered and shook his head. "Doesn't this wheelchair answer your question? I'm physically, not mentally impaired."

Palmer was done with his questioning of Drummond.

The next witness was Glen Myers, another deputy present at the crime scene, who gave his account of the investigation. He was cross-examined by Palmer, who eventually questioned Myers on the type of medication he was currently receiving. Myers volunteered, "I'm not on any type of medication for dementia, Alzheimer's, or any other mental disorder, if that's what you want to know. I only take over-the-counter medication for my arthritis."

****

On the second day of the trial, Clay Jackson smiled at his family as he walked to the defense table. The only family member returning the smile was his wife.

Baldwin called Sean Sullivan to the stand. Sean gave his account of the chain of events leading up to reopening the murder case. The evidence found at the crime scene was also presented, after which Baldwin asked Sullivan, "From this evidence what is your conclusion?"

"Objection! Your Honor," cried Palmer. "It's not the detective's job to reach any conclusion regarding this evidence."

"Objection overruled. Mr. Palmer, Detective Sullivan can give his professional opinion regarding the evidence. Detective Sullivan, please answer the question."

"The DNA on Ida Mae Cunningham's bedding matches that of Claude Jordan. In short, Claude Jordan raped and sodomized the dead body of Ida Mae Cunningham."

Again, the audience broke into a plethora of noise and commotion, making it difficult for the judge to maintain order.

When the audience was quiet again, Baldwin called Joel to the stand, who recounted how Danielle and he had discovered the existence of William Cunningham. The letter Clay Jackson had written to Ida Mae Gunderson, his original birth certificate, and his adoption papers were also submitted into evidence. In addition, Joel described how Fitzsimmons' fingerprints were a perfect match with those of Claude Jordan.

Captain Ray Graham was then called to the stand, giving his reasons for originally assigning Sean and Joel to the case.

DANI:

I was summoned to the courtroom on the third day of the trial. My voice trembled when I was sworn in, but I got hold of myself and listened intently to the questions. Mr. Baldwin asked me about my original encounter with Uncle Bill on his property. I went into considerable detail regarding Uncle Bill's physical appearance, thinking he was some kind of creature. Next, I spoke of how Uncle Bill came to live with us, bringing tears to my eyes as I described how my family had grown to love him.

When Mr. Baldwin finished, Gary Palmer led off his questioning. "Danielle, may I call you Danielle?"

I guess I was a bit prejudiced. I didn't like Gary Palmer from the moment I observed his sardonic attitude. My left nostril turned up in a sneer. "I guess so, since that's my name. But you know that, don't you?"

I heard chuckles from the audience.

He was ridiculous in his cross examining of me. He basically accused me of befriending Uncle Bill because I wanted his money. Dad and I were leeches, needing help in paying for my education. In his harassing manner, Palmer asked, "Would you say your family is struggling financially?"

"No, not at all. My father is a successful business man, and I'm working because I feel obliged to assist with the family finances. If you're insinuating our friendship with Mr. Cunningham is a result of us wanting to get him to pay for my college education or any of our financial obligations, you're sadly mistaken. I feel sorry for you if you think everyone is as sick and demented as the man on trial today."

Oh, my gosh. Did I get myself in trouble? And the courtroom was in an uproar. Judge Marchese was getting angry. The noise finally subsided. "This is your final warning. One more outburst and the entire courtroom will be vacated. As for you, Miss Reynolds, you may have been offended by Mr. Palmer's line of questioning, but you are not a member of the jury, and as such, it is not your place to decide the guilt or innocence of Mr. Jordan. Juror's, please disregard Miss Reynolds last remark.

"Mr. Palmer, are you finished with this witness?"

"Not quite, Your Honor." He again started badgering me. "Danielle, I understand you've recently come into a large sum of money. Is that correct?"

At first, I was confused. What was he talking about? Then it registered. He was referring to the trust fund Uncle Bill had set up for me. How the heck did he know about that? I stared at him, belligerently. "Yes."

"Would you tell the court how you came about receiving that money?"

I looked at the judge. "Your Honor, do I need to answer that question?"

"Yes, Miss Reynolds."

"It was a Christmas gift."

"Who gave you that gift?"

"Mr. William Cunningham, the kindest man I've ever known."

The judge reprimanded me again. "Miss Reynolds, I must remind you to simply answer the questions. Do not add your personal opinions unless you are asked."

"Yes, Your Honor, but it's difficult to just say yes or no when I know what Mr. Palmer is trying to get me to say."

"Just answer the question, please." Turning to Palmer, the judge said, "Mr. Palmer, get to the point."

"How much money did you receive from Mr. Cunningham?" asked Palmer.

"Objection! That is not relevant to this case. Miss Reynolds has already agreed she received money from Mr. Cunningham. The amount she has received is of no concern."

"Objection sustained. Mr. Palmer, it's time for you to move on."

Palmer looked at me as if I were the scum of the earth. "I'm done with this witness, Your Honor."

I was excused from the witness stand, and we broke for lunch.

Dad was the first afternoon witness. Baldwin asked him to recount his first meeting with Uncle Bill and to describe their current relationship. Dad related how I got him involved, describing our various trips to the Cunningham property. He explained how he assisted Uncle Bill in acclimating to his new life. Baldwin asked Dad, "Are you absolutely sure the man claiming to be William Cunningham is who he says he is?"

"I'm positive the William Cunningham I know is the same man who had been severely injured and left for dead back in 1971."

"How can you be so sure?" Baldwin asked.

"For starters, he has all the identification needed to claim his identity: birth certificate, baptismal record, knowledge of the orange growing business, and most of all, every detail about his family."

"Do you not think an imposter would be able to produce the identification documents if he had found them on the property?"

"I suppose that's possible for a man who might be of the same general age and physic to impersonate him, but there is no way that person would have the knowledge about his life and family. William Cunningham is a very astute and intelligent man with an exceptional memory."

"Did William Cunningham have any difficulties in

establishing his identity with the financial institutes where he had kept his finances?"

"None. He had all the necessary paperwork. His signature also matched those the bank had on file."

Palmer then started his cross examination. "If, as the prosecution claims, Daniel Reynolds was murdered inside the Cunningham residence instead of William Cunningham, how old were you at the time of his death?"

"I was six years old."

"Would you say a six-year-old could identify a person who he hadn't seen for over forty years?"

Dad rolled his eyes. "I may not have recognized the postman or the grocery store clerk after forty years, but we're talking about my father. Of course, I'd recognize him. Not only would I recognize him, but the DNA evidence found at the scene has proven the male adult body bludgeoned in the Cunningham House was my father. William Cunningham's DNA has also been tested, proving he is who he claims to be."

Palmer looked at Dad for a few seconds, then addressed the judge. "I have no further questions for this witness."

For the remainder of the day, Baldwin called several other witnesses. Bobby Cooper gave a very glowing account of Uncle Bill as a boss, an owner, and a friend. The DNA evidence was also presented to verify Uncle Bill's and my grandfather's identity. With that settled, the judge adjourned the court until the next day.

Chapter Forty-Seven
The Trial

Bill

This trial meant more to me than anyone. Maybe not quite anyone. Clay Jackson. He had a bigger stake in it than even I. Then, if it hadn't been for him, we wouldn't be in this ghastly situation.

Before Baldwin came forward to question me, I scanned the room and came to stare at Clay Jackson. As soon as he saw me focus on him, he quickly looked down at his folded hands.

Baldwin began, "Are you the William Cunningham, former owner of Gunderson Groves Limited and the husband of Mary Cunningham, the son of Ida Mae Cunningham who were murdered on October 31, 1971 and the father of Mary Cunningham's children who were also murdered on that date?"

I focused my gaze on Clay Jackson, for I knew he'd eventually look at me. "Yes, I am."

"Can you describe to the court the events of the night of October 31, 1971?"

"It was a Sunday evening…"

I continued telling the court about that fateful night—the noise I heard, being knocked unconscious, beaten, and awakening in the crawlspace of my own home, and then struggling to get into my locked house.

I reiterated my arduous task entering the house through the crawlspace. I described the horrific scenes in the kitchen and my mother's bedroom. At that point I had to stop my testimony. As I was narrating, against my will, I was revisiting those horrid scenes, and I found myself struggling to speak. Baldwin realized my predicament and requested a short recess. Instead, the judge ordered a lunch break.

Our group gathered outside in the courtyard. Danielle remarked about my emotional state. "Will you be able to finish your testimony?"

"This is more difficult than I thought. I've tried to block out the memories for so long, and now I have to remember every detail."

Danielle put her arm tightly around me and laid her head on my shoulder. Andrew, seated on the other side of me, grabbed my arm and clasped my hand in his. I took deep breaths to help relax.

Andrew suggested, "Maybe we can get Baldwin to postpone the rest of your testimony until tomorrow."

"No, I don't want to wait another day. The dread and anticipation would only make it worse."

Frankie was quietly observing this emotional difficulty. "Grandpa, if every time you feel you're having a hard time talking, how about if you look at me? I can make a funny face so you won't feel so bad. Do you think that'll work?"

I smiled at this precious lad. "Son, your idea might work. I'm just not sure how the judge will react to it."

"If I get in trouble, I'll just stop. What do you think, Dad?"

"It's worth a try. If the judge reprimands you, stop immediately. Otherwise, he'll send you out of the courtroom."

Upon reentering the courtroom, I was called back to the witness stand. "Mr. Cunningham, can you continue your testimony?"

I looked at Frankie. He puckered up his lips and opened his eyes wide, giving me an example of what was to come. "Yes, I'm ready."

I described the scene in the living room. As I told in detail what I saw, I began to tremble. I looked at Frankie. He was sticking his tongue out and raising his eyebrows up and down. I couldn't help but smile at the sight of him.

I next recounted the condition of each of my children's bedrooms. With each description, Frankie gave me a different comical face. Just as I was about to describe Travis' bedroom, the judge stopped me. I saw him look at me, then at Frankie.

"Mr. Cunningham, what is that young man in the front row doing?"

I cleared my throat. "Your Honor, Frank Reynolds is helping me get through this testimony. This is very difficult for me. Frankie suggested a way to get me through it. Neither he nor I mean any disrespect to you or anyone. It's just our way to cope with this challenging task."

"Mr. Baldwin, did you know about this arrangement?"

I answered for Baldwin before he had a chance. "If I may, Your Honor, he didn't know. We decided this on the lunch break. Please let us continue. With his help, I know I can finish my testimony."

At first the judge didn't respond. Then he affirmed, "It's unconventional, but I suppose there's no harm.

Mr. Cunningham, you may continue."

I told the courtroom about the murder scenes of the rest of my children, getting through my testimony with Frankie's unique assistance.

Next, I told how I finally realized I was assumed killed in that massacre and my best friend was a suspect in the murders. For the rest of the testimony I described how I had lived for the last forty plus years.

When I completed my testimony, Baldwin asked, "How did you find out you had a half-brother?"

I took a deep breath, envisioning when Frankie and I had found the letter Clay Jackson had sent my mother. I told of Frankie's unique discovery. Then I told of finding Clay Jackson's birth certificate.

Baldwin interrupted me to enter into evidence Jackson's letter. Then he asked, "Are you telling this court Claude Jordan is your half-brother?"

"Yes."

After Baldwin was seated, Gary Palmer sauntered over toward me. His mannerism showed he planned to do his best to discredit everything I said.

"Mr. Cunningham. I understand you're on some pretty heavy medication. Am I correct?"

"I'm on medication for my heart."

"Do you take any type of prescriptions for memory loss or any other mental disorder?"

"Objection! The witness has already stated he only takes medication for a heart condition, *not* a mental disorder."

The judge agreed. "Mr. Palmer, you seem to be fixated on mental diseases. The witness does not need to answer that question. Move on."

Palmer paced around the gallery for a few seconds

before questioning me again. Then he asked, "I understand your wife was pregnant at the time of her death. Is that correct?"

"Yes." I answered with my eyes cast downward.

"Were you aware of the rumor the baby may not have been your child?"

This man was getting on my nerves. "No. I was not aware of such rumors."

"The rumor was your wife was having an affair with your best friend, Daniel Reynolds."

"Objection!" Baldwin proclaimed. "Can Mr. Palmer substantiate these so-called rumors?"

"Your Honor, I intend to present witnesses to that effect."

"I will allow the line of questioning for now, but Mr. Palmer, you'd better be sure you can provide those witnesses."

Palmer continued in his irritating manner. "Mr. Cunningham, were you aware of these rumors?"

I was seething. Not only was my wife and best friend murdered, but this man was trying to tarnish my memory of them. It wouldn't work. I held my temper as best I could. "No. I was not aware of any such rumors. Even if I were, I would know they were false. Just because in this world there are monsters like the man who murdered my family does not mean my wife or my best friend were capable of such a despicable act. You are reaching for straws, Mr. Palmer."

The judge reminded me, "Mr. Cunningham, please just answer the question."

Heatedly, I repeated, "No, Mr. Palmer. I was not aware of any such rumors."

Palmer then really hit a nerve. "Do you think that

being unfaithful to one's spouse could be a reason for killing him or her?"

"Objection! Objection. That question is absurd."

"Mr. Palmer, that's enough." reprimanded the judge.

I felt my face turning red and my body starting to sweat. Luckily, as I looked into the audience, Frankie was putting his thumbs in his ears, wiggling his hands, and sticking his tongue in and out as fast as he could. I kept staring at that funny face until I was able to control my emotions.

Then the judge said, "This witness is excused."

Chapter Forty-Eight
The Trial

When Dean Baldwin called Beatrice Jackson Willis to the stand, he pointed toward Claude Jordan, "Are you related to the defendant?"

"Yayes, I aim. He my 'dopted brother."

"By what name do you know him?"

"He Clay Jackson."

"Does he have any identifying birthmarks or tattoos that you know about?"

"Yayes, he do. He got dis ol' tattatoo on his back. It be dis skull wit a knife stuck in da eyeball and blood jist a drippin' from the skull."

"Your Honor, at this time I'd like to present into evidence these photographs taken this morning of Claude Jordan."

The bailiff gave the photos to the judge. When the judge was finished reviewing them, Baldwin said, "If the jurors will look at the white screen, my assistant will project the photos onto it."

All photos were marked with the current day's date. The first showed a front view of Jackson stripped to the waist. The next photo was Jackson with his back to the camera. A skull, a knife plunged into the eye socket, and dripping blood from the skull were displayed on the left side of his back. Several other poses were shown. On each pose the gory tattoo was visible.

After the spectators calmed down, Baldwin asked Beatrice Willis several more questions regarding Clay Jackson. Palmer did not cross examine her.

Next Baldwin called Horace McIntire to the witness stand. "Mr. McIntire, is it true in the early seventies you were friends with Deputy Sheriff Edgar Fitzsimmons?"

McIntire, looking around the courtroom, found Claude Jordan sitting at the defendant's table. A look of confusion was on his face.

Baldwin asked, "Mr. McIntire, did you hear the question?"

McIntire looked at Baldwin, still confused, and responded, "Uh, yayes. I knewed Ed Fitzsimmons."

"Do you see Edgar Fitzsimmons in this courtroom today?"

"Uh, yayes."

"Can you point him out to the court?"

McIntire looked around the room, very muddled. Then he raised his hand and pointed to Claude Jordan. "That man right thar be Ed Fitzsimmons."

"Let the court note that Mr. McIntire has pointed to Claude Jordan."

Baldwin finished his questioning of McIntire, and Palmer began his cross examination. He tried to discredit McIntire's testimony because of his past dealings with the law, but the judge wouldn't allow it.

The judge then asked, "Mr. Baldwin, do you have any other witness to present in the case?"

"No, Your Honor. The prosecution rests."

"We will adjourn until ten a.m. tomorrow.

Chapter Forty-Nine
The Trial

Dani

Kudos to Mr. Palmer. I think he found every living person who had resided in Nawinah at the time of the murders. He was doing his best to discredit Uncle Bill and possibly give him a motive to kill his entire family. None of it was believable. Probably if anyone was the slightest bit credible, it was John Ramsey, the son of Mitch Ramsey, Gunderson Groves' foreman when Uncle Bill's mother was overseeing the company. John Ramsey told the court his father now suffered from Alzheimer's. Since all of John Ramsey's testimony was basically hearsay, the judge declared it inadmissible.

Palmer also called back Phil Drummond and Glen Myers, trying unsuccessfully to wrench something out of their testimonies that would be detrimental to Uncle Bill and to the advantage of Edgar Fitzsimmons.

Claude Jordan's neighbors and business acquaintances were called as character witnesses. The neighbors gave glowing accounts of his generosity and community activism. The business associates told the court Claude Jordan was an intelligent and savvy businessman much respected in Ocala's business community.

A man named Ronald Jordan from Pennsylvania

took the stand and claimed his great grandfather was a first cousin to Claude Jordan's grandfather. When cross-examined by Mr. Baldwin, who asked this Ronald Jordan, how he became aware of the relationship, Ronald Jordan told him he had subscribed to an online service that traced historical family backgrounds.

Palmer called a man who supposedly served in Viet Nam with Claude Jordan. He testified Jordan had rescued several men in his platoon. Mr. Baldwin objected to this man's testimony, stating they presented no record verifying Claude Jordan's military status.

Palmer called witness after witness, each trying to vouch for the good character of Claude Jordan. To our minds he did not disprove any of the hard evidence presented by Baldwin. On the following days, it was more of the same. Palmer and his witnesses painted a glowing picture of Claude Jordan. If I only had to consider Jordan's life, perhaps I would've agreed. According to the witnesses, he was friendly, charitable, respectable, and successful. He was an honorable veteran and an asset to his community. The big issue, however, was no matter how Claude Jordan lived his life, he was still Clay Jackson and Edgar Fitzsimmons, a cold, calculating murderer who committed unspeakable acts because of greed and jealousy.

Thus, we sat through the radiant testimonies of all these acquaintances of Claude Jordan, knowing these people didn't know the true persona of the man. We knew the truth, and truth had to prevail.

Chapter Fifty
The Verdict

Bill

We went back to Andrew's house after the jury retired. Dean Baldwin had done his best. It was now in the hands of those twelve men and women. During the days of the trial, I was full of anticipation and dread, knowing this was my only shot to get what little retribution was left for me. It was now a waiting game, a very tense and stressful waiting game. I needed to be alone to put it all in perspective. I went for a walk in the woods behind Andrew's house. Everyone offered to walk with me, but they understood my need for solitude.

The sun was hot and bright as I meandered through the trees, trying to clear all thoughts from my mind. I wasn't having much success. Long ago images of my family kept flashing in front of me. Finally, I gave in to them. I lowered my body onto a nearby fallen tree trunk and closed my eyes to allow their access. I envisioned Mary with outstretched arms reaching to the sky, her eyes sparkling as she gently smiled at me. I imagined all my children huddled around her with their arms open and smiles on their angelic, childhood faces. It was then I knew I'd be okay. Yes, I had lost their closeness, their physical touch, but no one, not even

Clay Jackson, could ever take away my love for them. They will always be a part of me, but I think I finally came to terms with their deaths. I don't mean the pain will magically go away. That'll never happen. I'll always second guess every action I took that horrifying night, wondering if I could've done anything to change their fate. But I knew they'd want me to move on, to live my life for them as best I could.

I sat on the tree trunk for several more minutes, then I walked deeper into the woods, listening to the sounds of life. Wonderful life of shivering leaves in the whispering breeze, small wild animals scurrying across the ground, a distant horn beeping from the far away road, and my own footsteps on the trampled foliage beneath my feet. Yes, life would go on. I'd make the best of it. I had no doubt one way or another, Clay Jackson would pay for what he had done.

I ambled back to the house. Everyone was seated in the living room, watching the television news. The newscaster was discussing the trial with two attorneys. I sat on the sofa next to Evelyn. She gently took my hand as we listened to their conversation.

Both attorneys had been surprised at how short the trial had been. One attorney stated that most murder trials often stretched on for weeks. They then discussed some of the tactics and key issues brought up. However, when asked by the newscaster how they thought the jury would rule, neither attorney would commit to an opinion. Since the world was now aware of his crimes, it was simply unthinkable that Jackson could ever get away with what he'd done.

We stayed glued to the television for several hours, hearing the many different viewpoints on the trial on different channels from various specialists. Danielle and Joel ordered chicken for dinner. We ate as we remained in the living room watching the television and waiting for a verdict.

Doug Plimpton called me shortly after nine o'clock. "Bill, the jury has retired for the night without reaching a verdict. Let me assure you, this means nothing, one way or another."

Disappointed, we watched the television for a little longer, then dispersed.

At ten the next morning, Andrew came home from work and suggested we get a hotel room near the courthouse to be nearby to await Doug's call. In the hotel room, we had lunch delivered and turned on the television for any updates. About one o'clock, Grace and Evelyn joined us.

At exactly three seventeen p.m., Doug called to say the jury had reached a verdict. We hurried to the courthouse, taking our seats behind the prosecution. My heart was racing as I sat twisting my hands. Before leaving the hotel, I had taken some medication to calm myself.

The Jordan family arrived shortly after our group. Craig's eyes and mine met as he took his seat. I could see both pain and sadness in them. No matter what, Clay Jackson was his father. Though evil and cruel, the man had raised him, sheltered him, and provided a home for him for many years. Craig had to be pulled in two directions. Knowing what his father had done, he knew he deserved whatever punishment he received. But he was his father, his own flesh and blood. Then I told myself Jackson was also my flesh and blood, my brother. So was our mother. Look what he had done to us.

Looking old and defeated, Jackson was led into the courtroom by two guards. He was again dressed very fashionably, clean shaven with his hair neatly cut and combed. No matter how nicely dressed he appeared, he still looked like a despicable, old man.

The courtroom filled up quickly. Shuffles and whispers were heard as those standing were vying for a good space. Anxious looks of anticipation graced everyone's face. The bailiff led the jurors into the courtroom. They moved to their seats in the order they had been in throughout the trial. I heard the scuffle of their feet on the wooden floor and the rustle of their clothing as they sat. Judge Marchese entered, and all noise and movement ceased throughout the courtroom as the bailiff called the court in session. Judge Marchese looked toward the jury. "Ladies and gentlemen of the jury, have you reached a verdict?"

"We have, Your Honor," spoke the foreman as he stood and faced the judge.

The judge looked at Jackson. "The defendant will rise and face the jury."

With Gary Palmer's assistance, Clay Jackson struggled from his seat and turned toward the jury. His eyes were wide open, staring at the foreman. I was staring at Jackson, as was probably everyone else in the courtroom. I wanted to see the look on his face when the foreman read the verdict.

Judge Marchese spoke to the jury foreman, "In case #9946, the State of Florida, Orange County versus Claude Hiram Jordan, how say you?"

The tension in the courtroom was as solid as a block of cheese. My hands and forehead dripped with sweat. I could feel Frankie trembling as he held my hand. Evelyn pulled a little closer to me.

The foreman stood tall. He looked directly at Jackson and recited the verdict. "We, the jury, find the defendant, Claude Hiram Jordan, *guilty* of ten counts of murder in the first degree, seven counts of child abuse, one count of rape and sodomy, and one count of arson."

Pandemonium broke loose. It was difficult to hear what the foreman said after the word *guilty*. Jackson's entire body relaxed as the attorneys on both sides grabbed him to keep him from crumpling. Poor Arna Jordan was screaming and crying all at once while Craig tried to comfort her as he slowly shook his head. Marcella Hinkle was gently crying into her husband's chest. While I was celebrating with such elation, this family was suffering deeply.

The judge tried to restore order to the courtroom, but his attempt was futile. Amid the chaos, he shouted, "This court is adjourned and will reconvene in one week for the sentencing."

I dropped into my seat. At last! At last! Mary? Dan? Mom? Did you hear? He is guilty! Now you can truly rest in peace.

The guards took Jackson from the two attorneys and led him away. He would never live as a free man again. I couldn't help but sit on that seat and indulge in the recent outcome. So long… So many years…

Epilogue

Two Years Later, Dani

Much has changed since the conviction of Clay Jackson. Dad and Grace were married in a lovely ceremony in December after the trial. Grace looked stunning in her lace and satin wedding dress with its delicate, waist length veil. Uncle Bill and Frankie were both Dad's best men. Uncle Bill had a dual role, for he also walked Grace down the aisle.

Uncle Bill and Evelyn got married last spring. He had the Gunderson House renovated to Evelyn's specifications, and he and Aunt Evelyn have moved into it. They look so cute, sitting and holding hands on the now pristine, white porch, looking out at Lake Gossette.

Frankie also has a girlfriend, a little French girl named Gabrielle, who moved to this country last year. Frankie adores her with her deep brown hair and brilliant blue eyes. Although she knew English before moving here, Frankie is teaching her the *real* English. Who knows if this is serious? They're both so young.

Uncle Bill had the Cunningham House demolished after removing any keepsakes and other items he wanted to save. Recovering those things had been another disturbing experience for him. Then he had every brick and every board destroyed and hauled away. He wanted all reminders of what had occurred in that house gone forever. In its place he had a beautiful home built for Dad and Grace. It took a lot of convincing, but Dad finally accepted the gracious gift.

On the opposite side of Dad's new house, Uncle Bill is building a house for Joel and me. We're getting married in October. I'm having Uncle Bill's mother's gorgeous wedding dress altered for me. Mary had also worn it for her wedding too. It's a tea length dress with both satin and lace fabric and a scooped neckline with tiny cap sleeves and pearl beading on the bodice.

As for me, I oftentimes think about the nightmares. I know my grandfather didn't want to spend eternity where his spirit was held captive. Looking back and knowing what I know now, I guess he was trying to shock me into action. I think the man in my nightmares wasn't just one man. Sometimes he was my grandfather; sometimes he was Uncle Bill; sometimes he may even have been Clay Jackson. Confusing as that may seem, maybe it was the only way my grandfather could ask for my help.

I have also moved on career wise. I received my Associates Degree in Criminal Justice from Valencia. I had finished my case study involving the Cunningham murders with straight A's. I'm now continuing my education at the University of Central Florida, hoping to get my bachelor's degree soon. I have also begun the Florida Law Enforcement recruit training program. I'd like to join the Nawinah Police Department.

As for Joel, he made detective last year. I'm so proud of him. He and Sean are partners now and have become great friends.

To our dismay, Clay Jackson cheated us by dying

six months after his incarceration at the Florida State Prison. The judge had sentenced him to death by lethal injection, but he didn't make it to that long-awaited event. Uncle Bill didn't say much when he learned of his death. He simply said, "So be it. May he burn in hell!"

Sometimes I see Uncle Bill sitting on the Gunderson House porch all alone, sadly staring out at Lake Gossette. I think he realizes he can't change what has occurred in the past, and he has forgiven himself, though no one ever thought he had anything to forgive. I know he'll never forgive Clay Jackson. That's okay because he has at least come to terms with all that has happened.

Among the few pieces of the past he has preserved are the paintings of his family he and Frankie had found in the house. To this day, Uncle Bill doesn't know who saved them and buried them in that closet. He had a small addition put on the Gunderson House, where the portraits are displayed with perfect placement and lighting and a plush, round stool sits in the middle of the room. Aunt Evelyn knows he needs their presence.

Members of the Jordan family were originally shunned by their community, ostracizing them because of Claude Jordan's deeds. They weathered the storm and eventually established themselves in good standing with their friends and associates. I guess they realized, as we did, that just because you're related to a monster doesn't mean you are a monster too. Surprisingly, we have all become very good friends. We went to Casey Jordan's high school graduation last year. He was accepted at the University of Florida, Uncle Bill's alma mater. Casey received a baseball scholarship.

Frankie has become good friends with Casey, Jason, and Justin. They're always skyping, texting, or talking to one another. As often as they can, they get together and include Dylan in their gatherings.

Little Nicole has become Uncle Bill's sidekick. Whenever she visits or he visits the family in Ocala, she never leaves his side.

Dad said he went with Uncle Bill to Doug Plimpton's office to change his will once more. Uncle Bill keeps no secrets from us. He told us he had previously changed it, adding the three of us as his beneficiaries. With the new change, he has also included the Jordan and Hinkle families, and Evelyn, his new wife. As for all the property he still owns, he has not yet decided what to do with it. Several developers have approached him to sell large acreage for housing or business developments. He has also talked about having some of it made into a children's park and a baseball field to be named Travis Field after his son.

I have asked Marcella Hinkle and Linda Jordan to be in my wedding. Of course, Emily will be my maid of honor. Emily got engaged to Troy last year, but they haven't set the wedding date yet.

Financially, Uncle Bill has promised to pay for Craig and Marcella's children's college educations. Craig is a proud man. It took a lot of convincing for him to agree. Dad told them Uncle Bill felt he had to do this. He was devastated a brother of his could let his own family suffer because of his actions. He wanted to reimburse them somehow for their pain. Dad told me Uncle Bill has also set up trust funds for the children.

Clay Jackson would turn over in his grave if he

only knew how close we have all become with the Jordan and Hinkle families. Perhaps this is the way Uncle Bill is getting his revenge. Perhaps out friendship has also brought us all a little more closure.

Arna Jordan is still having difficulty reconciling with the kind of man her husband was. She and Evelyn have become close friends, and Grace is helping Arna work through her issues.

I felt a need to see Nafia Celik one more time. Dad and Grace went with me. I sat in the same brocade chair where I had sat on my prior visits. The small table was covered with a forest green cloth. The same eerie light was dimly lit in the corner of the room, casting those spooky shadows across the ceiling.

After the four of us were seated, Nafia started to connect with my grandfather. She called on him, then began to communicate in that gibberish tongue, half chanting and half speaking. Eventually, I heard the familiar sound like a train whistle getting closer and closer until it enveloped the entire room. When the room became silent again, Nafia listened attentively. Then she softly spoke in cryptic babble as she moved her head and upper body in crooked circles with her eyes closed and her face and arms pointed upward. Next, she was still and quiet, all her frenzied movements stopped, and the atmosphere in the room returned to normal.

She dropped her head to her chest and slowly opened her eyes. She raised her head to stare directly at me. "Your grandfather is content. He wishes to thank you and expresses his love for you, your brother, and your father. He has now escaped the chains binding him to misery in his spirit world. He is pleased with the three of you and knows you will be happy with the lives you have chosen."

Nafia paused. From across the table she gently clasped my hands. "One last, very important thing. He wants you to tell William Cunningham he is looking after William Cunningham's family, Mary, all his children, and his mother and father, in the spirit world just as William Cunningham is looking after your grandfather's family; you, your father, and your brother, in this world."

A word from the author...

I have recently moved from Florida to Ohio to be close to family, and just in time for eighteen inches of snow and temperatures below zero. Some might say I'm crazy. Graduating summa cum laude from Youngstown State University, I was an art teacher for several years and have recently retired from a staff accountant position with a CPA firm. My daughter, Wendelin Saunders, collaborated with me in the writing of our first novel, *Let Freedom Ring*. Wendy passed away from cancer in 2009.